THE ART OF LOOKING FOR TROUBLE

A NOVEL

TOM COSENTINO

ISBN #: 979-8-8690-7940-4
The Art of Looking for Trouble
©2023 by Tom Cosentino
All Rights Reserved
Cover design by The Paper House

www.thepaperhousebooks.com
Published in the United States of America

For my wife Caye for always believing and for my children Genevieve and Dominic. A special thanks to Laura Kepner and all the Safety Harbor writing community that lent support and encouragement. Also Steve Lee, Joe Lane, my sister Chris Gellert, Ron Simpson; my Beta readers and friends. From the publication of my first short story to the release of this novel you have been there supporting and believing in my work.

THE ART OF LOOKING FOR TROUBLE: A NOVEL

PROLOGUE

FOUR SEDANS with US government plates assembled on a side street in the pre-dawn chill in the upstate city of Genesee, New York, a few blocks from the front door they were going to take. They donned their vests and FBI windbreakers while they went over their plan for the arrest. One agent could easily handle this assignment but taking down a public figure drew a crowd. The size of the FBI team sent a message not to forget that they were really in charge. The target was also going to get a perp walk for the cameras, which meant the number of agents was in direct proportion to how big the Bureau regarded this investigation.

"I saw this mope on that political show on HBO," an agent reading the warrant commented.

They got back in their cars and went to their designated positions. Two agents walked up the steps and knocked on the door and waited.

PART I: FALL

CHAPTER 1

MADAM MAYOR

MAYOR LEONA LERNER thought that her re-election campaign was completely under control. She had a token, hand-picked challenger that was supposed to serve her up softball opposition that would make her look better to the State party and at the same time keep the press interested in the race. But that easy adversary had decided to take a city manager job down in snowless South Carolina, leaving her running unopposed.

She waited in the conference room before any of her staff for the first time since she took the oath of office, which shook them when they saw her sitting at the head of the table. She glared at each person as they took their seats, daring them to state the extent of the bad news and the plans they better have to fix this mess.

"Well, Madam Mayor," Carter stammered, knowing he had to start because he was the Chief of Staff.

She insisted on being called 'Madam Mayor' by everyone on her staff, even her husband called her 'Madam Mayor' – when he was actually in town. She longed to shake this dying city's dust from her designer clothes and for the Madam to be dropped so she could hear the genderless title of Governor or Senator.

"Without an opponent we lose money from the State party, matching funds from national headquarters and the special funds that were being filtered through both," Carter said looking at his notes.

"Special funds?" the mayor asked, feigning ignorance to the rest of the staff, while looking straight at Carter.

Lerner never took the time to bother herself with details like fundraising or money funneled and cleaned to adhere to campaign finance laws. She left that to Carter. But she knew every side deal and knew enough that they could be dangerous to her future.

"Yes, the donations from our friends that have already given the max amount. They donate to the State party or the national committee and then it is filtered back to us. We don't really need the money for this race, but we are building our war chest for the next race, either Senate, if McGivern retires or Governor, if Russo decides to run for president."

"Is there anyone else we can put into the race at this point?"

The staff looked around the table to see if anyone had the guts – or the stupidity – to deliver the news.

Carter finally continued when he knew no one would take the ball.

"Well, Madam Mayor, at this point it would be expensive. We would have to fund their campaign and there really isn't anyone that has enough distance from us, far enough where it wouldn't be obvious to everyone they were a plant."

"I want some answers now," the mayor shouted through clenched teeth.

Nancy Elliot had just recently joined the mayor's staff. A product of a Genesee suburb with her eyes on City Hall, she planned to follow the same path that Lerner had taken to the precipice of real power. She had a plan for this problem and this was her chance to lay it all on the line. If it worked, she would cut years off of her ascent. If it failed, she would have to move to DC and start all over on someone else's staff.

"I have an idea," Nancy broke in.

All heads in the room turned to her. Carter shot her a cold look of disapproval.

"I have a great candidate, if we can convince him to run. He'll give us plenty to hit him on and that will create a lot of press. He'll be perfect to motivate our local base, get access to the state and national resources and we won't have to give him a penny for his campaign."

Nancy waited for all she had said to sink in and savored the anticipation that her pause was creating.

"Who?" Carter asked in a wimpy whine, humiliated at his loss of control.

"Mike Lee, the owner of Quinn's Bar up on Liberty Hill."

Carter emitted a loud, fake laugh before responding.

"He's a local nobody, sure he's been involved in opposing some of the mayor's initiatives, but he hasn't shown any indication of seeking office. He could win the city council seat for Liberty Hill without even trying, but he's never shown interest."

Nancy stood up and stared across the table at Carter.

"I have a source that tells me he is thinking about running."

Carter stood to face her.

"Source, what source?"

"A very good source. And I know what we can do to give us a ninety percent chance he'd run. We have a couple development ideas for the old Grover Cleveland Middle School on Liberty Hill. If we change the development to something I have in mind, he'll have no choice but to run."

The mayor turned in her chair. "I like this, what should we do with the school?"

Nancy smiled and put both hands on the table as she leaned in the mayor's direction.

"Public housing."

———

Nancy's real source was that she had been talked into going to Quinn's to listen to some local Irish band featuring her friend's boyfriend. When she was waiting at the bar to be served, she saw Mike Lee sitting with a bunch of other men and they were all imploring him to run for mayor. He was non-committal, but Nancy had seen more than her fair share of politicians in her short tenure and saw something in his expression that made her think that he was really considering running. Not just considering, but that he had already made up his mind to run.

After the conversation between Mike and his friends

broke up, Nancy sidled up to the loudest member of the group that was begging him to run. He was a tall, gregarious man with a distinct Irish accent.

"Hi, I'm Nancy."

"Seamus Corrigan, pleased to meet you."

"Who was that gentleman you guys were pushing to run for mayor?"

"Oh, that's Mikey Lee, he owns this place."

"Did anyone ever tell you that you look like Liam Neeson? Especially with that accent," Nancy said laying on her charm.

"Yeah, all the time," Seamus replied without hesitation.

"What makes you think your buddy should be mayor?"

"Well, he knows half of the people in the city, he owns half of Liberty Hill and he thinks the mayor is a horse's arse. She's running the city into the fecking ground and now she's running unopposed. He thinks somebody should run, just to give people some kind of choice."

"She isn't that bad."

Seamus raised one eyebrow and looked down on Nancy. She sensed she was losing the initiative.

"I mean, what are you going to do? Politicians are all the same. So, is your friend serious?"

Seamus sensed something was going on with her overanxious curiosity. "What's your name again?"

"Nancy, sorry I see my friends need me. It was nice talking to you Seamus," she said before retreating to her friends.

When Nancy got home, she went online and found everything that was ever written about Mike Lee. When she saw light, she took a shower and changed before starting to call the people who would know how to fill in the blank spots in the information she had pulled. She needed to know about Mr. Lee, his friends, and what would make him run.

Nancy opened her briefcase and took out copies of an outline for her plan to persuade Mike Lee to throw his hat into the ring. She passed them around the table and then walked a copy over to Mayor Lerner.

"We have a big news conference about converting the old school into public housing. We show how we are compassionate and that we truly care about poverty in the city. Any opposition to this project from the neighborhood would show them as short-sighted and anti-poor. If that doesn't get Lee to run, we can take another step. We send in a reporter from the *Herald* under the pretense that they are writing some kind of detailed story about the impact on the neighborhood. Lee will object to the project and we can have the reporter say that the best way to fight against the public housing would be to enter and win the election. The reporter's job will be to push Lee into running, at the very least they will plant a seed that we can exploit. Make him think it is his civic duty. Maybe even shame him into running. Use his friends that already want him to run to help us without then even knowing what they are doing."

Nancy had been watching the mayor since she stared down Carter when she began to explain the details of her plan, looking for some reaction, but the mayor hadn't flinched.

She swallowed and continued.

"Mike Lee inherited Quinn's Irish Bar from his father-in-law Jimmy Quinn, who opened it right after he returned from World War II. Mr. Lee was the center for St. Patrick's High School county championship basketball team in 1983 and is a fixture in the Liberty Hill neighborhood. Besides Quinn's, he owns several two-family rentals and flats, commercial property, and a corner convenience store. He is married to Helen Quinn Lee and they have one daughter, an English professor down in Florida."

"He's a nobody, surrounded by nobodies. He won't be able to solicit enough money to be a serious candidate and I doubt he'll want to use his own money when he knows he's gonna lose," Carter countered.

"He's a rank amateur. I agree.," Nancy said. "He has a weakness though, he thinks he actually cares about the city, especially Liberty Hill and public housing in his neighborhood will be his issue."

Carter scoffed but Nancy continued with more intensity.

"We can get him to enter the race and once he does, we'll portray him as so far to the Right that he'll be a Gen-X reincarnation of Barry Goldwater. The *Herald* will help in every step of the process. He's bound to make huge mistakes we can exploit. In the end we'll win eighty percent of the vote and look unstoppable." Nancy stepped closer to the mayor. "We'll look like not just the natural, but, the *only* choice for the Senate or Albany, whichever opens."

The mayor flipped through the proposal. Nancy tried to remain confident but could feel a trickle of sweat run down her temple.

"Go on," the mayor said without any tone of approval or disapproval.

"Mr. Lee also has two friends that we can approach with operatives, I know that they want Mr. Lee to run, so we can exploit that. The first man is Seamus Corrigan, fifty-two of 223 Hudson Street on Liberty Hill. Mr. Corrigan is Mr. Lee's closest friend. Mr. Corrigan immigrated from Dublin, Ireland in 1984 and started working at the Chrysler plant that closed a few years ago. I've already sent feelers out to our friends in Homeland Security to check on his status, to make sure he is here legally. He took the offer of the early retirement package a few months before the plant was closed and his current source of income is his pension. He does odd jobs for Mr. Lee. He is not married."

"The other close friend we can approach is Vincent DiPietro, fifty-three of 1010 East Avenue, Liberty Hill. Mr. DiPietro also worked at the Chrysler plant and is retired and drawing a pension. Mr. DiPietro is married to Katherine O'Hearn DiPietro, she's a nurse at University Hospital. They have three grown children. Mr. DiPietro also does work for Mr. Lee."

The mayor turned in her chair, facing away from her staff, she disappeared behind the big executive chair. Her disembodied voice resonated in the conference room.

"Carter, do you have something better?"

Carter mumbled without answering.

"Then we go with..."

"Nancy Elliot."

"Ms. Elliot's plan. I want daily updates until I see Mr. Lee on the news announcing his candidacy. Carter, make an appointment with Turnbull, he's the Governor's contact on development funds. I think it'll be fairly easy to get state and federal funds for public housing. The Governor will love that we are developing that property, yes, I like this idea. Thank you everyone, please leave except for Carter, you stay."

The room emptied quickly; Nancy smirked at Carter as she walked by him on the way out.

"Carter, what impact would this have on the special funds?" the mayor asked once they were alone.

"The school has asbestos, so the abatement alone with the union contractors would be in the seven-figure range. The governor would give us the regular fee from the federal development funds, filtered through the construction union or the minority general contractor. This could be bigger than the other projects."

"Excellent, Carter, make all this happen," the mayor said turning again to the wall.

CHAPTER 2

QUINN'S

QUINN'S WAS a real Irish bar, cozy, with dark wood and polished brass, not the corporate Paddy McFunsters that pass as an Irish bar in most cities. It occupied a prominent corner in the Liberty Hill neighborhood in Genesee that up until the 1960s was exclusively Irish. They knew how to pour a proper pint at Quinn's and only Catholic whiskey was served. Ordering a Bushmills would only get you a history lesson.

Over sixty years of pictures of the bar's patrons and scenes from the neighborhood covered the walls. On another wall was a map of Ireland with pins in the towns that sired the ancestors that braved the ocean and ended up in Genesee to work in the factories, dig the canals, and fight the nation's wars.

Just as Nancy had outlined, Mike Lee's inner circle consisted of Seamus Corrigan and Vince Di Pietro. They served him as advisors, part-time help, occasional bouncers and were also his eyes around the neighborhood.

Rounding out Mike's team were two guys who also

worked at the plant before it closed. John "Murph" Murphy, was short and round, with reading glasses always perched on the end of his nose as he read the daily paper, making sure to editorialize on the news, especially local politics. He tried his best not to look like he was a blue-collar guy by wearing a tweed jacket and cap, but he never fooled anyone.

Pete Piontek was the last member of their group. He only had a few years at the plant before it closed and now worked at a Sears Automotive Center at the mall. He was about thirty years younger than the other guys, but they adopted him as sort of a mascot once his sister started coming to the bar. If you asked any regular to define the term "smoking hot" they would answer "Pete's sister" without a moment's hesitation.

When Seamus walked into Quinn's that evening, he took his regular seat at the corner of the bar where he could see everything, who was coming and going, and who was doing something that they weren't supposed to be doing. Before he could order his first pint, Pete and Murph accosted him with an urgent matter.

When Vince arrived, he was surprised to find his three friends huddled in conference and looking over their shoulders to make sure no one was eavesdropping.

"Who you planning to rob?" Vince asked as he pushed his way into the huddle.

"It's Mikey's 50th birthday and we wanted to throw him a party with gag gifts and maybe a stripper," Pete said in an excited whisper.

"Is your sister going to be the stripper?" Vince asked Pete.

Seamus laughed. "That would be a gift for all of us."

They both drew a malicious stare from Pete.

Murph brought the group back to their task, "We have to hurry, Mikey will be back from dinner with Helen any time. Now, I know a guy up on Morgan Hill that raises goats. We could buy one and plant him at the bar like he was a customer."

"Why a goat?" Vince asked.

"I went to a party, they had a goat, it was a funny gag, end of story," Murph said, annoyed at being questioned about his comedic ability.

"Well, I think we need a round before we can make any decisions," Vince suggested.

They broke their huddle which prompted Dave Moran, the part-time bartender and full-time city fire-fighter, to pour four pints of Guinness and bring them over.

"What's up, Davey?" Murph asked.

"Busy as hell at work, meth heads have burned down three houses this week cooking their shit. We have to treat the houses as a hazardous chemical site. It takes more paperwork per fire than it took me to get divorced from my first wife."

"That bitch," all the guys said in unison, as Dave had trained them to do at the mention of his first wife.

"I thought that problem was just out in the sticks," Vince asked.

"Nah, just in the past month it's moved into some vacants here in the city, there's so many empty houses that they can practically cook the meth in plain sight."

"This fecking city is going to hell," Seamus added.

Murph cleared his throat and rapped his knuckles on

the bar. "Screw the meth cooks, we have a party to plan. Davey, what's the schedule like around Mikey's birthday? We want to throw him a surprise party."

Of course, the party would be held at Quinn's so Mike could reap the profits and not protest too much about the gag gifts and the ball busting he was going to receive all night. Davey confirmed a Saturday when he knew Mike had nothing else going on and helped the guys set their plans in motion. Word was passed of the details of the party and the strict rules of silence were put in place, that if broken would result in the wrath of Seamus and Vince.

Murph and Seamus secured the goat. They had to explain to the cops what the goat was doing tied up behind Murph's house when one of his old lady neighbors called in a complaint.

"What's with the goat?" the officer asked.

"That's me cousin Bart, he's just arrived from Dublin, he's a wee indisposed, jet lag from the trip ya know," Seamus said to the officer who was a regular at Quinn's.

"And what is the purpose of Bart's visit?"

"He's here for a birthday party. Tomorrow, Quinn's, starts at nine."

"Make sure you have him scrubbed and presentable then."

"Yeah, will do, officer, thanks for the advice."

Pete visited Barone and Sons Funeral Home at Seamus's suggestion that they needed a casket for a proper Irish wake. He talked his buddy Dominic Barone into letting him borrow one of the floor models for the night, all it cost him was his sister's cell number.

CHAPTER 3

THE MAYOR'S HIT TEAM

NANCY ELLIOT WAS GIVEN a team and a sizable budget from the City's Public Works fund for street repairs. They began a rotation of visiting Quinn's so that no one person became too noticeable. They were supposed to sit near enough to eavesdrop on Mike and his friends.

Nancy and Peter Gibbons were scheduled to go to Quinn's on Saturday night for their first weekend shift. So far, the team had made seven visits to Quinn's without anything being said about Mike and the mayor's race. Nancy was beginning to worry their efforts would become a complete failure, but the plan really hinged on when the mayor made the announcement about the public housing project on Liberty Hill.

They walked into Quinn's and saw that it was packed because there was a birthday party for Mike Lee. They were handed a t-shirt to put on for the party and luckily found a table near the door, not close enough to hear anything but at least they were in.

"Is that a goat?" Peter asked, pointing to the bar.

CHAPTER 4

BART THE GOAT

THE BIG NIGHT arrived and Mike was securely called away for an intentional water leak at one of his rental flats a few doors down from the bar. Murph was dispatched to pick up Mike's wife Helen.

Pete's sister arrived wearing a tight sweater and a very short skirt. Seamus took a five-dollar bill and folded it in half and started waving it in her direction.

"Seamus! She's not a stripper," Pete protested as he grabbed the cash.

"If you take my money, you have to dance," Seamus responded.

Pete stuffed the five bucks into his pocket, turned around, and shook his worthless rear end in Seamus's direction.

"Jaysus that's an ugly site, I don't know how you share the same genes as that sister of yours, because her arse and your arse can't be related."

"Put on your birthday shirts everyone," Davey yelled

over the crowd, saving Seamus from having to watch Pete do any more dancing.

The crowd donned their party t-shirts, even the goat. On the front was printed "Mike Lee - Memorial Wake". On the back was the bar logo, "Quinn's - A Fine Neighborhood Establishment since 1946". Since Seamus ordered the shirts, he added a line he was constantly trying to get Mike to adopt: "Where they all look good at last call."

Black banners and balloons decorated the bar. Gifts of all sorts were piled high on a big table in the corner. A poster-sized framed photo of Mike from a past St. Patrick's Day—where he looked a little worse for wear—sat in front of the casket, propped centerstage on the pool table.

The goat sat positioned in a chair in the middle of the bar and was given a dog bowl of beer to keep him happy. He lapped up bowl after bowl as Pete kept the refills flowing.

Donal Maroney, a Quinn's regular over the last thirty or so years and Dublin import, took the stool next to the goat. He put a drink chip in front of his neighbor and patted the goat's head.

"Here's a drink on me, welcome to Quinn's."

After five bowls, Seamus was the first to point out the obvious.

"The goat's twice the size he was before he started drinking."

It was true; all of the beer had distended the goat's ample belly to dangerous dimensions.

"He's starting to look like my first wife," Davey added.

"That bitch!" the bar responded.

"Let the goat have his fun, it's his only night out," Pete said. He poured another pitcher into the goat's bowl.

"That belly is growing three inches per bowl, the pressure from all the CO_2 in the beer, a few more pints and we might have a volatile situation here," Seamus laughed, using his fingers to gauge the goat's circumference.

Vince came through the front door and gave the signal that Mike was coming. As soon as Mike took one step into the bar a huge chorus of "Surprise" rang out from the crowd. The goat, scared by the noise, proceeded to defecate jellybean-shaped projectiles with surprising force, scattering the patrons' unfortunate to be near his chair. Unfazed by his faux pas, the goat resumed drinking from his bowl of beer.

Laughter rolled through the bar at the sight of the incontinent goat. Donal put another drink chip in front of his new drinking buddy. Murph went to get a broom.

Before Murph could get to the backroom, the door banged open again, loud enough for the crowd to turn their attention to the new arrivals.

Two masked, tweaking meth heads, burst into the bar, shotguns pointed. The sweaty men shook and screamed for the money.

"Open the register now!" they yelled in unison to Davey, who was closest to the register.

Seamus took a slight move toward the intruders with Vince a half an inch behind.

"Just calm down," Davey yelled from behind the bar, "I'll get the money and you can leave."

Time had stopped; no one breathed or made a sound.

Seamus made eye contact with Vince as he moved

another half inch toward the taller meth head. Vince nodded and made his imperceptible move toward the other.

Davey filled a bag while the robbers continued to yell for the money.

Mike located Helen. Thank God, she's off to the side and not in the line of fire, he thought.

The unbearable tension was suddenly shattered by the goat, when he let out an unearthly combination bleat and belch that shook the windows.

Meth Head One, closest to the cash register jumped a foot in the air. He barely got out a "What the f—" before he pulled the trigger and the bar reverberated with the concussion of a shotgun blast.

Blood and guts rained all over the room as the patrons hit the floor and dove under tables. People screamed.

Seamus took advantage of the chaos to grab Meth Head One, disarming him of the shotgun and any future use of his right arm.

At the same time, Vince took out Meth Head Two, but in the process, another shot rang out and hit the ceiling, showering dust and debris, causing more panic in the room.

Mike yelled through the confusion, "Call 911! Who's hurt?" He ran to Helen to make sure she was alright.

As the smoke cleared patrons wiped flecks of guts and spurts of blood from their eyes. The panic eased somewhat when the people realized they were not hurt and the meth heads had been subdued.

"Oh no!" Murph cried as he pointed at the bar.

Heads turned and a shocked groan resounded through the crowd.

All that remained of the one and only victim of the attempted robbery was a smiling goat head still lip deep in a dog bowl full of beer and four goat legs, scattered throughout the room. The rest of the goat had exploded when the shot gun blast hit his gassed-filled torso.

A nearby city cop, that had heard the shots, burst in.

"What the hell happened?" he yelled.

"Meth heads tried to rob us, they shot the goat, the goat exploded," Vince said as if it was a daily occurrence.

"Donal, you're hit," Davey yelled as he grabbed Donal's right arm to inspect the wound. "It's not bad, you're a lucky man."

Donal laughed and grabbed the drink chips from the bar, "I don't think you'll be needing these," he said waving toward the remains of the goat.

Mike tried to rally the stunned crowd as more cops arrived and dragged the meth heads out of the bar.

"It's all over everyone, thank God only one minor wound and no one else was hurt too bad... well, except the goat." He looked at Seamus, "what now?"

Seamus thought for a second and jumped up on a chair. "Do we know how to throw a fecking party or what?" he yelled.

The crowd cheered in response.

"A round on the house," Mike shouted to even more applause.

Seamus jumped down from the chair and grabbed Pete's sister, dipped her like he was Fred Astaire and gave her a long, deep kiss as the crowd shouted and clapped their approval.

"Somebody get a mop and some paper towels," Murph said looking at the remains of the poor goat.

"Seamus, we need a toast," Vince cheered.

Pints were handed out and glasses were raised. Seamus cleared his throat:

"There are many good reasons for drinking,
One has just entered me head—
If a man doesn't drink when he's living,
How the hell can he drink when he's dead?
So, here's to our good host and friend
May his years wear like a warm winter coat,
And may God hold him tight in His hand
So he won't end up like our friend here, the goat."

CHAPTER 5

THE PLAN STARTS

NANCY STARED at the chunk of the goat that had landed on the table while she fumbled in her pocket for her cell phone. The crowd was still in a panic and the police hadn't arrived but she saw that Seamus and Vince had subdued the robbers. Peter had his hand over his mouth, gagging as he tried to wipe flecks of goat meat off of his Mike Lee Memorial t-shirt.

She hit the number for her contact at Channel 9 and waited as Peter lost his battle with nausea and ran to the bathroom.

"Send a crew to Quinn's on Liberty Hill," Nancy said when her contact answered. "There was an attempted robbery and a shooting... well no *person* was hurt... a live truck, yeah that'll be great. Make sure the reporter asks about what the mayor is doing about crime and her re-election campaign... yeah, Turnstone is okay... no she doesn't need to know anything about our arrangement... Thanks."

CHAPTER 6

IN THE NEWS

THE CHANNEL 9 news truck showed up shortly after one ambulance left with Donal and another headed off with the meth heads. Mike saw the young reporter come in the door after Seamus finished his toast. Parts of the poor goat still clung to the ceiling.

"How the hell did they hear about this?" Mike asked Seamus who had also spotted the reporter and her camera man.

Helen grabbed Mike's hand.

"Sorry about all this on your birthday. Don't tangle with the reporter, you don't have anything to gain," she said squeezing his hand for emphasis.

Nancy was in just the right position to hear the reporter without being on camera. This was perfect she thought.

"You want me to get rid of them?" Seamus asked. "I still have another broken arm in me tonight."

"No, I have something worse. Murph, come here," Mike yelled to Murph who was still surveying the cleanup job for the remnants of the goat, which he felt responsible for, since it was his idea to bring him to the party.

"Where's the ladder? We have goat on the ceiling," Murph said. "Or do you have a power washer?"

"Don't worry about that right now, I have a more important job for you, do you want to be my spokesman?" He leaned in to whisper in Murph's ear as he pointed over to the reporter.

A smile grew on Murph's face, happy with what he was hearing, as Mike continued to talk into his ear. When Mike finished, Murph nodded to acknowledge he understood Mike's instructions about what to do with the reporter. He straightened his jacket and took a deep breath.

"How's my hair?" he asked.

Seamus laughed. "What's left of it you mean?"

"You look wonderful," Helen said as she shot Seamus a look of disapproval.

Murph ignored him as Mike gave him a thumbs-up. He strode over to the reporter like a man of importance as she and the cameraman were taking shots of the shotgun damage and the chalk outline of the goat.

"John Murphy, spokesman for Quinn's." he said, extending his hand.

The reporter put her microphone under her arm and with a shortened reach, offered her hand. Murph had to lean forward to meet her reluctant handshake.

"Lacy Turnstone," she said in an obviously practiced reporter's voice. "I'd like to speak to Mr. Lee, the owner."

"He's not available, I'm the spokesman," Murph asserted again.

"Okay, but we really want at least a short statement from him," Lacy conceded, "So, what happened here?"

"Well, two males in their twenties came into this establishment at approximately 9:30 p.m., carrying shotguns and attempted to rob the bar, but they were overwhelmed by two of the patrons. In the process of being disarmed they discharged their guns shooting a, uh, a goat that was sitting at the bar."

"A goat? Why was there a goat sitting at the bar?"

Murph started to answer but the reporter's phone rang and she turned to answer.

"Yeah just an attempted robbery... nah, one slight injury and the perps were arrested... well, a goat was shot... I don't know why there was a goat in the bar... Yes, I'll try to talk to Mr. Lee... okay, I'll call back if there's more."

She turned back to Murph. "Okay, just like you told it to me a minute ago. Mr..."

"Murphy, John Murphy."

She nodded to the cameraman who turned on the spotlight on the camera and hoisted it to his shoulder, he counted her down. She did not notice Murph's knees buckle slightly when he saw the camera lights turn on.

"Lacy Turnstone here on Liberty Hill at Quinn's Bar, the site of an attempted robbery that was thwarted by brave patrons. I have with me a spokesman for the bar, John Murphy. Mr. Murphy, can you explain what happened here this evening?"

Murph froze. Luckily, Mike and Seamus had eased up behind him to hear what was going on. Mike poked Murph in the back which broke the spell of the camera lights.

"Ah, well, there was a goat at the bar and naturally he

was drinking, we got him a dog bowl," Murph stammered. A typhoon of sweat broke out on his forehead.

"What about the attempted robbery, Mr. Murphy?" she said, obviously trying to salvage the interview.

"Two meth heads came in the place to rob us and we took them out, but they shot our goat."

Lacy Turnstone let the microphone drop to her side as she waved her index finger across her throat. The lights went dark. Murph stood blinking away the spots in his eyes.

"Now John," she said, her reporter's voice was replaced with the slow pacing of a grammar schoolteacher telling the student that just peed their pants that everything was okay.

"Now, John, you told the story to me soooo well when you first came up to me. Do you think you can do it exactly like you did that time?"

Murph nodded as he wiped his forehead with the back of his sleeve.

The cameraman redid the count and she lowered her head like an actor getting ready for a scene. The lights came back on.

Nancy's hopes were starting to fade that this would turn out the way she hoped.

"Lacy Turnstone here on Liberty Hill at Quinn's Bar, the site of an attempted robbery that was thwarted by brave patrons. I have with me a spokesman for the bar, John Murphy. Mr. Murphy, can you explain what happened here this evening?"

"Sure, Lacy," a now miraculously composed Murph said as he replayed his version of the attempted robbery.

Seamus took his foot off Murph's toes when Murph finished the story. Lacy turned to the camera.

"Just another night of drug-fueled crime in the Center City. This is Lacy Turnstone for Channel 9 News," she said enunciating her name and the station.

"That's it?" Seamus asked Lacy as she was checking her phone.

"We would have stayed for a live shot for the 11 o'clock news if anyone really cared about this kind of thing."

"So, the city is full of people cooking meth in plain sight, their customers are committing strong arm robberies so they can afford their product and that isn't news?"

"Meth is new to the city, it's still mostly out in the sticks, up in the north country, besides the city doesn't have the money to address it. The cops are busy cleaning up after all the gang shootings. So, for right now it isn't on the top of the list of local stories."

"As we hear it, the mayor is handcuffing the police and not letting them go in and clean up the crime," Seamus said, feeling his anger rise past where he usually let it go.

"So, Mister..."

"Corrigan, Seamus Corrigan."

"So, Mr. Corrigan are you a retired policeman? You think we should go back to the old days when Irish cops could beat confessions out of people and crack skulls to keep order? Was that broken arm on one of the suspects your handy work?"

"Where the hell did that come from?" Mike said, pushing Seamus aside to face the reporter. Helen tried to grab his arm but missed. "What do you have against the cops? All we did here was protect ourselves."

"Mr. Lee?"

"Yes."

"Great, you are the person I needed to talk to. Mr. Lee, do you agree with the mayor's position that we live in a more diverse city now and we need a different strategy with the police that is more cognizant of the cultural influences on crime?" she said without emotion as if she was reading prepared talking points from the mayor's office.

Nancy smiled and leaned in closer to the conversation. "What a load of horse shyte," Seamus said as he tapped Mike on the shoulder to show him that the cameraman had turned on the camera.

"I'm Mike Lee and I own Quinn's Bar and other businesses in the neighborhood. I care about the people that live here and I am tired of watching the city go downhill. And we have to sit here and watch mayor after mayor do nothing about it."

"So, Mr. Lee, you are not supporting Mayor Lerner in her reelection?"

"I didn't support her election. She has done nothing except pursue policies that look good in a college classroom but mean nothing to the people trying to earn a living in a city that doesn't care about them anymore."

"That's a strong statement, Mr. Lee. Do you think you are in the minority in your opinion? Mayor Lerner is running unopposed, so it really doesn't matter does it?"

"Her opponent was just another version of her. He wasn't a choice anyway," Mike said.

"So, what is the answer to the problems that you feel Mayor Lerner's current strategy is not addressing?"

Mike waved her off.

"Do you think you could do a better job of running the city Mr. Lee?"

"I most certainly could. I have more common sense in my big toe than the last three mayors have shown. They are doing the exact opposite of what should be done."

"Care to elaborate on what you would do as mayor Mr. Lee? Why don't you run since you feel strongly that the people of the city need a choice?"

"I'm not going to take anymore bait, or any more of this BS, Miss Turnstone, have a nice evening," Mike said as he turned away and walked back behind the bar.

Lacy stood there for a minute then waved to the cameraman to follow her as she started to walk toward Mike, who leaned against the back of the bar, drinking a fresh pint.

"Let's finish this Mr. Lee," she called out. "You seem to have a strong opinion about the mayor and I'm willing to put it on the air."

"I don't want that right now. Besides, you'll take it back to the station and edit it to make me look like the local idiot," Mike growled.

"This is your chance, Mike." She smiled, putting the microphone in front of Mike and giving a signal to her cameraman to resume shooting.

"Goodnight, Miss Turnstone," Mike said taking a long swig from his pint.

"Okay Mr. Lee, it's your place and if you don't want to talk, that's okay. I'll take what I have back and edit it as you say. You can watch the morning news and see how it turns out. Thank you for talking and if this story has legs, I'll be back."

Mike walked over to the table where Helen had taken a seat during Mike's tangle with the reporter.

"I told you that would happen," she sighed

"Why didn't you hit me over the head with a bottle?"

"I think the reporter got more than enough; she didn't need more theatrics."

Nancy was still watching all the action. She got out her phone and texted her contact at Channel 9: *Keep Turnstone on this story she's perfect.*

CHAPTER 7

THE WRONG ANSWERS

"I DON'T THINK that anyone could have predicted a more eventful evening," Mike said as he sipped a glass of Jameson's after closing.

Seamus and Vince were still there, along with Pat Quilty, a city police sergeant that had joined them after his shift, having heard about what had taken place at the bar. They were discussing why crime was getting worse, especially the actions that the mayor had taken to handcuff the police.

"Almost everyone on the force hates her," Pat said after Mike asked him about the state of the department. "Her policies were implemented to 'address systemic inequities' in the city, but what they really did was to provide the criminals throughout the city with every excuse imaginable." Pat used air quotes for "address systemic inequities."

"They know how far they can push us before we have to react and it's pretty far. We have to stand there and take it. It doesn't matter if it's trailer park meth heads from the sticks cooking on the west side or gang bangers on the south side. We have to file a hundred-page Department of Justice report anytime our total arrests exceed the racial profile of the city. That means we are filling that out every week."

"So, you guys are doing paperwork instead of police work?" Vince asked.

"Yeah, and the worst part is we have to let people do things that would have gotten them arrested in any common-sense way, but now we have to let them scream in our faces and pound on our cars. We actually had to sit in a classroom and listen to some consultant, that has never worn a badge, say that they aren't criminals at all, they have been exploited by an unfair society and therefore weren't responsible for their actions. To reduce crime the police have to embrace this fact. The worst part is that she volunteered to do all this with the Justice Department. There are rumors there are FBI agents here too, don't know what for but there are Feds everywhere."

Pat sounded like a beaten man.

"And once you guys do this, crime was somehow going to magically stop?" Mike asked.

Pat just laughed and shook his head. "I just have five more years until I retire, I'm going to keep my mouth shut and take it. I can't do anything else at this point."

"So, she doesn't care about the increase in crime?" Seamus asked.

"Well, actually the crime rate is down because in some neighborhoods the people know it is useless to even report some crimes. No report, no crime, rate goes down. Or we can't arrest because of stats. No arrests, crime goes down," Pat laughed.

"You have to be kidding me? Ray Charles can see that crime is worse," Mike said standing up and walking over to the window as he looked out into the street.

"Can we start a neighborhood watch?" Vince asked.

"You can, but you'll have to be careful about why you call us. If you call us for a suspicious person and it turns out to be nothing, then that person can claim harassment or profiling. Then someone from a TV station or the paper does a story about you being crazed vigilantes."

"So, what about what you said to the reporter Mike?" Seamus asked. "Are you serious about possibly running for mayor? You know we all think you should."

"I would if I thought I could win. But I don't have the money she has; I don't have the machine she has. And she can use that machine in a lot more ways than just winning an election. But it does piss me off that the other guy dropped out. He wasn't going to win but he was better than nothing."

"Well, let's forget all that shyte. Mikey, that was quite a birthday. And the best part was that kiss I had with Pete's sister. I haven't felt that much of a tingle since I went under Molly O'Brien's sweater behind the playground back in Dublin."

They all laughed at Seamus' joke as Mike passed the bottle for another round.

"Is it time to sell the bar, cash out and move to Florida?" Mike asked.

"If you do, you'd have half the neighborhood follow you. You'd have to buy a pretty big house," Vince added.

"We aren't going to solve this tonight, so finish your drinks boys and we'll see if we can all make the walk home without getting mugged," Mike said draining his glass.

CHAPTER 8

NANCY GETS TO WORK

NANCY COULDN'T WAIT until Monday to start the next step of her plan, she had to take advantage of the gift she was given from the strung-out meth heads. She called the contact at the *Genesee Herald.*

"This is Nancy Elliot from Mayor Lerner's office. I wanted to give you a heads up about a potential story. And this is completely off the record, no one needs to know this came from me. Make it good and we will think about something above the standard fee."

"Since when are you calling the shots from City Hall?" the contact asked.

"That doesn't matter. Do you have anyone working a story on crime currently?"

"Crime is an everyday story."

Nancy ignored his comment and told him about what happened at Quinn's and Mike's statements about the mayor.

"This part has to stay confidential; it didn't come from

me and the reporter can know but not too much. Mike Lee is thinking about running for mayor."

"Why? He'll lose by eighty points."

"It doesn't matter, we would like him in the race, so your reporter needs to know that he should try to subtly push him in that direction if possible."

"Sure, her running unopposed is boring, we'd love to see even a patsy like Mike Lee in the race."

"Do what you can and we will be very appreciative."

CHAPTER 9

MORE REPORTERS?

WHEN MIKE WOKE he went downstairs and joined Helen in the kitchen to watch the news. His head was pounding a little and of course Helen had the coffee ready. He was on his second cup when the story about the robbery began. His cup waited an inch from his lips as he watched Lacy Turnstone wrapping up a commentary outside the bar where she had almost taken his side, she was *almost* a little bit critical of City Hall for not doing anything about the city's current meth problems. He let the cup meet his lips for a second then laughed to himself. "I'll be damned. She didn't edit it to make me look bad."

"What's that sweetheart?" Helen asked.

Before Mike could answer Helen and enjoy his small victory with the local press, his cell rang.

"Mike Lee."

"Hello Mr. Lee, I'm Devan Piersky from the *Herald*. I saw you on Channel 9 this morning and I wanted to talk to you about possibly doing a story on crime in the city, from the perspective of a businessman."

"How did you get this number?" Mike asked, annoyed by the intrusion.

"Another reporter that covers City Hall gave it to me, do you want me to ask him where he got it?"

"No, Mr. Piersky, no need. Are you calling so your paper can do another story about the drunken Irishmen of Liberty Hill, I almost liked the line that we lived in an 'all-white bubble from the 1950's.' I'm sure the term 'Neanderthals' was debated in the editorial room."

"Mr. Lee, I didn't have anything to do with that story and as I remember, I disagreed with its publication at our staff meeting."

"Be that as it may, I really don't want to talk to anyone; I said everything I needed to say to the reporter last night."

"I was actually doing a story on the meth epidemic in the city," Piersky said, hurrying his tone before Mike could hang up. "I started the story and when I saw you on the news. I just thought you could add a dimension that would really show the impact of this new local crime element on businesses, especially now that it has impacted you personally."

"You know I have a business phone number and I can be reached at Quinn's, if I'm not there, you can leave a message. Right now, I'm trying to enjoy my coffee."

"I apologize, Mr. Lee. Will you be at Quinn's today?"

"I'm at Quinn's almost every day, I can't guarantee that I'll have anything to say even if you get me. Good day, Mr. Piersky," he said hanging up.

"Who was that?" Helen asked.

"Another reporter. What have I started?"

"I don't know, but be careful," Helen warned.

CHAPTER 10

OPERATION GOAT

THE MAYOR OPENED her email titled "Local News" and watched the video of Mike's interview on Channel 9. She calmly let Mike disparage her approach to crime and his statement that he could be a better mayor. She closed the file and called Carter and Nancy into her office.

"Ms. Elliot, is this story with Mr. Lee I just watched part of your plan?"

"No Madam mayor, but I think we can exploit what happened on Saturday. It actually has moved up my time-line to get him into the race by a couple months."

The mayor nodded and turned back to her laptop. "Carter let's have some fun with Mr. Lee. Have the

Health Department do an inspection and call our contact at the State Liquor Authority and find out when his license is up for renewal. Put someone on this to keep a close eye on the bar. Rotate our compliance people through his business and see what's going on. None of that will interfere with your plan Ms. Elliot?"

"No Madam Mayor, it will actually help. I think if you

get him mad it may goad him into running out of spite. I was actually counting on that as part of the plan to get him into the race. After the attempted robbery I think we should start that now. We need to have the news conference as soon as we can announcing the public housing project to really get him mad at us."

"Well Ms. Elliot, I think you will see that I am very good at making the people I don't like mad. Carter, when is the meeting with Turnbull?"

"Next week Madam Mayor, he'll be in town," Carter confirmed.

Nancy knew Turnbull would mean a lot of closed doors and meetings she wouldn't be invited to join. The thought ran through her mind that the mayor might be using her, but she dismissed it and tried to remain focused on Mike Lee.

CHAPTER 11

PIERSKY ARRIVES

PIERSKY SHOWED up at 2 p.m. just after Mike walked in to start preparing for dinner and the evening patrons.

"Devan Piersky, *Genesee Herald*," said the short man reaching his hand up to Mike.

Mike expected someone older. Piersky looked like he was in his early thirties. Mike shook his hand after looking at it for a second.

"Might as well get this over with if you're going to just show up, why don't we sit over at a table. Do you want a beer, Piersky?"

"No thank you, I don't drink."

"Of course, you don't," Mike said, regretting his decision to talk to Piersky.

Mike walked him to the table that he used for all meetings and where he sat with his friends when he wasn't working. He took his regular seat and Piersky sat down on the opposite side of the table.

"So, Mr. Lee—"

"Since I can't get rid of you, you can call me Mike."

"Mike, let me tell you about my project."

Piersky launched into a description of what he wanted to accomplish in writing about the growing crime in the city. He talked long enough for Davey to bring Mike a pint and for Mike to finish it before Piersky stopped to ask a question.

"So, Mike, you have lived in the city all your life?"

"Born at St. Joseph's, brought home to the same house I still live in. St. Patrick's from kindergarten all the way to high school graduation. Stayed home and went to St. Benedict's College and have been here, working in the neighborhood almost my whole life. I've seen Liberty Hill at its best when I was a kid and what it is now."

"And what is it now?"

"A neighborhood that is barely holding on. Every other house is owned by someone close to eighty. There isn't a young person with a good enough job to buy it once they pass on. So, I buy as many as I can afford, fix them up and try to rent to people that will not wreck the place and will be good members of the neighborhood. I don't make a profit on my rental properties, but I keep buying them, just to keep landlords out that wouldn't care."

"Would you consider yourself the reason Liberty Hill hasn't suffered the same fate as the other working-class neighborhoods, say on the northside, that were unable to stay stable as the city has lost jobs and population?"

"I'm a very small part." Mike sighed. "I have friends that help me keep the properties going. The fact that Quinn's is a city institution helps a lot. We try to make the bar more than a destination on St. Patrick's Day and the Irish Music Fest. We have live music and we try to create a welcoming atmosphere, like a pub in Ireland, where the neighborhood gathers to meet and talk, not just drink. I try to talk to everyone who comes in. I try to get to know them, at least a little, and make them feel at home."

"So that they will come back?"

"More so that we have a community. Like I said, we have people that come in just to talk or listen to the music. A lot of people come in for the comradery. If you come in and take a table, you won't feel pushed to buy a drink, or hurry and finish eating so the waitress can turn her section."

Mike looked around the bar he called home before continuing. He breathed every inch of Quinn's; it was as much a part of him as his blood.

"You'll be more likely to have someone ask if they can join you and strike up a conversation, if you are sitting alone or if you are new to the bar. That is the atmosphere that we have built here and I would defend, Quinn's, the neighborhood, with everything I have because it keeps me alive."

"So, how do you feel when drug addicts try to rob you? Where they could have possibly killed someone?"

"Isn't that obvious? Those punks were robbing my family. Not of money, but of safety, they were attacking everything Quinn's is about and that's worse. If people don't feel safe, they won't come here. They won't rent my flats. They won't patronize my businesses or the businesses I rent to in my commercial property. That's just the business side. On the personal side, I know everyone within a five-block radius. I knew their parents, most of their grandparents. I saw their kids christened. I helped plant their family in Assumption Cemetery. They are my family."

"This is about money then? Because if all of that happens, then you don't make money," Piersky asked, flipping to a new page in his notebook.

Mike leaned in closer. "Mr. Piersky, you aren't listening. I do all that I do to keep Liberty Hill a neighborhood, not to just make money. I've had high six figure offers from national chains for Quinn's alone. I could sell what I could and head to Florida for an easy life, but then Liberty Hill would be just like the other neighborhoods in the city. But the people you see here in the bar, the people out in the neighborhood, as I said, they are my family."

Piersky looked at Mike again without saying anything.

"Do you have enough, Piersky?" Mike asked.

"We haven't really even started," Piersky said, pulling out his phone from his messenger bag. "That was so I would know what questions to ask you for the article. If you don't mind, I'll record what you say and I'll send you a copy so you won't have to worry about being misquoted."

"And what's in it for me?"

"People need to hear your story, Mike. I think if they do, you'll be surprised at how much support you would gain."

Mike thought he detected Piersky's tone shift from detached reporter to advocate.

"What do I need support for, exactly?"

"Because the people who run this city don't care about you or your friends anymore. You are just a tax base for their glamorized programs that they think are saving the world, with their over-the-top, self-righteous caring. They love you because you will never leave, no matter how much they raise your taxes and no matter how their programs never accomplish anything. You vote against them but there aren't enough of you to make a difference and they know it. So, they ignore you, because to them, you are irrelevant."

"Stop sugarcoating it, Piersky." Mike laughed. "You don't sound like a member of the press. What's your angle?"

"It's getting tougher every day to stay a member of the press. We don't make waves because we'll get shut out of local politics. We don't listen to people like you or tell your story, because as I said, you are irrelevant. Now, if you have the time, this will take a few hours to do it right."

"Okay, Piersky. I'll talk to you. Just because I'm curious." Mike waved to Davey for another pint.

"Good, because I needed to get in your good graces to ask you this next question."

"Go ahead Piersky, you're dug in like a tick now."

"I hear a rumor that you are considering running for mayor."

"Did you hear that from that reporter from the other night? She's a nice girl, but she doesn't know what she's talking about."

"From her and from others. Rumors get around the city faster than you would think. Between me and you Mike, it makes me sick that the mayor will run unopposed. No one is keeping her honest. The press certainly isn't at this point."

"And you think me getting my head handed to me, spending a lot of money that could go to better things and possibly pissing the mayor off so she makes my life miserable with the forces of city government at her disposal? Well then, sign me up."

Piersky looked down at his notes.

"Well Mike, I'm from a little town outside of Cooperstown. I got a job with the *Herald* right out a college even though I planned on going somewhere else. I don't have many reasons to stay and if Genesee doesn't start showing some signs of life, I'm going to pack it in."

"Join the crowd, Genesee had a population of almost two-hundred fifty thousand when I was born, it'll probably be under one-fifty when they do the next census."

"So do something Mike."

"I told you everything I'm doing here on Liberty Hill."

"You're right Mike, I won't bring it up again. But the city needs someone like you, maybe not as mayor, but if you were cloned and placed in each of the neighborhoods, more progress could be made than a thousand politicians could accomplish. Maybe the next Mike Lee on the south side or north will be inspired by your story."

"You're dreaming. What you said may be true Piersky, but the rest of the city has no idea that I exist."

"That's what I'm here for."

"I think you are overestimating the readership of the *Herald.*"

"We'll see Mike, we'll just have to wait and see."

CHAPTER 12

SUNDAY PAPERS

THE PICTURE in the *Genesee Herald* for Piersky's big article was of three young men in handcuffs bent over the trunk of a police car. Mike opened the Sunday paper and scanned for his name. On the third page of the front section he saw the paragraph header, Local Business Impact. Two paragraphs down he saw his name and began reading. Piersky used a lot of what he had said. He didn't take any of Mike's quotes out of context and he didn't editorialize. When he flipped the page to continue reading, he saw the picture that Piersky had taken of him leaning on the bar, it wasn't half bad he thought, trying not to smile.

Mike got his phone, saw that it was just a few minutes past seven in the morning and called Piersky.

"Hello Mike," Piersky said in an unused voice.

Mike smiled knowing he had woken up the reporter. "You did a great job with the article; I won't have to send my friends to beat you up."

"You woke me up to tell me that?" Piersky asked, his voice a little clearer.

"I thought you'd want to know."

Piersky coughed a couple times to the side of his phone before he replied.

"Well Mike, you tell a great story. There was no reason for me to change anything. Did you like the rest of the article?"

"I haven't read it all yet, just the part about me."

"Do me a favor and read the entire article. I'm hoping to get a reaction from City Hall and I may want a quote from you with a reaction to their reaction."

"Where does this all end then?"

"It doesn't, you should know that. The mayor will come out with some stupid program, probably some educational program for the police that shows them that all the crime is really their fault because their mere presence in the neigh-borhoods causes people to feel oppressed and lash out."

"I know you're joking, but you know what you said is probably not that far from what she'll end up doing, and that's the real problem." Mike sighed.

"This city has turned me into a cynic. I used to believe in all the same things that the mayor does, but they just don't work. Now can I go back to sleep?" Piersky asked.

"What made you change your mind?"

"A lot of dead kids and lives that have no chance. Kids having kids, human beings that have little to no chance of having any kind of life. You don't keep seeing them as I do with my job, the never-ending cycle of poverty and violence and it's getting worse, not better. It's almost all over the city, regardless of race, it's the same pathology of failure. After a while you really want to see the killing end, the neglect, the abuse and it just keeps getting worse."

"Well what a great start to the day, thanks for the cheery thoughts. Go back to sleep, Piersky. I'll read the entire article over coffee and my bagel."

"Thanks, Mike, my editor didn't push back like I thought. I have a million conspiracy theories on that alone. I'll call you if I need you. When I need you. The mayor will be all over my article before lunch."

"I'm sure you will Piersky. I'm sure she will too."

CHAPTER 13

STEP TWO

CARTER CALLED Nancy into his office twenty minutes before they had to brief the mayor.

"So, what's the plan," Nancy asked, even though she had her own plan on what to tell the mayor.

"The mayor comes out acknowledging that the economic disparities caused by institutional racism in the system are the real issues that need to be addressed and that the article was naïve and lacked a deep understanding of the causes of crime. She's already met with the governor prior to the article and she had already obtained funding for and inclusion for Genesee in a study on how to combat racism and poverty being conducted by the University of Albany."

Nancy turned toward the window, hoping that Carter wouldn't see her smile. She knew that was exactly the type of non-response that would get Mike Lee even more fired up about his conviction that the mayor was doing nothing about the problems in the city.

"I think that's great. The mayor will love it. She's

already committing to addressing the issue and has found the solution even before the paper found that the topic was worthy of a six-page in-depth report."

"Good, I'll see you in her office in fifteen. Let me do the talking," Carter instructed as she stood to leave.

"How about we have the press conference up on Liberty Hill, that's where all this started."

"Yeah, we could do that, good idea, rub it in that bartender's face. The mayor will love that."

"One more thing," Carter said as Nancy was about to leave, "call this number at the City Health Department and tell them the we got an anonymous tip about our friend on Liberty Hill."

Nancy laughed, "again, aren't we overplaying our hand?"

"Don't you want him to run?"

"Yes, of course, but I want to be in on these decisions."

"Don't overplay your hand Ms. Elliot," Carter said waving her out of his office.

CHAPTER 14

HAZMAT SUITS

MIKE'S PAYBACK for badmouthing the mayor on television and in the paper showed up right before Quinn's was going to open up for lunch. A van from the City Health Department pulled into the parking lot and three municipal employees got out in hazmat suits. One person started to roll out yellow tape around the bar as the other two went inside and found Mike.

"We had an anonymous report of a hazardous chemical spill that we have to investigate," he explained in a voice muffled by the respirator he wore.

Mike thought for a second about throwing them out, but he knew he couldn't fight this one.

The bar was evacuated as the health department set up monitors and began removing various objects in sealed biohazard bags for show. Mike realized who the show was for when two remote news trucks showed up for a live shot at noon of Quinn's sealed off and workers in suits acting as if someone was at the bar with a raging case of Ebola.

Of course, all of the live reports were pure conjecture

because there was nothing to report, but the pictures showed a shocking story, telling everyone in the viewing area that something terrible had happened at Quinn's.

After an hour of finding nothing and especially after the news trucks left, the health department packed up, giving Mike a report that nothing was found and a certificate of occupancy that he had to display on the front door for the next thirty days.

"Well that was for talking to the news," Mike said as he walked over to Seamus and Vince to let them know it was safe to go inside for a much-needed beer.

CHAPTER 15

HELEN QUINN LEE

MIKE SAT at the breakfast table watching Helen making him coffee, which he told her he was perfectly capable of doing himself, but she insisted. She was still the girl from high school that he climbed the bleachers to ask on a date.

If he was going to seriously tangle with the mayor would it impact Helen? Would the mayor go after his friends? They had a great life and it was only a few more years before they could seriously think about retiring. He needed to start grooming someone to take over the bar. Davey was ready if he wanted the job, he was set to retire from the Fire Department in two years. Mike's thoughts stopped racing as Helen placed the cup on the table and leaned in to kiss him. She was the best part of his life.

He thought about how lucky his life had been to this point. He had starred on the St. Patrick's High School basketball team, leading them to the 1983 county championship in the waning years of the Parochial High School league. Each neighborhood had their own Catholic high school and St. Patrick's had been the doormat of the league until Mike and his friends entered their freshman year.

They had been playing together since they could hold a basketball. They knew who was going to cut to the basket, when someone was going to go to the corner and could pass to the spots, they knew from years of playing together where they would be on the court. By their senior year, they were undefeated and on their way to beating St. John the Baptist by fifteen points to hoist the first trophy for the Gaels.

The entire school attended every home game for the championship season, cheering on their team to victory. Everyone screamed and went crazy with every score except a quiet sophomore named Helen Quinn. She spent the games in the very last row of the bleachers reading. Of all the wild fans, yelling and waving signs, the one-person Mike noticed was Helen Quinn.

Mike, at 6'5", was the tallest person in the school. Helen was 5'3", on the thin side, with curly red hair and to Mike she was the most beautiful girl he had ever seen. Every cheerleader in the school would have killed for Mike to ask them to the championship dance but Mike walked up to the top of the bleachers and asked Helen Quinn as everyone celebrated the victory.

"Would you like to go to the championship dance with me?" he asked as the crowd watched, pulled away from their celebration by his surprise trip up to the top of the bleachers.

Helen looked up from her book and blinked.

"I would like it if you'd be my date for the dance," he said again.

"You'll have to ask my father," she replied, still a little stunned by the invitation.

The next day after school he followed her to her father's bar to ask his permission. When Mike walked into the bar, he received a hero's welcome. The neighborhood men had followed the team closely and to them Mike was near royalty. There was no way Jimmy Quinn could say no to the school hero that wanted to take his daughter to a dance.

Helen's mom took her downtown to the best stores on Genesee Street to look for a dress. Jimmy had told them to "buy whatever you want, don't even look at the price tags."

When Mike knocked on the door of the Quinn house, he was ushered into the living room to wait with Jimmy, while Helen finished getting ready.

"You boys winning that championship was the biggest thing in this neighborhood since Jack Kennedy was elected president," Jimmy said as Mike glanced at his watch.

"Thank you, sir, it really was something special. I'm still having a hard time believing we did it."

"Well you know..." Jimmy started to say when his wife walked in.

"She's ready," Mrs. Quinn said as she held out her hands like a game show model.

Mike and Jimmy stood for her grand entrance.

Helen walked in a green satin dress, her hair was up in a coif and high heels that made her almost reach Mike's shoulder.

Mike was stunned by her transformation. She looked like a completely different person, a Cinderella like change. She had curves under her bulking school sweatshirt that he did not know existed. He handed the corsage out to Helen.

Helen looked up at Mike. "You're supposed to put it on me."

"Oh, right, sorry." Mike tried to open the box, that at this point was as secure as Fort Knox. He couldn't get the plastic open and was close to crushing the flowers.

Get a hold of yourself, you weren't this nervous in the game, he thought.

"Jimmy, can you get my camera while I help Mike with the corsage?" Mrs. Quinn asked.

Jimmy left the room as he was instructed, as Mrs.

Quinn easily opened the box.

The corsage was pinned and three packs of film in the instamatic later, Mike and Helen were in the car heading for the Knights of Columbus Hall on West Salina Street.

The beginnings of spring highlighted an unusually warm night for late March. The remnants of snowbanks lined the parking lot as Mike ran around to the passenger side to open the door for Helen.

He held out his hand to help her out and was surprised that she did not let go as they walked into the hall.

They found their seats at the head table reserved for the players and their dates. Mike pulled out Helen's chair for her to sit down. He had taken all the lessons in etiquette his mother had taught him and they had carried him well up to this point. Now he was sitting there with her and didn't know what to do next.

Helen spoke first. "They did a nice job with the deco-rations."

"Yes, they are nice," he agreed without looking. "The flowers are really beautiful, thank you again."

"Mrs. MacPherson at the florist helped me out, I had no idea what to get."

"Well, she did a great job in helping you."

The program started with the introduction of the players as each stood to cheers. Mike was the last one announced and with his name, the room stood and applauded.

Mike couldn't hide his embarrassment as he waved and smiled.

Dinner was served and as the night progressed their initial awkwardness faded. They began to talk about more than pleasantries and to Mike it seemed like they were the only ones in the hall. After dessert, the lights were lowered and the music started. Couples slowly drifted to the dance floor.

"Would you like to dance," Mike asked. He pushed his chair back and held out his hand.

"Of course," Helen said taking his hand.

They danced as the floor became more crowded with couples. By the time they slow danced to the Bee Gees' "How Deep Is Your Love," they both knew that they would be in love for the rest of their lives.

Mike wanted to kiss her right there on the dance floor but knew that would be frowned upon by the chaperones, so he bent down and whispered in Helen's ear, "Thank you for being my date."

"Thank you for asking me. What made you climb up the bleachers?"

"You," Mike said and squeezed her a little closer.

On Helen's front porch he waited for her to climb the steps while he stayed two steps from the top. They were face to face.

"Helen, I had a great time, would you like to do something tomorrow, maybe go get lunch or something?"

"I would love to; can you pick me up at noon?"

"Of course."

They stood there looking at each other until Mike finally leaned in and kissed her gently on the lips, then pulled back to make sure that it was okay to kiss her. She smiled.

"You can kiss me again if you want."

Mike kissed her again, this time with a little more pressure and he let it last a little longer.

They were together every day for the rest of the school year and into the summer. They spent a lot of time sitting in a booth at Quinn's doing homework and talking.

"Your coffee's getting cold," Helen said bringing Mike back to the present.

Mike smiled and took a sip.

"Helen, do you think we should start slowing down, maybe retire early? We could join Kit down in Florida. Maybe travel."

"You'll never leave Genesee and I wouldn't want you to. We can take a trip to Ireland, that would be great, but you need to stay put. What would everyone do without you?"

CHAPTER 16

CLINGING

THE PRESS WAS ASSEMBLED outside the old Grover Cleveland School waiting for the mayor. Murph had seen the commotion from his house and joined the small crowd on the sidewalk. A caravan of city vehicles pulled up, the staff getting out of the cars put on a show worthy of the Secret Service casing a scene before they let the president get out of the limo.

Carter tapped on the mayor's window signaling it was time for the mayor's grand entrance. He opened the door and pretended to talk into a microphone in his lapel.

Mayor Lerner walked to the podium waving to the cameras. She stepped up on the podium in front of the microphones set up by the local press.

"The way to confront institutional racism is to break down the barriers of the past represented by neighborhoods such as Liberty Hill. We need to teach everyone that neighborhoods are not just for one group but for everyone. To ensure that these lessons are learned we are taking proactive steps to do what people that hold on to the past will not do for themselves. That is why we are announcing today a project for the Grover Cleveland School. We are going to build this public housing project, intended for single mothers, to break down the walls of oppression and show the people that cling to their antiquated notions of justice and oppressive ideas that they will no longer be tolerated."

Murph stood wide-eyed as the mayor finished her press conference. Before the mayor could get back into her car Murph was running as fast as his middle-aged legs could carry him, up the street and heading for Quinn's.

CHAPTER 17

THE GERMANS?

MURPH STUMBLED through the front door gasping for air, his combover falling in a heap of sweat across his forehead.

"Where's Mike? I have to tell Mike," he wheezed between breaths.

"What is it?" Seamus asked.

"The school, its… its…"

Vince returned from the bathroom to the sight of Seamus holding up a sweaty, hyperventilating Murph.

"What's wrong? The Germans bomb Pearl Harbor again?" Vince teased.

"The school…" Murph tried to speak again. "Call Mike."

"This is what he's talking about," Davey said pointing at the television as he turned up the sound.

The guys watched the mayor's press conference in silence.

"All this because of Mike talking to the paper and that TV reporter?" Vince said.

"Murph's right," Seamus said taking out his phone, "call Mike."

By the time Mike got to Quinn's his phone was already ringing. It was Piersky.

"What's going on now, Piersky?" Mike said, sounding annoyed because that was now their routine.

"Just when you thought she was ruining the schools and the police department with bad ideas; the mayor is at it again."

"What now?"

"Well if I wasn't a cynic, I'd say she is going after you personally since everyone knows you are going to run against her, even though you refuse to realize that you are. That is why I wanted to get a react quote from you as an unofficial candidate and neighborhood leader, to a proposal the mayor just announced."

"Jesus, Mary and Joseph, that lady. The guys called me about something important, I'm sure it's the same thing. What is it?"

"It's part of what you signed up for Mike so get used to it."

"Okay, sorry, what is her highness going to do this time? Let's see, you want to talk to a neighborhood leader so she's going to double the property taxes in Liberty Hill?"

"Well, it definitely will make the neighborhood unhappy. You've heard a lot of rumors about what was going to happen to the old Cleveland Middle School. She's just announced that they are going to redevelop the building into over fifty units of public housing."

Mike closed his eyes and tried not to blame himself. "Mike? Still there?"

"It'll kill the neighborhood. People will leave in droves," Mike said, shaking his head.

"She already has the governor involved and there's a promise of Federal funds."

"We'll fight it with everything we have, there's my reaction."

"Since you are an unofficial candidate here's some unofficial advice. She's making this personal, she's building issues to hit you on once you announce. She needs an opponent to beat up on and you volunteered to stand up against her, remember?"

"Well I haven't made up my mind about running."

"I'm a reporter, I'm supposed to know things about what's going on. You're a perfect opponent for her, white male, rich by Genesee standards. You fight homes for poor people and she'll have even more to hit you with. She's pushing you so you fight back. That's what she wants."

"Thanks for the heads up. I'll talk to you later, sorry Piersky I know you're just the messenger," Mike said hanging up.

Mike walked into Quinn's as he put his phone away.

"I take it you already know?" Seamus asked, seeing the look on Mike's face.

"I wish I didn't, but I know."

CHAPTER 18
RUN, MIKE, RUN

"CAN we take a walk around the neighborhood?" Mike asked Helen after they finished eating dinner.

"Sure, what's wrong?"

"I just have a lot on my mind and I thought I could use both the fresh air and the company."

They walked a few blocks holding hands, Mike was still thinking and Helen was still waiting for him to say something.

"It's a lot colder than I thought it would be," Helen said, trying to get him started.

"We can go to St. Patrick's and get warmed up," Mike offered.

Mike had the keys to the front doors and the gym. Father Gualtieri made him a set for emergencies.

They went into the gym as Mike turned on the lights.

"How many memories are in this place?" he asked.

"More than anyone can count. What is it, honey? What's on your mind."

Mike was still lost in the memories that the gym held.

The winning baskets, hoisting the championship trophy.

Helen quietly stepped away and went up to the top of the bleachers, to the place where Mike had first asked her to the championship dance. When he realized she had left his side, he spun around looking for her, finally spotting her sitting in the bleachers. He climbed up and sat next to her.

"Helen Quinn, would you go out with me? I'm captain of the basketball team, a good guy and I think you are the prettiest girl in the entire school."

"You'll have to ask my father."

Mike looked up to heaven.

"Hey, Jimmy Quinn, can I date your daughter?"

Mike waited for an answer.

"I think he said yes," Mike said, turning to his wife.

"What is it, Mike? Is it bad news?"

"It could be."

"What?"

"Potentially, I mean, I don't know. Helen, I think it is a sacrilege that Lerner is running unopposed. And now the thing with public housing in the neighborhood. It's all because of me, my stupid pride. I think I should run against her. Just to give people a choice and maybe stopping the neighborhood from being ruined. She might try to ruin us too, but I think she underestimates how many friends we have in the city. I really think I need to do this."

"I think you need to run. I want you to run. I have wanted you to run for a while, but I wanted you to reach the decision yourself."

Mike smiled.

"I love you Helen Quinn."

CHAPTER 19

PARTY OF NONE

MURPH WALKED IN, looked over at Mike at the corner table, looked down at the ground, then continued to the bar and got a beer before heading over to join Mike.

"What's the verdict?" Mike asked as Murph sat down in a heap.

Mike had sent Murph out to talk to the Chairman of the City Republican Party, Wayne Garrett. Mike wasn't a registered Republican, but if he was going to run against the mayor and have any chance, he thought it would be important to have the backing of a party.

"No dice," Murph sighed.

"No consideration at all?"

"None," Murph said taking a long drink. "Garrett said that running a novice with no money of his own to put into the race, draining what little money they had in their election war chest was not going to happen. He said letting the mayor run unopposed was a better solution than backing you."

"To hell with them then," Mike scoffed but he knew

that without a party his slim chances became almost non-existent.

"He also said that they are still trying to persuade one of the few high-profile Republicans that are left in the city to run, just to show that they can still be a factor in city politics."

"So, if we go ahead and announce and the Republicans put up a candidate, all we can do is take half of their twenty percent. Our slim chance becomes no chance in hell."

"That's a pretty good summary," Murph conceded.

"Well, what do we do now?" Mike asked.

"If you run, at least you can get some press and try to squash the housing project."

"But she gets re-elected and the health department shows up once a month, our liquor license gets suspended and they build a nuclear power plant to replace St. Patrick's. No, if we run, we have to win, and if we don't win, we have to be close enough that she is at least a little afraid of us. But can we do that?"

Murph shook his head, he didn't have an answer for Mike.

CHAPTER 20

A FAVOR FROM PIERSKY?

MIKE HADN'T BEEN able to sleep through the night since he began his deliberations about running for mayor. Now that Helen had expressed her support for a run, Mike still needed one more piece of advice before he could fully commit. Everyone around him meant well, but he knew he needed to bring in someone who knew a lot about local politics, someone seasoned, who couldn't be bought or intimidated by the mayor. Someone who knew where all the bodies were buried in the city. That was an awfully short list unfortunately, since the mayor specialized in squashing people who weren't for sale.

Mike knew he had only one person who could give him this kind of information. He thumbed through the numbers on his phone and called Piersky.

"Finally calling to tell me you're in the race and you are going to give me an exclusive?" Piersky said without saying hello.

"Maybe, if you can do me a favor."

"Really? You want to owe me? You know that's not a great place for a politician to be in the debt of a reporter."

"I know, but I need a number and an introduction and you are the only person I know that can do both," Mike conceded. "I need to talk to someone."

Mike explained who he needed to speak with and why.

"Fine," Piersky responded, "If only to make the election an election and not a coronation, but you'll owe me and you cannot tell anyone I'm the guy who gave you his contact information."

"I thought you were the guys who couldn't reveal their sources," Mike said.

"Yeah, yeah, you politicians and the Constitution. Don't you know that the First Amendment has nothing to do with local politics, especially in this city."

"Can you help?" Mike asked, getting mad at himself because he thought he was coming off as desperate.

"I think it's a fifty-fifty shot he'll talk to you, but those are the best odds you'll ever see if you do this."

"Thanks, Piersky."

"Holy cow, I think you mean it."

CHAPTER 21

BRINGING IN A REAL MAYOR

MIKE CALLED a meeting of all the people he trusted, those whose opinions he wanted as input into the decision to run. Helen greeted everyone as they came into their living room. Extra chairs were brought in from the dining room, Seamus took a spot standing by the door.

Mike took his place in front of his friends and was about to start when there was a knock at the door.

"I thought everyone was here," Seamus said, alerted by the knock.

"I asked one more person to come. I wasn't sure if he would show," Mike said, motioning to Seamus to open the door.

Seamus did as he was instructed and there was a palpable breath from the group when former Mayor "Happy" Dan Halligan walked into the living room. Dan was now in his eighties and been the last mayor before the economy and the people started to head south.

Mike walked over and shook the former mayor's hand.

"Everyone, you recognize Dan Halligan. I reached out

to him earlier in the week because I thought he would have a unique insight into this decision and I want to thank him for helping us out."

Vince gave Dan his seat and joined Seamus by the door.

"Okay," Mike said with a smile, "Let's start with the pros of me running. Anyone can start."

"She's ruining the city."

"She's focusing on the wrong problems."

"She's arrogant."

"No, no," Mike stopped them. "I wanted the pros for me, those are the cons for her."

The group was silent for a moment.

Dan spoke up, "Because you love the city."

"Yes," the group agreed.

"You want to fix, instead of blame," Vince added.

"Because you will focus on the city and not promoting yourself."

"Yes, you won't spend all your time sucking up to the governor so you can get an easy six-figure state job when you are tired of being mayor," Murph chimed in.

"Good," Mike responded, "keep going."

"You can be the mayor for everyone, not just the people that get you headlines or the people that contribute to your campaign."

The pros kept going for a few more minutes until there was silence.

"Great, now the cons. Let me start. I don't have a snow-ball's chance." Mike laughed.

"It doesn't matter. At least you have the chance to make people think there is another way to run the city.

Even when... if she wins, she will have to change her governance with your new position. You will have the opportunity to be the official opposition, if you get at least forty, maybe forty-five percent of the votes," Dan said.

Mike stepped forward and shook Dan's hand.

"She'll make the race personal and go after you," Seamus added.

"She already has and I haven't announced," Mike responded.

"A Republican can enter the race," Murph said louder than he intended.

Everyone in the room turned and looked at him. The lively discussion came to a halt.

"I can make sure that doesn't happen," Dan Halligan said breaking the silence.

The room clapped as he acknowledged their appreciation.

"Okay, let's keep going then," Mike said, nodding to Dan in thanks.

"It'll be a lot worse and she may go after your friends, maybe even Helen," Seamus continued.

"That could backfire," Dan said. "How?" Mike asked.

"It would show her as petty, that the office was beneath her. You could use it against her in the press and in a debate, if she has the guts to debate you. And if she does something egregious enough, I will come out of retirement and condemn her in the press."

"You don't have to do that for me, Dan."

"I want to, Mike, I don't have anything to lose. I'm never going to run again. I live half the year in Florida. She can't get to me. I have thought a lot about this since you called me. I still love the city and it's selfish of me to sit on the side- lines, collecting my pension and watching how bad things are getting."

"Thanks, Dan, that means a lot. Your support will make a huge difference."

Mike opened the meeting to any other comments which went on for about a half hour until everyone had offered their opinion.

"Okay, then, I think I have everything Helen and I need to make this decision. Let me see a show of hands, remember if you vote yes, you will be in this with me every step of the way. Who thinks I should run?"

Mike watched as every hand in the room went up, including Dan and Helen's.

"Great, we will all be in this together then," Mike said, turning and smiling at Helen.

The group applauded.

"What should I do now, Dan?" Mike asked.

"I would wait to announce. March or April. If you announce too soon, you'll lose any momentum you get from the initial announcement. You announce now and she just has more time to go after you in a big way. It's a tough balance but you have to be patient. You can talk to people you trust but only people you trust. But be assured word will probably leak and that's okay too. Deny, deny, deny until you are ready Whether you are running will be a story we'll want to keep in the news until you really do announce."

"Thanks Dan, anything else?"

"Don't let anyone leave the house without writing you a check for the campaign, you're a politician now."

CHAPTER 22

PIERSKY IN THE KNOW

MIKE CALLED Piersky after the meeting and told him, just to make sure that he didn't find out from anyone else. Piersky was very excited at the news which unnerved Mike.

"You want me to lose and see the mayor ruin me Piersky?"

"No, I want you to run. First, I think it'll be a good story and second, I think you have a chance," Piersky chuckled.

"I know I can't win, so you can forget about that. I just want people to see that they can have a choice. Good night Piersky."

"There's something else I'm hearing that you should know."

"What now?"

"I heard they want you in the race."

"Then why are they going after me?"

"To make you pay for challenging her," Piersky admitted.

"I think politics is too confusing, I'm going to stick to drunks. Good night Piersky."

"Mike," Piersky said before Mike could hang up.

"Yes, I'm here."

"Mike, I need your word that no one knows I'm helping you. Not even your wife. This has to be between only me and you."

"You have my word."

"Okay then, thanks Mike."

"Secret meetings, informants, what else is there going to be."

"A lot more, just wait Mike, 'stiffen the sinews, disguise fair nature'."

"I hope you have a lot more than just Shakespeare Piersky. I'm going to need it."

CHAPTER 23

THE GOAT IS IN THE PASTURE

MIKE KNEW that word would get out, especially since he hadn't sworn everyone at the meeting to secrecy. They were prepared for that inevitability, as Dan said, "deny, deny, deny."

It didn't take long for Murph to burst at the seams and whisper to someone at the bar that Mike was going to run. Of course, Murph swore that person to secrecy which lasted all of an hour and a half , enough time for that person to have three more pints and whisper the secret to his friend that just came in and sat down.

Nancy found out from the person on her team who overheard the third person in line after Murph let the word out about Mike during their shift of spying at Quinn's.

Nancy heard her phone buzz and saw the text: *The Goat is in the pasture*

Mike was the Goat.

CHAPTER 24

SHARP DRESSED MAN

AS WORD of Mike's decision spread through the bar, Pete slunk in, still in his grease-stained Sears Auto Center uniform, sat down at his regular seat without saying hello to anyone, and asked Davey for a shot of the house whiskey and a Bud.

"Lose a patient during an oil change, doctor?" Murph asked, then laughed at his own joke.

Pete downed his shot and then directed his glare at Murph.

"Sears shutting down?" Vince asked, sounding concerned.

"No, worse," Pete said. He pointed to the shot glass, motioning to Davey who was still standing in front of him with the bottle of whiskey.

Pete downed his refill. "It's my mother."

"She sick, in trouble maybe?" Seamus asked.

"Worse, she's moving back to Genesee," he said and hung his head even lower.

"That's it? What's wrong with that?" Murph said,

coming back to the conversation after no one laughed at his attempt at a joke.

"She moved to Florida ten years ago. She was always on my case about doing something with my life, which I could take when she was a thousand miles away. Now she says she wants to be back home and I'll be getting the lecture every day."

"Oh, come on, she's just your mom and she wants the best for you," Vince said.

"She can't be that bad, by the way do you take after her or does your sister favor her?" Seamus asked.

"You can see for yourself in about a half hour. My sister is bringing her here to the bar."

At the mention of Pete's sister, with Pavlovian precision, Murph combed what was left of his hair with his fingers, Seamus tucked in his shirt, and Vince checked his watch to see if he had enough time to stay until she got there.

The guys spent the next thirty minutes alternatively drinking their pints, checking the clock and turning around every time someone came in the door, except for Murph. He watched the door like a polar bear waiting at the edge of the ice floe for a seal to pop his head out of the water.

"They're here," Murph finally announced with an adolescent crack in his voice.

They walked into Quinn's like the women in a ZZ Top '80's music video, in step and backlit by the afternoon sun. At least that was the scene playing in Seamus' mind as he watched Pete's mom walk into his life.

Pete's mom was a carbon copy of his sister, or the other way around, but the guys wouldn't have been able to answer that question if asked, they were thunderstruck. Pete's mom looked slightly older than her daughter, with a few extra curves that made her seem a lot more dangerous.

Pete's mom was wearing a tight sweater and a skirt even shorter than her daughter's, that showed off her long-tanned legs that stood out even more amongst the pasty and sunstarved native Genesseans.

Seamus was the first to break the spell of the shock of seeing Pete's mom.

"Seamus Corrigan," he said, extending his hand, "Davey, please get these young ladies whatever they want to drink and put it on my tab."

"Roxanne," Pete's mom said, taking Seamus' hand.

"Of course you are," Seamus said. He moved in front of his friends to block her view of them and stood there shaking her hand until Vince finally stepped in.

"I'm Vince Di Pietro," he said taking her hand from Seamus. "That guy there holding in his gut is John Murphy, the guy behind the bar with his mouth hanging open is Davey Moran and the guy who won't turn around, you already know, that's your son, Pete."

"Why don't we take our drinks over to a table," Seamus said as he retook Roxanne's hand and walked her over to the big corner table.

The rest of the group hesitated.

"He means all of us," Vince said, grabbing his pint and following Seamus.

They all took their seats while Vince walked back over to the bar and grabbed Pete by the arm and dragged him over to the table.

Seamus radiated in his seat between Roxanne and

Angela. Pete slouched in his chair, facing towards the bar, away from his mother. Vince alternated between watching Seamus try to be charming and Pete trying to disappear.

"Angela has told me all about this place," she said in a voice that sounded more like a purr.

"Angela?" Murph asked.

"Pete's sister," Vince whispered near his ear, "she's right on the other side of Seamus you idiot".

"Oh," Murph said as he reddened.

"So, Roxanne, what brings you back to sunless, cold Genesee?" Vince asked seeing Murph's embarrassment.

"Oh, I just want to be near my kids, maybe one of them will get in gear and make me a grandmother," she laughed.

The guys laughed in unison along with her.

"No one would ever believe you were a grandmother, even if your kids got themselves to the altar and procreated," Seamus said, patting Roxanne's hand.

"Oh, you're sweet," Roxanne said. She laid her hand on top of Seamus'.

"Procreated?" Vince whispered to himself.

"I have to use the can," Pete said, stomping off.

"So where are you staying?" Vince asked.

"I'm going to bunk with Angela for a while until I can find a job and get settled in."

"What kind of job are you looking for?" Vince asked. "Oh, I'm a hair stylist, just like Angela, so it should be pretty easy."

"Yes, easy," Seamus repeated.

Seamus waved at Davey for another round. Davey stood unmoved by Seamus' command, so Vince went up to the bar and got the drinks.

"Does she smell as good as she looks? And I don't appreciate being waved at like a servant, especially since I can't join you at the table. Have you ever seen Seamus like this?" Davey asked without waiting for answers.

"Never," Vince replied. "He's always played the field and has been happy with a carousel of girlfriends. This is something completely different, he looks smitten."

"Seamus? Smitten?" Davey shook his head.

"I'll start planning the bachelor party," Vince said and looked back at the table.

Seamus bought drinks all night and stayed with Roxanne even after Angela left because she had to work the next day. Pete never got out of his funk and no one noticed when he stumbled out.

Vince tried to stay, to keep Seamus out of trouble but his wife called and told him he had to come home. Murph tried to hang in with Seamus but he got tired of being completely ignored by the newly joined couple and finally left without either of them pausing from their conversation to say goodbye.

When Davey yelled out last call, Seamus and Roxanne were the only ones left in the bar.

"Well I guess we need to leave," she said with an exhale.

"I'll be walking you home safe then," Seamus said getting up and extending his hand as he had done hours earlier.

They walked down Kilkenny Street a few blocks to Angela's apartment, a two-family that Mike owned and stood looking at each other.

Seamus finally spoke.

"Would you do me an honor and join me for dinner tomorrow, can I pick you up at six?"

"Sure, that sounds fun."

She leaned forward and kissed him on the cheek.

"Goodnight, Seamus, thank you for a wonderful evening."

"Goodnight, Roxanne," he let her name linger on his tongue, "see you tomorrow."

He watched her go inside and loitered for a minute, waiting for the lights to be turned off before he headed back up the hill to his house.

CHAPTER 25

DEPARTMENT OF WHAT?

CITY HALL WAS a flurry of activity. The Governor was in town to join Mayor Lerner at a ceremony and press conference celebrating an award the city schools were getting from the Department of Education because of the dramatic turnaround of student suspension rates. Even the mayor's seldom seen husband was there for the photo op.

The schools had adopted the Department's program of "restorative justice" at the mayor's insistence, that was supposed to end the "school to prison" pipeline. Just as the police were responsible for crime, insensitive teachers were responsible for the record suspension rates of the students, as the program asserted. The thought was if the school administration and teachers understood the kids better and reasoned with them on why they were acting out, then an unruly student could stay in the classroom instead of being suspended and sent home. Suspending them for let's say, punching a teacher, would only take them out of the classroom so they couldn't learn, so it was better to keep them in the building.

The suspension rate in the city schools had gone from over thirty percent to less than ten percent. It was a miracle by government standards.

A functionary from the DOE handed a certificate to the mayor, who stood on the steps of City Hall so that she was at eye level with the governor, who was three steps below. A staffer had checked all the television cameras to make sure that the mayor's position on the steps was not visible in the shot.

The governor told the assembled crowd that Mayor Lerner was doing a great job and he implored other mayors and school districts in the state to adopt this "cutting edge" DOE program. Combining this program in the city schools with social justice programs like the public housing project in the Liberty Hill neighborhood was exactly the right plan to bring "fairness and to break down the old walls of oppression."

The mayor beamed as she took the podium and thanked the governor for sharing in this great day for the city and then proceeded to go through all of the city's accomplishments. She gave one of the best performances she had ever given before the cameras, hoping that at least one national network was going to run with the story.

When the ceremony was over, the governor and Mayor Lerner went into the back seat of the Governor's limo as all the staff pushed the media back. Carter could see the governor emphatically making a point with his hands as he heard the mayor's high pitch voice escaping the cracks in the bullet-proof limo. Carter winced, knowing there was going to be some unsavory mess for him to clean up later.

When the mayor exited the back seat she stormed

towards her staff. Carter exhaled when she went straight to Nancy and pulled her aside.

"I need an opponent in the election. I am on a roll and if I don't win big in November it'll all be a waste."

"As a matter of fact, I heard today that Mr. Lee met with his friends and is unofficially in the race. You have been so busy with the Governor I didn't have a chance to tell you," Nancy said savoring her victory.

"Good, I want to know right away when it's official and if any polls show him over forty percent, I want your resignation on my desk that day."

CHAPTER 26

HOOK, LINE AND SINKER

SEAMUS SHOWED up at six o'clock sharp, dressed in new clothes and sporting a haircut from Vince's cousin who owned a barbershop on the north side. He even took his truck to the car wash, going for the Pina Colada air freshener. He regretted his choice on the drive home because it smelled too "girly." He stopped at a florist and got a small bouquet of six red roses; he thought a dozen would be overkill. He didn't want to seem too easy, because he was.

He rang the doorbell and waited nervously for Roxanne to answer. After a minute, he rang again. He heard footsteps running to the door, but when it opened, it was Angela in a tank top and a pair of shorts.

"Is your mom ready?" he asked looking up at the sky to check for rain and not look too long at Angela's tank top.

"C'mon in, she's still getting ready."

Seamus followed Angela into the living room, checking the ceiling for water spots so he wouldn't notice Angela's shorts.

He took a seat on the couch.

"You should ask Mike for a window air conditioner, it's hot in here," he said feeling a bead of sweat run down his forehead.

"I'm going to go back and help my mom. There's beer in the fridge if you want one."

Seamus started to decline the offer of the beer, but Angela had already disappeared down the hallway. If he had been looking at her and not at the ceiling, he would have seen that she left.

After ten minutes of waiting he heard footsteps running down the hallway and this time he knew it was Angela again, probably to tell him that Roxanne had changed her mind about dinner.

"She's ready," Angela cheered with a bounce that had Seamus searching the ceiling again.

He heard the sound of high heels clicking down the hallway. He stood and held up the roses and waited. Roxanne emerged and without realizing it, he dropped the flowers to his side.

"Wow," was all he could say. He couldn't have imagined Roxanne looking better than she did last night when she walked into Quinn's, but she was stunning in a tight blue dress.

"Thank you. Are those for me?" Roxanne pointed to the roses.

Seamus snapped back from being stunned. "Yes, they are for you, just a little token."

"Angela, can you put these in some water please?" Roxanne asked.

"Sure, Mom," she said taking them from Seamus as he

held them out. He didn't have to look at the ceiling because his eyes were glued to Roxanne.

"You look gorgeous," Seamus said, extending his hand. "I got us reservations at Caroma's. It's not fancy but it's the best Italian food in Genesee. If that's okay with you?"

"Sure, that's fine. And you are looking especially handsome this evening."

"This?" Seamus asked, looking at his new clothes.

They walked out to the truck and as they did Seamus thought he should have borrowed Mike's Cadillac or even Murph's Chrysler. His date was barely eye level with the door handle.

He helped Roxanne step up into the seat, which was a little difficult given how tight her dress was and he didn't know where he should put his hands.

"Sorry about the step up," he said before he closed the door.

"Don't worry about that, I'm used to it after all those years in Florida, lots of pickups down there."

"Sure, sure," he said but he was still mad at himself for not thinking of borrowing a car.

On the drive to Caroma's, Seamus pointed out different places of interest and Roxanne made comments about how much the city had changed in the years that she had been gone.

"Yeah, there really are parts of the city that have gone to hell. We are trying our best to keep Liberty Hill from suffering the same fate. Since me and Vince are retired, we help out a lot of the older people keeping their houses in good shape."

"That's very nice of you."

"Helping out is just the way the neighborhood has always been. Everybody watching out for each other. Mike is really the one holding the neighborhood together. You'll meet him soon."

"Mike owns Quinn's?"

"Yeah, he owns a lot more than that. Me and Vince do a lot of work on his properties too."

Seamus found a spot right near the door and ran around to the passenger side to help Roxanne down.

"Do you mind?" Seamus asked holding out his big hands to show her that he was going to lift her down.

"Not at all."

Seamus grabbed Roxanne under her arms and she put her hands on his shoulders as he lifted her down. He was surprised at how light she was and the smell of her perfume made him swoon just a bit.

Seamus had called Frankie Gigliante earlier in the day, to make sure that he held the best booth for the date. There were fresh flowers on the table and a bottle of Caparzo Brunello waiting for them.

Frankie came over as they settled in.

"Seamus, good to see you, and who is this lovely lady that you brought with you?"

"Frankie, this is Roxanne, she just moved back to Genesee, she's been in Florida."

"Very pleased to meet you, Roxanne. Welcome to Caroma's. I have a special just for you guys, Veal Braciola Alla Cacciatora. I'll have Anthony come over with the house special antipasto and he'll open your wine. If you need anything just ask."

"Thanks, Frankie," Seamus said. "Wow, I'm impressed," Roxanne said.

Anthony brought the appetizer and opened and poured the wine for Seamus to taste.

"I have to thank Vince, he's the one who taught me all about real Italian food. I was a meat and potato guy forever, until Vince brought me here. Now I'm probably here once a week. Wait until you taste the ricotta Gnocchi."

The food started to arrive. Seamus explained what each plate was as Roxanne tried them with enthusiasm.

Seamus ordered a second bottle of wine as they slowly made their way through the amazing dinner. They shared a hazelnut torte for dessert, Seamus had a glass of Vin Santo and Roxanne had an espresso. They felt like they were the only people in the restaurant.

"Come here," Roxanne said, motioning Seamus across the table with her index finger.

When Seamus was close enough, she leaned forward and kissed him on the lips. Once lightly and then a second time that lingered.

"That was the best part of the meal," Seamus said. He settled back into his seat.

"Thank you for going all out, if you were trying to impress me, you more than succeeded."

"I'm glad, that was my intent all along. How about we go back to Quinn's for a night cap?" Seamus reached across the table and took her hand.

"That sounds lovely."

They held hands as they walked out to the truck.

Seamus lifted her into the seat without asking. As they drove back to Quinn's, Roxanne leaned across the seat and put her head on his shoulder. Seamus kept looking at her in the rear-view mirror to make sure she was real.

CHAPTER 27

THE OTHER HERALD

MIKE WALKED into Quinn's after having lunch with Helen. He grabbed the mail that was on the bar and flipped through the stack as he walked back to his office.

"Some reporter from the *Herald* called, he'll be here in a few minutes," Davey informed him.

"Piersky?" Mike mumbled.

Mike was already in his office and didn't hear Davey say, "no some other guy." When Davey poked his head in and told him the reporter was here, Mike walked out and scanned the bar for Piersky.

"Where's Piersky?" Mike asked Davey.

"Haven't seen him, but that guy is here to see you," Davey said pointing over to a table by the window.

Mike walked over, thinking the reporter looked more like a kid who was there looking for a job.

"Sorry, we don't have any openings right now," Mike teased.

"Excuse me?"

"I'm full right now, but I'll take your application if anything opens. Dishwasher, right?"

"Mr. Lee I'm Neil Myers from the *Herald*. I'm here to talk to you about your possible candidacy."

"What?"

"We are hearing that you plan to enter the race for mayor and I'm here to confirm those rumors and hopefully talk to you, ask some questions, so I can do an article for Sunday."

Mike laughed.

"I don't know what you are talking about, but if I was running it would be because the city's in bad shape and the current mayor isn't doing a thing about it. Actually, she's making it worse with things like that idiotic public housing project up the street."

"So, you won't confirm the rumors?

"Sorry Mr. Myers but you were misinformed, I would be happy to get you a beer, but I would have to see some ID first."

"No thank you Mr. Lee. We are going to run a story, so it would be better if we had some quotes."

"Sorry, that's all I have to say."

Myers thanked Mike and left the bar. Mike called Piersky to tell him about what had just happened.

"Sorry, I didn't know we were sending someone to talk to you."

"If you were on the payroll, I'd have to fire you."

"Very funny Mike."

"I'm going to keep denying for the time being, I really need to figure out how I'm going to announce," Mike said more to himself.

"The story they'll run will be full of conjecture. I'm sure they'll throw in stuff about you being unqualified and that you don't stand a chance. They'll throw in your opposition to the housing project."

"I wouldn't expect anything else from that fish wrapper of a paper you work for Piersky."

"I'll do the story when you do announce, and I'll be fair, but I can't believe I'm saying this, you need to do a news conference when you finally do announce."

"Piersky I'm shocked, my respect for you just went up a notch."

"You mean you now have some respect for me?"

"I guess you're growing on me."

CHAPTER 28

RUNNING?

THE HEADLINE SAID IT ALL, "Political Novice Running For Mayor – No Chance At All." The story was on the front page, below the fold. There weren't any quotes from Mike or anyone from the neighborhood. There were dozens of quotes from the political class of Genesee and the surrounding area, saying Mike had no idea what he is getting himself into by running against a successful mayor, with statewide support and the potential for higher office.

The article cited all the accomplishments of Mayor Lerner, all of which were reasons Mike felt she was beatable. They were all fake and meaningless. You could say that the schools had improved and crime was under control, but the people who were paying attention knew better. Mike knew he had to reach those people and get them to the polls.

Mike walked into Quinn's just before lunch and everyone in the bar had a paper in front of their faces. The headline on each paper had been changed to "Political Novice is Going to Kick the Mayor's ASS."

CHAPTER 29

OLD LADY BLUE DYE NO. 5

ROXANNE AND SEAMUS were inseparable from that first night at Quinn's. They went out to dinner a couple nights each week, had been taking day trips to Rochester and Saratoga and even a few overnight trips to New York City.

"I thought this would never happen to Seamus," Mike said to Vince as they looked at the happy couple spooning in a booth by the window.

"I'm surprised too, but very happy for him. I kind of had an idea that once he fell, he would fall hard," Vince replied.

"What made you think that?"

"Well, he resisted getting serious with almost every woman he dated. He would run for the hills at the slightest hint of a clinger. I knew once those defenses fell, it would be all over."

"So, what do you think will happen?" Mike asked as he raised his eyebrows because they were now making out like teenagers.

"She's moved in without him even realizing it. Oh, and I forgot he wanted to talk to you about the empty storefront on Emerson."

"What for?"

"He is thinking of helping Roxanne open her own salon," Vince said with a shrug.

"Actually, that's not a bad idea. There isn't any place in the neighborhood for the old ladies to go. If she buys senior lady blue dye number 5 in bulk, she'll be able to make a good profit."

"Well if he ever stops groping her in public, he'll probably come over and ask you about it."

"I can give her a good rent, that place has been empty for over a year. I'd rather have fifty bucks coming in than nothing. How much start up does she have?"

"More than enough from what Seamus told me. She already has a few of the other stylists ready to revolt at the place she's working now and of course Angela too. They will work for her if she opens something up."

"Well then, I think we can do this thing," Mike said impressed at how quickly they formed the business, even while the prospective owners were still in the booth making out.

"Wow, she's a natural businesswoman. Planned, financed and started a business, all while never coming up for air," Vince said as Seamus and Roxanne continued to kiss.

"Let me get some guys to clean the shop out. Maybe I'll have the entire strip redone and try to rent out the other two stores."

"Should we plan their wedding before they start taking their clothes off?"

"I've always been partial to a fall wedding, with the leaves changing and it's a little cooler so you don't sweat to death in a tux," Mike said as Murph walked up.

"Who's getting married?"

Vince nodded towards the happy couple.

"Mazel Tov," Murph said lifting his glass.

CHAPTER 30

BUILDING A NEIGHBORHOOD

DONAL MARONEY HAD SPENT NEARLY every day of the past thirty years at Quinn's Bar since he moved to Genesee from North Dublin. He worked construction but if you looked at him in his rumpled tweed jacket and cap, both of which seemed too big for his thin frame, you would never guess he worked a trade. He never married, although one time he mentioned a girl back in Ireland that he had loved. He came in around 7 and stayed until 10, slowly drinking his pints, as he became part of the décor like a framed picture of the "auld" country that no one noticed until it was taken down.

He paid close attention to the conversations and about once every few months he would actually say something witty that would surprise everyone and it would take a few seconds for people to laugh or agree. If the conversation had been about Irish literature, he would have talked all night. If Joyce had been brought up, Donal would have been on the edge of his stool, showing off his degree from Trinity that no one knew he had. Even if someone had mentioned Roddy Doyle, Colm Tóibín or Sebastian Barry, he would have perked up and given you his opinion about their novels.

But the conversations, were mostly about sports and when they weren't, they were about the dying local economy and the feckless politicians that the city seemed to hate but kept electing.

Donal didn't tell anyone what they found in his blood-work when he went to the hospital after catching a little buckshot in his arm when the meth heads ruined Mike's birthday party. He didn't say anything about the visits to his doctor and the weeks of tests that followed. No one knew that Donal had been given the worst news of his hard life, news that left him numb and reminded him of the day decades ago on St. Stephen's Green, when she said she did not love him and he decided to leave Ireland because of her rejection.

No one noticed for a few days that he was missing from the bar. Someone would come in and look around knowing something was out of place and after a few minutes would ask "where's Donal?"

When he finally showed up back at Quinn's he walked in and went straight up to Seamus who was reading the paper.

"Seamus, can I talk to you outside for a minute if you can spare some time?"

"Donal, we thought you packed up and went back to Ireland, sure let's go outside. How's the arm."

"Well my arm is grand, thanks for asking."

Seamus looked at Vince, furrowing his brow as if to ask, "what could this be about?"

Vince replied with a shrug.

They walked out into the back-parking lot that Mike used for overflow on big holidays like St. Patrick's Day.

"I'm going to die," he told Seamus without any lead-up.

Seamus, for once, was at a loss for words. Finally asking, "From the gunshot?"

"Nah, that was a scratch, but they found something else when I was at the hospital. I have a few months at the most. Cancer. Nothing they can do, really."

"Jesus Donal. Jesus. I'm sorry to hear that. What can I do for you? Anything, really," Seamus said placing his hand on Donal's shoulder.

"I don't have family here and for some reason the thought of my casket in an empty church is too much to bear."

"That's not gonna happen, Donal. I'll be there, Mikey'll come too, Vince, Davey, Murph and Pete, the whole lot of them."

"Seamus, if you ask people, they'll come."

"Aye, Donal, they will. I'll make sure the place will look like it's a holy day of obligation."

"One more thing," Donal started to say but his voice caught with emotion. He dropped his head and toed the gravel in the parking lot until he regained his voice.

"I want a proper wake the night before the mass and I would like for you to say a few words. I know there's not much to say about me, but I know you can handle it."

"Aye, don't worry about a thing, I'll take care of it."

"Here," Donal said, handing an envelope to Seamus. "There's five-grand in here for the drink and the food. I'm sure Mikey will let you use the bar. I have more if you think it's not enough."

"Of course, we can use the bar, Donal, but I can't take your money."

"I've no use for it now. I want everyone to have a good time, a grand affair. And if they don't remember Donal the man, maybe they'll remember the sendoff you gave me. I don't want a dry eye in the place if that's possible. I'm sorry for the imposition of putting this all on you Seamus, but I know you are the only man that could pull this off. It's selfish of me so I'm sorry and I'll understand if you say no."

"No, Donal, don't worry, I can do this for you. I know what it's like not to have my family around me. I know that the people inside are my family now and if I was in your place, I'd be asking Vince or Mike for the exact same thing."

"Thank you, Seamus. You're a grand man and I know the Lord will bless you for this."

"Well, at least he'll have one reason then."

Donal laughed, then coughed. When he finally stopped, he looked up at Seamus. "Let's go have a little Irish medicine, my treat. Doctor's orders."

CHAPTER 31

WARNING

VINCE AND SEAMUS were returning from taking the three widowed Gleason sisters to the Walmart in East Genesee, for their monthly drag race on the motorized carts through the aisles, without regard to the other shoppers. Vince and Seamus tried to keep up and shout warnings to anyone that didn't see them coming. The sisters were now safely in the back of Kate's minivan talking about something from their childhood. Each one had a different version of the story. The discussion had turned into an argument and Vince had tried vainly to calm them down by throwing out new topics for discussion. With the tumult in the back of the minivan reaching the decibel level of a busy night at Quinn's, Vince didn't hear the police car now on his tail, signaling with short blasts from its siren.

Seamus was also oblivious to the cop behind them, as well as the arguing old ladies, because he was busy sexting with Roxanne. When the ladies suddenly became silent, Vince looked in the rear-view mirror because he was worried that all three had simultaneously suffered a stroke and had all died in his care. Instead of lifeless widows he

saw that the ladies were looking out of the back window at the flashing lights.

"Was I speeding?" Vince asked toward the speedometer.

Seamus giggled, sounding like a schoolboy in love. Only when Vince put his hand over the phone's screen did Seamus realize that they were slowing down and pulling over to the curb.

Vince and Seamus stared in the rear-view mirror waiting for the policeman to get out of his car.

"Why were you speeding with these young ladies in the car? I hope we know this guy." Seamus said without taking his eyes off the mirror.

"FRONT SEAT PASSENGER, PLEASE EXIT THE CAR," blared from the cop's loudspeaker.

"That's you, boyo," Vince said laughing. "I wish I had known you were wanted; I would have turned you in for the reward."

Seamus unclicked his seat belt and opened the door. The sun reflected on the cop's windshield so Seamus couldn't make out who was in the car. He held his hands up because he thought that's what he needed to do and slowly walked back toward the police car.

"STOP THERE AND PUT YOUR HANDS ON TOP OF THE CAR."

Seamus did as he was instructed. He heard the door on the police car open and heard the officer walking toward him.

"That's Pat, why is he fuh, I am mean why is he

screwing with Seamus?" Vince said. The widows looked at him with disapproval after his almost use of the F word.

"Seamus Corrigan, you mick bastard, did I hear you are banging Pete's mother?"

Seamus took his hands off the top of the van and turned around.

"Pat? What the hell is this all about? I should kick your ass for scaring these old ladies."

Pat Quilty laughed and pushed Seamus back into the van, spreading his legs with his foot in the process.

"I wanted to make this look real in case anyone happened to drive by and see what's going on. If they see you in handcuffs, they'll think it's as natural as seeing fat ladies in tube tops at a country bar."

"What's going on, Pat?" Seamus asked struggling to stay serious.

"It's the mayor," Pat said, lowering his voice.

"Ah, Jaysus, what's that piece of work up to now?"

"She's after Mikey again, she's sending an undercover team with an underage kid into Quinn's to see if he gets served so she can try to have the State take away Mikey's liquor license."

"Man oh man, she's fighting dirty. Do you know who they are?"

"I don't know their names, but I saw them in a conference room with one of the mayor's assistants when I was at City Hall dropping off a report. I asked a friend in the office and he told me what was going on. He's a skinny tall kid with a hipster goatee and one of those stupid man buns. She's a pretty blond that in real life would never be seen with a punk guy like that. You'll easily spot them. She's actually twenty-one so she'll try to buy drinks for both of them or she'll try to sweet talk the bartender, so he won't pay attention when the guy tries to buy a drink. I heard that they are going to be in this Saturday, make sure Mikey throws them out and doesn't serve the guy."

"Thanks, Pat, we'll take care of this."

Pat pushed Seamus up against the car and patted him down once more for show.

"If I wasn't spoken for, I might enjoy being felt up," Seamus said, this time unable to hold in a laugh.

"Just take care of this. Tell Mikey I don't expect to pay for drinks for a while and I would appreciate it if you forget this ever happened," Pat said. He stepped back and loud enough for even the Gleason sisters to hear, "Sorry for the inconvenience Mr. Corrigan, you fit the description of the person we were looking for. Have a nice day." He then walked back to his cruiser, turned off the lights and sped away.

Seamus got back in the car.

"What the hell was that all about?" Vince asked.

"There was a bank robbery on Monroe Street, two guys in masks, I fit the description," Seamus said as the widows gasped in horror that Seamus even looked like a criminal.

Vince looked at Seamus. "What's going on?"

"We need to go to Quinn's when we drop the ladies off," Seamus whispered.

Vince nodded, "Pat warning us?"

Seamus grimaced, "Unfortunately," he said as he got out his phone and called Mike.

"Meet us at the bar in a half hour, it's important, it's the mayor again," Seamus said and hung up.

Twenty minutes later Mike was waiting by the front door.

"We shouldn't take any chances talking about this out in the bar, let's go over to the empty rental across the street," Mike said, the keys in his hand.

"So, we throw them out? Rough the guy up?" Vince asked once they were settled in the empty apartment and

Seamus had informed Mike what Pat had told him about what was going to happen.

"No," Mike said, looking out the window at the bar, his home really, he thought. "We do that and someone will end up in jail and the mayor will use that as a reason to shut us down. She's really after me, the public housing move and now this, she's intent on hurting me and the neighborhood."

Mike turned back to face his friends.

"So, I know what we have to do to win this thing. We need to make an example of them. We also need to show her that there are people in the city that are on our side and that we are tougher than she thinks"

"How about we announce that you are running and in the news conference you talk about all these dirty tricks? Seamus offered.

"No, we'd look weak. She can deny everything, there's no proof she's after me personally, it certainly looks that way, but people won't really care at this point."

"Okay Mike," Seamus and Vince said together. "So, what are they throwing at us again?"

"A team of two kids, a guy and a girl," Seamus said.

"And Pat told you what they looked like?" Mike asked

"She's legal and Pat says she's really good looking. He's a skinny hipster punk," Vince added.

"Okay," Mike said as he thought for a moment. "If she wants to buy a drink we'll let her have more than a few. But we have to keep them separated so he doesn't get any. We'll need to bring in a few people to help us."

"Sounds good," Seamus said. "Make sure Davey is tending bar then."

"And I have a plan to keep the guy occupied and away from any drinks," Vince said with a laugh. "Seamus, what's the name of your t-shirt guy?"

"Billy Cosgrove up on Marshall Street." Seamus answered.

"What's the plan then?" Mike asked.

"This is what we'll do." Seamus said as Mike and Vince leaned in to listen.

CHAPTER 32

DOUBLE D'S

AROUND 9:30 p.m. the undercover pair walked in and just as Pat said, they were very easy to spot. The boy took a seat at a table and the woman went up to the bar. She stood there waiting to be served. Pat had understated how gorgeous she was – super-model pretty with stylish blond hair, the perfect distraction for any male bartender.

Three young guys who Seamus had recruited, sidled up on either side of her as she waited to be served. They were neighborhood guys, Tom Hogan, Buz Holliday and Don Cook.

They yelled in unison, "Birthday shots!"

On queue Davey Moran had a tray of four shots in front of them. Donnie handed them out, giving the one that actu- ally contained alcohol to the girl.

She smiled and took the shot as they downed them and cheered for another, then another until she had three shots. She cheered for the fourth round.

"So, beautiful, what's your name?" Tom asked her.

"Alison," she slurred a little.

"I'm Tom, this is Buz and that's Donnie."

"Who's the birthday boy?" she asked.

"I am." Buz responded, "Ready for another one?"

Seamus and Vince were watching everything that was going on and could see the male half of the undercover team getting more and more anxious as his partner continued to party with the group of birthday guys. Seamus gave Buz the signal that the male partner of the undercover team was ready for the part of the plan they had for him.

"Who's the guy that came in with you?" Buz asked Alison.

She looked around the bar, "Guy?" she asked.

"The skinny dude over there with the man-bun," Buz said, pointing.

"Oh, him, he's..." she paused for another moment, "Trevor!" she yelled.

She motioned for him to come over and join them. He reluctantly got up from the table and walked over to the birthday party. He stood there with his hands in his pockets and stared at Alison.

"Alison, we need to go, we only came here for one drink," he said in a tone as perturbed as he looked.

"Join the party, have a drink," Alison said pointing to the bar.

This perked him up.

"Yes, a drink, I'll take a drink," he said taking his hands out of his pockets and leaning into the bar and waving to Davey.

As soon as Davey got over to the group, Tom and

Donnie sandwiched Trevor, picked him up by his elbows and held him a few inches off the ground.

"Davey this is Bob, he's our designated driver for the birthday party," Donnie said.

"My name is Trevor, put me dow..."

Before Trevor could finish his sentence, Davey threw a t-shirt over to Tom.

"Here's your DD t-shirt, Bob, you put that on and you get free cokes all night for being the designated driver," Davey said nodding his approval.

Tom caught the t-shirt and with the other guys wrestled the shirt onto Trevor over his futile protests. On the shirt was a picture of the mayor from the waist up. Over her chest were the capital letters "D" tilted at a slight angle to visually enhance what the good Lord failed to give the mayor. On the back of the shirt was printed, "Mayor Learner's Designated Driver Program Don't Drink and Drive."

Seamus fell over laughing, nearly spitting out his beer in the process.

"What gave you the idea to add her picture, Vince?" Seamus was barely able to ask.

"Well I thought the only thing that could make the mayor almost palatable was if she was sporting double D's," Vince said with a big smile.

The birthday group picked Trevor up and laid him out flat on their shoulders and carried him around the bar chanting, "Bob, Bob, Bob."

Trevor flailed in protest but was no match against the three of them.

After a couple laps the entire bar was chanting "Bob," even Alison.

The guys put Trevor down next to Alison as she continued to chant "Bob."

Trevor tried to compose himself as the guys took more shots of tea while Alison had more shots of Jack Daniels.

"Alison, we came here for a couple drinks," Trevor said, grabbing her by the arm.

"She is drinking," Donnie said pushing Trevor away from her.

Seamus stood up. He had told the guys no rough stuff. Donnie saw him and waved an apology and put his arm around Trevor like they were best friends.

Trevor sloughed off Donnie's arm and went up to the bar where Davey was standing on the other side.

"Can I have a beer please?" Trevor whined.

"Bob, you know you are the DD. Here, I'll pour you a Coke," Davey said, grabbing a glass off the shelf.

Trevor stood there with his head down and took the Coke when it was handed to him. He drank it down and put the glass on the bar.

He turned to Alison. "We need to go. You know we have people waiting for us," he said, pointing to the door with his eyes.

"Ease up, Bob. I'm having a great time," Alison said as she swayed a little trying to keep her eyes on Trevor.

"I'm out of here. And I'm going to make sure they hear all about this," he said taking off the shirt and throwing it on the floor as he walked out the front door to more chants of "Bob, Bob, Bob".

CHAPTER 33

STUPID AND FUTILE GESTURES

THE NEXT MORNING Mike met Vince at the Liberty Hill Diner for breakfast.

"That was quite a scene last night," Vince said. He sipped his coffee.

"When is she going to give up this vendetta? She knows she's going to win by a landslide, why is she making it so personal? Public housing projects, the health inspections and now she's trying to take my liquor license?"

"Well, Mikey, that's the kind of person her side admires. It isn't enough to win on ideas; she has to crush the soul of her opponent because they don't have her same beliefs."

"She has no idea what I believe," Mike scoffed.

"Doesn't matter," Vince replied, "kiss ass or get squashed."

"I have a feeling now that this will continue after the election. I've taken up permanent residence on her shit list," Mike said, grabbing a menu even though he had ordered the same thing since the diner opened.

"That's a possibility. So, after the election you are going to have to say that you support the mayor and will work with her if you don't want it to continue."

"I would rather ride through the St. Patrick's Day parade as Grand Marshall in my birthday suit."

"You could do that too, but it's still a little chilly in March and you know, shrinkage," Vince teased.

"You think that's the flaw in that statement?"

"You do have a reputation to maintain, you are a big guy in the neighborhood."

"That's true," Mike conceded. "So, what are you going to do?"

"I'm going to eat my frittata, drink my coffee, say hello to the people I know that are here..."

"And shake their hands like a candidate for mayor that you are going to be," Vince said finishing Mike's thought.

"Not yet, besides, everyone here is going to vote for me anyway. Okay, but both of us know I have to do this. It's a stupid and futile gesture but what better way to get her off my back than by letting her beat me by sixty points at the polls. She'll get the press she wants, look like a potential gubernatorial candidate and then we can get back to our lives. I won't support her in my concession, but I'll say that I hope we can work together because we both have the same goal of a better Genesee. And then, hopefully, she'll leave us alone after the election."

Vince looked at Mike and leaned across the table.

"Who says you'll be the one giving the concession speech?"

"Vince, c'mon now..."

The waitress saved Mike by coming over to take their order.

"Why do you always get the frittata, Mikey?"

"Cause I like it. Why do you always get the peppers and eggs?"

"Cause Mikey," Vince said sounding defiant. "Nothing's ever gonna change, is it? That is nothing will change unless we make it change. We are going to win this thing Mikey. I can feel it."

Vince turned to the waitress.

"I'll have the Corned Beef hash, two eggs over easy and Italian toast."

"The same," Mike said handing the menu to the waitress.

"Game on?" Vince asked. "It's on." Mike said smiling.

"Then let's do it. Let's win this thing."

"But I want to wait until we take care of Donal, all our efforts will go towards taking care of him. We have plenty of time to start campaigning."

Vince shook his head in agreement.

"Yes, Donal first, you're right. But at least keep in touch with Piersky and Mayor Halligan. We can continue working behind the scenes, maybe line up some money?"

"You're right, we can run to make a point or we can run to try to win, no matter the odds."

"You can win Mikey, I feel it in my bones," Vince said leaning across the table again. "Win."

PART II: WINTER

CHAPTER 34

THE DEAD

AS MUCH AS Donal had brought the neighborhood together to support him, his sickness also leant an underlying sadness as everyone accepted the fact that he wasn't going to get better and that he would soon be departing this world.

Seamus spent the bulk of his time after their conversation behind Quinn's, driving Donal to his appointments, bringing him food, and making sure he was never alone more than he had to be. Without being asked, people from the bar joined in, helping with meals and shopping.

When the time came, Mike arranged for the hospital bed to be put in Donal's flat and made sure the hospice was the best in the city.

They put a signup sheet in the bar to go sit with Donal and read to him. What to read was not an issue because Donal had shelves full of what seemed to be everything Irish authors had ever put on paper.

Seamus walked through the beginnings of a storm that

would bring a foot of snow in early November to Genesee for his shift to sit with Donal.

Helen sat in the recliner next to the hospital bed and raised her index finger to her lips when Seamus opened the door.

"He's just fallen asleep," she whispered and folded the blanket she had draped across her lap. "The nurse will be here in an hour; he was in a lot of pain earlier."

"Thanks, Helen." Seamus gave her a hug and helped her with her coat. "I appreciate you helping out."

"My pleasure, he's such a sweet man, I wish he hadn't been so shy all these years."

"Be careful in the snow now, do you want me to get Mike up here to drive you home?" he asked as he held the door for her.

"No thanks, it's only a few blocks and I like to watch the snow."

"Okay then, love. Make sure you tell Mike I offered when he wants to yell at me."

"Will do, Seamus." She glanced toward Donal. "Take care of him."

"I will."

Seamus was about to sit in the chair when he heard Donal move and looked to see his eyes open and a smile on his face.

"It's snowing, ah I love the first snow. Open the curtains more so I can see."

"Sure, and how about a fire?"

"Aye, that'd be grand."

Seamus built a good fire, went to the fridge, and

grabbed a Guinness from the six-pack he had hidden behind a pot of stew.

"What do you want to hear today?" he asked as he walked to the bookshelves.

"Joyce of course. *The Dead.* Always a good read on a snowy day."

Seamus easily found the first edition that was one of Donal's prized possessions.

"Give us a sip," Donal asked after Seamus put the bottle on the side table.

"The nurse'll skin me alive if she finds out I let you have a pint. She'll be here at two."

"Not a pint, just a wee sip."

"Not a word then."

"I'll be as quiet as a Provo in a room full of Brits."

"Or as quiet as Donal Maroney in Quinn's for thirty years."

"Aye, don't make me laugh," Donal said, holding his side.

Seamus handed him the bottle and guided it to his lips. "Ah, I hope they have that in heaven."

"It's a well-known fact that the angels are mostly Irish so there's bound to be a pub just inside the pearly gates."

"I said don't make me laugh. One more sip and then read, we can't keep Joyce waiting."

"Have all you want," Seamus said as he poured the bottle into a cup with a straw, "I'll get another."

The snow was falling hard and the fire snapped while Seamus made his way through *The Dead.* He glanced at Donal every now and then to see if he was awake, and every time he looked, Donal was smiling and watching the snow.

When Seamus heard the nurse on the front steps, he grabbed the empty bottles and hurried to the kitchen to get rid of the evidence.

Luckily the nurse turned out to be Kate.

"It's good to see you in some place other than Quinn's corrupting my husband," Kate said. She gave him a hug.

"Hey, Katie, I'm glad it's you, that last nurse yesterday gave me the stink eye the entire time."

"And that surprised you?

"Yeah, I guess you're right. Need any help?"

"Can you go get the box of supplies out of my car?" She handed him the keys.

"Hello, Donal, I hope Seamus isn't being too much of a pain in the ass. How are you feeling, sweetie? Any pain other than Seamus?"

"Nah, he's grand company. Joyce is a thousand times better when he's read aloud with an Irish accent."

Seamus returned with the box and opened it up on the dining room table. Kate checked Donal's IV and hung a new morphine drip.

She finished and gave Donal a kiss on the forehead.

Seamus helped her with her coat and followed her to the car, grabbed her snow brush and cleaned her windshield.

"Call my cell, not the service if he needs anything," she said and got into the car.

"Of course," Seamus said as he finished brushing the snow off her car and put the brush on the floor of the front seat. "Be careful driving home."

She started to pull away from the curb but stopped and rolled down the window.

"Seamus, don't give him any more beer or I'll have you arrested."

"Beer? I don't know what you're talking about, Kate," he said, smiling.

"No more beer," she said again and rolled up the window.

Seamus went back inside and put a few more logs on the fire and grabbed another Guinness for himself,

shaking his head no when Donal glanced at his empty cup.

"Now, where were we then?"

"They were passing the sweets," Donal said.

"Aye, the sweets." Seamus found the place where he left off.

He glanced over after a few pages and Donal's eyes were closed. He stopped reading.

"Keep going, I'm still here," Donal whispered.

Seamus started back up and kept going until he finished.

"Read that last paragraph again and don't spare the Irish."

Seamus started to read again with the thickest brogue he could muster.

A few light taps upon the pane made him turn to the window. It had begun to snow again. He watched sleepily the flakes, silver and dark, falling obliquely against the lamp- light. The time had come for him to set out on his journey westward. Yes, the newspapers were right: snow was general all over Ireland. It was falling on every part of the dark central plain, on the treeless hills, falling softly upon the Bog of Allen and, farther westward, softly falling into the dark mutinous Shannon waves. It was falling, too, upon every part of the lonely churchyard on the hill where Michael Furey lay buried. It lay thickly drifted on the crooked crosses and headstones, on the spears of the little gate, on the barren thorns. His soul swooned slowly as he heard the snow falling faintly through the universe and faintly falling, like the descent of their last end, upon all the living and the dead.

"That was grand Donal, I know why you love Joyce."

"I hope Father Cronin was wrong," Donal said, his eyes still closed.

"Father Cronin?"

"My parish priest in Dublin."

"Wrong about what?"

"That Joyce didn't go to heaven because he didn't have a proper Catholic mass and burial."

"Any man that writes like that will be in heaven. And save me a seat in the Pearly Gates Pub, I figure after a couple hundred years in purgatory I'll be able to join you. I'd like to meet him too."

"Seamus, please take my Joyce collection after I'm gone."

"Are ya sure, Donal?"

"Aye, I know you'll take good care of them."

"Thanks, Donal, it'll be an honor."

"I want to thank you for all you've done, you've made these past months bearable."

"Well we should thank you for bringing the best out of

the people at the bar, you've made us feel more like a family."

"Nah, save that shyte for the speech at my wake."

Seamus laughed and patted Donal's hand a few times then held it gently. He turned his head and pretended to watch the snow.

"Donal do you mind if I ask you a question?"

"Sure, what is it?"

"You mentioned a girl once, a girl back in Dublin."

"Aye, Geraldine Carr, she was a beauty. I loved her but she didn't love me back. It's what made me pack up and move here. I was a true eejit. But once I got here and realized it was a mistake, I could never find the courage to go back home."

"Aye, I know the story well."

CHAPTER 35

MORE BAD IDEAS

NANCY KNEW why the mayor wanted to see her, Mike Lee had almost disappeared, the teams that were watching Quinn's only saw him on occasion. They told her that someone was sick and that no one was talking about the election, only this sick man.

Nancy knocked lightly and took a deep breath.

"Enter."

"You wanted to see me Madam Mayor?"

"Why am I not seeing headlines about your man, Mr. Lee? Why hasn't he formally announced? I thought you had this under control, Ms. Elliot."

"My team tells me that he is taking care of a sick friend."

"Sick friend? You are letting a sick friend get in the way of my campaign?"

"Well Madam Mayor, he is very loyal to his friends."

"Nonsense, we need to get him back in the game."

"We could make another announcement to draw him out," Nancy replied hoping the mayor would take the bait.

"Like what, Ms. Elliot?"

"You could add to your poverty and social justice initiatives. Mr. Lee is a landlord with several properties on Liberty Hill. Cities in Westchester County have come out with programs that force landlords to take Section 8 housing."

"And that has worked?"

"It certainly gained a lot of press. If Mr. Lee comes out against the housing and the Section 8 program, he's giving you more ammunition to hit him as uncaring during the election."

"Okay Ms. Elliot, tell Carter I want to see him. And Ms. Elliot, if anything backfires you'll be working a drive-up window somewhere."

Nancy nodded, "Yes Madam Mayor, I understand."

CHAPTER 36

PARADE FOR THE POPE

THE NEXT SNOWSTORM lasted three days and turned what had been a long, colorful fall into an instantaneous winter. Donal was fading and the doctor told Seamus that it wouldn't be more than a week before it was over.

"So this is it?" Donal whispered as he slid the oxygen mask to the side.

"Aye, Donal it is," Seamus answered, trying to smile.

"Time to get the priest close or just time to talk more about the wake close?" he said barely finishing the last words before replacing the mask.

"The wake, Donal, so I have everything ready. We'll have a full house at Quinn's and I have my eulogy mostly written. After I finish speaking, I'll raise a pint in a toast and then we'll play 'Parting Glass' to finish it off. There won't be a dry eye in the place."

Donal moved the mask. "Did you forget any of the other Irish clichés for a wake?"

"Naw, I think I got them all. I did want to ask you if you wanted Enya's version of 'Danny Boy' or Bing Crosby's?"

Donal laughed silently and reached for Seamus' hand which Seamus took and gently patted as Donal closed his eyes.

There was a light knock on the door and Vince let himself in. He took off his boots and coat, pokered the fire, added a log, and pulled a chair next to Seamus.

"How's he doing?" Vince whispered.

"He's getting weak. The doctor was here earlier. It won't be long."

"Jesus, this is going to be tough."

"Yeah, it is. This little guy here has changed us since we all started taking care of him. How everyone has rallied around to help and how it's spread to other things. We are better people, better neighbors because of Donal," Seamus said and he adjusted Donal's blanket which had slid a little. "Yes, it is amazing, how he's brought the neighborhood together."

"You know what else he's done, he put together the start of Mike's campaign organization."

"You're right, Donal you sly fox you."

"Beer?" Vince asked, standing up.

"How long have you known me now?"

"Let's see, you moved here in 1984, I had been at Chrysler already for a couple months so that makes it..."

"It makes it a rhetorical question, just get the beer."

Vince went into the kitchen. "Have you eaten anything?"

"Not since breakfast, why don't you call Caroma's and get a pie."

"Already on the way. I called right before I came in. And you think I don't know you, you dumb mick."

"So, I should have asked you to move in instead of Roxanne?" Seamus asked, laughing.

Vince walked in with the beers.

"Should I call Roxanne and tell her you're throwing her out and having me move in?"

"Ah no, I'm one-hundred percent sure that I'll stick with her," Seamus said taking the beer.

"I'm sure Kate wouldn't mind getting rid of me," Vince said.

"Did you talk to Dominic Barone?" Seamus asked. "Yeah, everything's set. The casket, the plot, it's all arranged. I also called Tom Tracy to make sure the will was filed. Everything is ready," Vince said.

"I never had to do this since all my family is back in Ireland. I just get that bad phone call and then I send money so one of my sisters can order flowers."

"My father had it all arranged and paid for. All we had to do was go to the funeral home and sign the final papers."

There was a hesitant knock at the door and Mike let himself in.

"How is he?" Mike asked.

"He's getting close," Seamus replied.

"I'm not dead yet," Donal whispered from behind the mask.

"Hey, boyo, how ya doing?" Mike leaned in and smiled.

"Ready for Christmas Eve at Quinn's. I'll buy the whiskey if we can sneak out for midnight mass."

"We always talk about midnight mass and before we know it the Jameson's is gone and the sun is coming up." Mike laughed.

"So, Mike, what's the latest from the witch of city hall?" Vince asked.

"This isn't the time or place." Mike nodded toward Donal.

"Right, right," Vince said. "What's this?" Donal asked.

'Nothing, just the mayor, she's pissed at me like usual," Mike replied, patting Donal's hand.

"Mike, I wish I could be around to watch you get sworn in," Donal said, his breath fogging his oxygen mask.

"No, Donal, they'd be giving the Pope a parade in Belfast before anyone ever sees me on the steps of city hall taking the oath."

"Nah, you're gonna win. I'm going to make sure of that," Donal said with more strength than he'd shown in weeks.

"He's right, Mike, you'll have help from the heavens," Vince said.

"Yes," Donal said grabbing Mike's sleeve. "You are gonna win, I know it. You, Mike Lee, are a good man. You have always thought about your friends before yourself and now it's time to do that for the city. The city needs you Mike."

"Donal, thanks, but the big question is does the city want me?"

Before Mike could say anything else, there was a loud knock at the door.

"Pizza's here," Vince said, getting up.

Mike leaned down and whispered in Donal's ear.

"Thanks Donal, thank you for everything."

CHAPTER 37

LAST RITES

DONAL'S BREATHS were slow and labored. It had been a day since he was conscious, the heavy morphine drip lingered at the side of the bed. The room was full of his friends, he would not die alone in a hospital.

Father Gualtieri had been to the flat the day before, to give him his last rites while he was still lucid. Donal smiled during the entire blessing. Perhaps he already saw the greats of Irish literature waiting for him in heaven.

Seamus read Joyce softly. Kate and Vince sat on the couch, Vince was looking out the window at the snow.

Mike prayed the rosary as Helen rested her head on his shoulder. The others just sat and waited for the end.

Death came quietly and only Seamus noticed at first, but he kept reading until he finished the final chapter.

"He's gone, everyone," he said, closing the book.

Mike went into the kitchen and brought back the bottle of Jameson and a tray of glasses. He filled them all and passed them around.

They sipped and waited for the hearse from Barone's to come and take away their friend.

CHAPTER 38

THE EULOGY

SEAMUS SAT QUIETLY at his regular spot, looking over all the notes he had written in the past week on what he should say in the eulogy, all the things that Donal had suggested. He flipped through the pages looking for something, anything, that he thought was right.

"This is all shyte," he whispered.

Vince heard him, stood up and put his arm around him. "Just talk about him. If it comes from your heart, it will be the right thing to say."

"I know, speak from the heart," he said shaking his head. "Just say a Hail Mary for me."

"Will do," Vince said as Seamus stood up and they embraced.

Seamus grabbed the microphone from behind the bar and walked over in front of the small stage where the bands played every week, bands that Donal had enjoyed so much and where a quartet stood by in their black suits ready to play their dirge.

"Hello, everyone, thank you so much for coming

tonight to say goodbye to our good friend Donal Maroney. Donal was worried that no one would show up for his wake and here we are in a packed house, so thank you again.

"We knew Donal for thirty or more years, yet we really didn't know him until he got sick. And then something really special happened, he had an extraordinary effect on the entire neighborhood. We all rallied around to help him out and, in the process, we went from a group of people who knew each other, into a better neighborhood and then into a family. He brought out the best in everyone. We signed up to take turns helping him and that grew into helping out each other in other ways. Taking people who couldn't drive to the store, fixing a window, raking leaves or just sitting on a porch and talking for a couple minutes.

"I spent a lot of time with Donal in his last weeks. The way everyone united around him made him so happy, he felt he was part of a big family. He was so happy at the end. A couple days before he died, while he could still talk, he even found the time to tell me a joke. Here it is:

"An American tourist was travelling through Ireland and it was a grey, rainy day so he thought he would spend the day at the local pub. As he walked to the pub, he saw an old man standing in the rain holding a stick with a string tied onto it. He was casting the string into a puddle. 'What are you doing?' the Yank asked. 'Fishing,' the old man replied. The Yank felt sorry for this feeble old man, maybe his mind had gone soft. 'Why don't you come out of the rain and come with me and I'll buy you a whiskey.' 'Okay,' said the old man. They went in and sat at the bar. After a couple drinks the Yank asked the old man, 'So fishing?

How many did you catch?' The old man picked up his glass and inspected his whiskey in the light. 'Yank, you're the third one today.'"

A quiet laugh filled the bar.

"That was Donal. He was a quiet man but once he went fishing, he caught us all. He made me a better person. He made the neighborhood a better place to live. So, everyone please raise your glasses in a toast to our dear friend Donal. May God hold him close and I know that is so because of all your prayers. I know that he was talking to St. Peter an hour before the devil knew he was dead. He's having his pint with Mr. James Joyce as we are having our pints in his honor. So Donal, watch over us, help us to be better people in your memory. To Donal."

Everyone raised their glasses and drank. Seamus gave the queue to the quartet on the stage and they started to play "The Parting Glass". They all sang with the band, slowly and beautifully until there was "not a dry eye in the place," as Seamus had promised Donal out on the patio.

"This is exactly how he wanted it," Seamus said to Vince after the song.

"Send me off the same way," Vince said, putting his arm around Seamus.

"Me too."

CHAPTER 39

DOUBLE D DO OVER

SEAMUS RECOGNIZED her as soon as she walked into the bar. Her blond hair was tied back in a ponytail and her great body was wrapped and hidden in a Seneca University sweatshirt. She had expensive sunglasses on top of her head and for some reason Seamus' first thought was why would anyone buy expensive sunglasses when you live in the city with the least amount of sunshine per year in the entire country.

I see a girl that pretty and all I think about is her sunglasses? Seamus thought as he took a long drink from his pint in anticipation of why the young lady had come into Quinn's.

It was the girl from the mayor's undercover team. The last time Seamus saw her, she was leaving the bar with Donnie at last call. His next thought was, lucky Donnie.

Alison Bradbury walked up to the bar and asked the bartender a question. Vince's nephew Joe was the daytime bartender and he shrugged his shoulders in response to her question and then pointed over to Seamus.

As she walked up to Seamus, he thought she looked like she wanted to kick somebody's ass. He looked over her shoulder, to Joe, to see if he could give some indication of her intentions but he just shrugged his shoulders again.

"I'm trying to find the owner," she said without any kind of introduction.

"Why are you asking?" Seamus responded trying to sound uninterested.

"Because he owes me," she said glaring at Seamus. "The guy at the bar told me you would know where he is."

"He's not here at the moment, but I'd be happy to pass along a message."

She pulled out her phone and thumbed through a few screens and then looked back at Seamus.

"I'll be back at two, make sure he's here."

"And what gives you the right to be bossing me around, missy?"

"My name is Alison Bradbury, I have something important I want to tell him, so he should be here when I come back at two."

"I'll try my best to let him know but I can't be making any promises, especially to a young lady that lacks in common manners."

"Well then, you'll get him here so you won't have to see me get mad, won't you?" she said before turning around and leaving the bar.

Seamus hit Mike's number and told him what had just happened.

"I'll be there at two then, just because I'm curious to hear what she has to say," Mike said.

Word got around about what had happened and there

wasn't an empty seat in Quinn's as the time neared for Alison's scheduled return.

True to her word, Alison was back at exactly 2 p.m. She stopped at the doorway and paused, she located Seamus and made a beeline for the corner table where he sat with Mike. She walked over to the table and sat down without any invitation.

"I'm Mike Lee, the owner of Quinn's," Mike said, extending his hand.

"Alison Bradbury." She shook his hand.

"So, Miss Bradbury, I hear that you are very determined to meet with me."

"First, I wanted to say that your little stunt got me fired. I had to sit there and listen to one of the mayor's flunkies scream at me for twenty minutes about how I am a stupid blond and that I couldn't handle an easy assignment like going into a bar and ordering one drink."

"It wasn't personal."

"I know you weren't after me, but you got me fired, I am here so that you can give me a job to replace the one you cost me."

Mike looked over at Seamus. Seamus raised his eyebrows and shook his head "yes" almost imperceptibly.

"And why should I trust you, Miss Bradbury?"

"Listen, I'm just a student at Seneca University and I am trying to pay for most of it myself, and now I don't have a job because of you."

"Well," Mike said slowly as he thought about what to say next. He looked again at Seamus.

"Give the kid a chance," Seamus said looking directly at Alison to see her reaction.

"Okay then," Mike said. "What can you do? Waitress? Bartender? Dishwasher? Or would you rather work at the corner store I have over on Hamilton Street?"

"I can be a waitress, I guess."

"So, you can be a waitress at a lot of places, why come back here?" Mike asked.

"Like I said, you owe me. And this place is close to my apartment and..."

"And what?" Mike asked.

"And I had a really great time here," she confessed.

"Okay, stay here and I'll get you an application to fill out" Mike got up from the table and went into the office to get the paperwork.

"Are you really Irish or are you part of the atmosphere?" Alison asked Seamus.

"I am 100% Irish, born and raised. Came over when I was about your age."

"So why did you guys do that to me and Trevor? Just because you hate the mayor? Cause I can totally understand that, she's a total bitch."

Seamus just looked at Alison.

"Is that the Irish or Mafia silence thing? Nobody knows nothing thing?" she asked.

"May I ask you a question, Miss Bradbury?"

"Sure...."

"Seamus"

"Of course, Seamus. You couldn't be Bill, that wouldn't be authentic."

"How much did those fancy sunglasses set you back?"

"Three hundred in New York."

"You paid that much for sunglasses in the cloudiest city in the country?"

Before Alison could answer, Mike returned with the application.

"You two getting to know each other?" Mike asked.

"Best friends," Seamus replied.

"Great, we're a family here," Mike said smiling at Alison.

"Sure, you are. When can I start?" Alison asked.

"You can work tonight, watch one of the other waitresses, train on the computer. We are going to be busy tonight. Wednesdays, we have live music," Mike said pointing to the small stage.

"Let me guess, Irish music?" Alison raised her eyebrows at Seamus.

"Of course," Mike said tapping the application. "Fill it out first and then we can talk some more."

CHAPTER 40

GRAND OPENING

MIKE, Seamus and Roxanne stood outside the Emerson Street storefront. The freshly painted row of shops was decked out with a big "Grand Opening" sign hung from the eaves. Mike even called Piersky and promised a future favor, maybe a heads up on something in the neighborhood, in exchange for a business reporter and a photographer so they could do a story for the business section. The three posed for pictures as they cut the red ribbon across the door. Vince drove a van around the neighborhood collecting widows so they could get their new hairdos for the senior citizens dinner that night at St. Patrick's, which was coincidentally scheduled for the same day as Roxanne's grand opening.

It had been years since there was a salon in the neighborhood, so Roxanne quickly built up a steady clientele. All the traffic into the salon helped Mike to rent out the shops on either side. One for a paint-your-own-pottery store and another for a small coffee shop, not an eggs and hash coffee shop that he hoped for though. One with espresso and lattes.

"This is how you revitalize a neighborhood. This should have been a campaign event," Mike said to Vince as they finished shaking hands and greeting the patrons.

"Maybe the city will see what you're doing here and put a program together to help that'll ruin everything," Vince deadpanned.

Mike laughed. "We can only hope."

CHAPTER 41

BACK IN THE GAME

WITH DONAL GONE it was time to start concentrating on the campaign.

Mike and Seamus sat in the waiting room of Gilman, Burns and Bertrand after the two hour drive down the Thruway to Albany. Dan Halligan made the call on Mike's behalf to get an appointment with one of most highpowered political consulting groups in the state. Dan also got them to waive their fee for the assessment.

They were meeting with Tom Burns to go over his evaluation of what Mike would need to run a campaign, strategy, money and organization. The part about how to win was also supposed to be included in the report and Mike was most curious to see what they had to say.

They were shown into a conference room with a great view of the capital steps. There was a coffee service on the table as well as binders with "Michael Lee, Genesee Mayoral Campaign Review" on the coversheet.

"This is going to be expensive, should we stay?" Mike whispered to Seamus.

"If you want to head back, go on then."

"No, we came this far, we need to hear them out," Mike conceded.

"Have some coffee, try to look political for the gentleman."

"We should have at least dressed up a little, do you even own a tie?"

Before Seamus could answer, Tom Burns walked into the room like he was an hour late even though he was a few minutes early.

"Tom Burns, nice to meet you," he said extending his hand.

"Mike Lee and this is my friend Seamus Corrigan. Thank you for seeing us, we appreciate you fitting us in to your schedule."

"Well, let's have a seat and go over our initial assessment, shall we?"

Tom Burns took a seat across the table and opened the binder.

"Okay, please open your binders to the index page, you'll see that we broke the assessment up into sections. If you don't mind, I'm going to skip around a little so that I can highlight what I feel is important."

Tom Burns spent the next hour talking about budgets, campaign literature themes, organizational structures and position papers. Mike waited for the simple words he wanted to hear but after an hour they had not been spoken.

"Mr. Burns, thanks, can I ask a question?"

"Sure, but please call me Tom."

"Thanks, Tom." Mike cleared his throat. "Can I win?"

"Well Mike, that assessment is in the last section, why don't we turn to that."

Tom waited for Mike and Seamus to find the section in the binder.

"Given the demographics of Genesee, the money Mayor Lerner has in her campaign war chest, the fact that you have not held any public office or even run for any public office, well..."

Mike waited for what he knew was coming.

"We have calculated the chances of you winning at approximately 10%."

"The other grim statistic that isn't in the binder is your fee for helping me in this long shot, no win situation."

Tom closed the binder.

"You would have the full resources of Gilman, Burns and Bertrand behind you. We have a proven track record of winning, although we have not had a candidate in your situation. Our initial fee would be $500,000 with additional costs based on what you choose from our services. There is also a $250,000 winner's bonus if we bring you across the line first."

Mike nodded without saying anything. He turned in his chair and looked at Seamus. Seamus raised his eyebrows to tell Mike that he didn't have an answer for him.

"I want to thank you and your firm for all of the work you put into this proposal," Mike began. "I will take this all back to Genesee and talk this over with my friends and family. I'll have to see if I can raise that level of money. But one more question Tom."

"Sure Mike, what is it?"

"What is your gut feeling about my prospects?"

"Well, we really aren't in the business of gut feelings, but ignoring all the computer models, I think you might have a shot. Lerner's negatives are very high, but you'll need to know how to exploit them."

"Exploit?" Mike asked.

"Well, to have any chance we think you'll have to go very negative. It'll be ugly, but we think that's the only way for you to have a chance."

"But I do have a chance?"

"If you listen to us, maybe."

"Thanks Tom, I appreciate your honesty, you'll be hearing from me shortly."

Mike and Seamus didn't speak on the way back to the car. Seamus kept looking over at Mike, but Mike was looking out the window. It wasn't until they got on the Thruway and started to head west that Mike finally turned and spoke.

"I know I can probably find that kind of money, if I sell some things and go hard at raising money outside of the city. But it just doesn't feel right. I think we wouldn't be in charge of the campaign and we would lose the reason I ran in the first place."

"Are you sure Mikey?"

"Yes, I know it. We'll find some other way than spending the money. We need somebody we can trust completely. These aren't the guys. Let's go home."

CHAPTER 42

RINGS AND THINGS

SEAMUS AND ROXANNE had been living together for a few months and they were getting along famously. The perpetual bachelor was now acting like a kid in love and thinking about getting married, which, since he was now in his early fifties, he felt it might be time. Roxanne was younger and at forty-four she was also ready to settle down now that she was back in Genesee. Her salon was thriving and she enjoyed the steady life of working, domestic bliss with Seamus and being part of the neighborhood.

Christmas was approaching and Seamus had made a decision about asking Roxanne to marry him.

He didn't know the first thing about diamonds, so he called Vince to go with him to pick out a ring. He figured since Vince had been married for over thirty years he was as good of an expert as anyone.

"Morning Vince, are you free today?" Seamus asked when Vince answered his phone.

"Sure, I just got back from the gym, I was going to take my snow blower in for service over on Erie Boulevard."

"Good, that's the part of town I need to go, can I tag along so we can make a stop after that?"

"Come over in an hour, you can help me load up the snow blower and we can head out. Where do you need to go?"

"I'm going to see Gerry Marra."

"Gerry Marra as in Gerry's Jewelry?" Vince asked. "Do you know any other Gerry?"

"A couple, but that doesn't matter. Are you getting Roxanne a necklace or something for Christmas?"

"Yes, the or something. A ring," Seamus said.

Vince had enough of the game, so he came right out with the ball busting.

"Are you sure you're ready? You're still a young man, what are you sixty-three now?"

"You know I am nearly the same age as you, and yes I'm ready."

"So you really want to be Pete's dad then?"

"Ha, me Pete's dad, I have to laugh every time I think about that."

"And you think she'll say yes?"

"Ah, I hadn't thought about that either. I think she will, but I guess I'll find out."

"When are you going to ask her?"

"At the Christmas Eve party. That's about as romantic as I can get," Seamus said, a little embarrassed that he had actually thought about being romantic.

"So she can't say 'no' in front of everyone?"

"Well, if she says 'no' at the party, there may be someone else in the crowd that'll say 'yes,' I hope."

"Yeah, I think Murph is tired of being single too."

"Ah feck off, I'll be there in an hour then."

Seamus dug out the shoe box he had hidden behind some suitcases in the back of his closet. He had been nervous since he withdrew the $7000 from the bank and was more relieved about getting all that cash out of his house than he was about spending the money or whether Roxanne would say yes. He put the cash inside an envelope and stuffed it inside his shirt, securely tucked into his belt so it couldn't move or fall out. He walked over to Vince's house paying attention to who was on the street, looking over his shoulder every few seconds.

"This is my neighborhood, why am I so worried?" he thought.

He was so busy looking around for potential criminals that he didn't see the patch of ice on the sidewalk.

Seamus felt his legs go out from under him and realized he was horizontal, looking up at the perpetually grey Genesee sky. He hit the sidewalk, luckily butt first, so his head didn't take all of the impact. But when his head hit, he did see stars for a second. He laid there on the ground, slowly taking inventory of his body with small movements to make sure nothing was broken.

The grey sky was suddenly replaced by Vince's face. "You okay, buddy? I heard you hit from halfway down the block."

"Give me a hand then," Seamus said as he sat up, feeling his head swirl a little.

When he finally got to his feet, he felt his side to make sure he hadn't blacked out, giving someone the opportunity to steal his money, but thankfully the envelope was still there.

Vince helped him stand up straight and held on to his elbow, just to make sure he didn't go down again.

"You're going to make Roxanne a widow before you even marry her," Vince said looking at Seamus to make sure he was okay.

"I'm good," Seamus said, brushing himself off. "I wasn't paying attention because I have all this cash on me and I was worrying like an eejit that I was going to get robbed."

"How much do you have on you?"

"Seven grand for a grand ring,"

"Holy cow, why do you have that much cash? They do have debit cards now."

"You know I don't care for any of that plastic shyte, I'm a strictly cash man," Seamus said checking again to make sure the envelope was still there.

"Okay, let's get on the road before anything else happens," Vince said still holding Seamus' arm as they headed down the block.

Seamus kicked a chunk of ice from a snowbank before they started walking and held it on the lump that was growing on the back of his head.

"Sit in the truck before we have to add the emergency room to our trip," Vince ordered once they got to the house.

"Okay, Ma."

They talked about anything other than engagement rings and weddings as they drove over to the east side.

"Seamus, stay here and watch the truck while I go get the guy I talked to this morning about the service," Vince said. He pulled into the parking lot of the Toro dealer and put the truck in park.

Partly because he didn't like being told what to do and partly because he wanted to prove he could do it, Seamus unloaded the snow blower by himself.

"You are an eejit," Vince said when he saw Seamus standing next to the snow blower in the parking lot.

Seamus paced the showroom the entire time that Vince was talking to the service manager. Vince signed the paperwork and motioned to Seamus it was time to go.

The jewelry store was only a few minutes from the Toro dealer and this time Seamus was unusually quiet as they approached the store.

"Are you sure you want to do this?" Vince asked when they parked near the front door.

"Absolutely," Seamus said. "I was just thinking about why I waited this long to get married. It would have been nice to have a couple kids."

"But you are going to be a dad. You are going to be Pete's dad," Vince laughed. "And don't forget Angela. You are going to be the father protecting the honor of the hottest girl in the neighborhood."

"Ah Jaysus, I know. I hope she hasn't told Roxanne about that kiss at Mike's 50th birthday party."

"I'm sure she hasn't told her mom, but that hasn't stopped the other hundred people from telling her."

"Well remember, that kiss has to compete with the story of an exploding goat," Seamus said. "Enough talk, let's go inside and do this."

"Any idea what you want to get her?"

"An engagement ring." Seamus said. "Gerry'll help me I hope."

They walked into the jewelry store and were greeted by an overly cheerful saleswoman.

"How can I help you gentlemen?" she asked. "Gentlemen," Vince laughed.

"I'm here to see Gerry," Seamus said giving Vince a sideways glance.

"He's with a customer right now, can I point you in the direction of what you are looking for?"

"He's looking for an engagement ring," Vince said pointing at Seamus.

"Well congratulations, Mister..."

"Corrigan."

"Mr. Corrigan, the engagement rings are over here and if you would like, you can also pick out a loose diamond and look at the different settings."

"This is going to be tougher than I thought," Seamus said.

They sat down in front of a huge case full of rings.

Seamus looked at Vince.

"How did you pick out Kate's ring?"

"Katie took me to the store and said buy me that one," Vince replied.

"Maybe I should have brought her instead of you."

"If you were smart, you would have."

Gerry interrupted their back and forth.

"Well Seamus Corrigan, I never thought I would ever have you in my store to buy an engagement ring. I was very surprised when you called. Who's the lucky girl?"

"Roxanne Johnston," Seamus said, smiling as he felt himself blush a little.

"That is the look of a man in love, I see it all the time. It keeps me in business. So, Seamus, how much in love are you?"

"Seven grand worth I'd say." Seamus said, reaching into his coat for the envelope.

"What are you looking for? Solitaire? Pear shaped? Round?"

"A diamond that she won't say no to," Vince chimed in. Seamus gave Vince another dirty look.

"Why did I ask you to come with me again?" Gerry brought them back to task.

"I have the perfect ring for you, Seamus, I can give you this at my cost, any place else it would cost you three times as much. You won't find a better diamond outside of New York City. Consider it my wedding gift."

Gerry went into the open safe behind the counter. He returned with a green velvet tray and placed it on the counter in front of Seamus. Vince tried to grab it, but Seamus slapped his hand away. He took the ring in his big hands and twirled it, watching all the colors shimmer in each of the facets.

"Wow, that was easier than I thought it would be," Seamus said.

"That is a 'beut. She won't be able to say no. I would marry you with that ring," Vince said, trying unsuccessfully to take the ring from Seamus again.

"Let's take care of the paperwork and I'll give you a box worthy of a ring of that quality. Once she says yes, she can bring it back in and get it sized."

"So, how exactly are you going to ask her?" Vince asked when they were back in the truck and on the way back home.

"I was thinking right before midnight, when Mikey closes the doors and it's just friends and family."

"That would be good. It's where you met. Women like that kind of stuff," Vince replied.

"I actually didn't plan it that way, but you're right, she'll think I'm being extra romantic."

"Yeah, you'll need all the help you can get."

"Even as nervous as I am about asking her, I'm still looking forward to the party. It's been a few weeks since Donal passed and I think everyone is ready for a good time," Seamus said, feeling his pocket to make sure the ring was still there.

Chapter 43

DID SHE SAY YES?

MIKE'S CHRISTMAS Eve party was legendary in the neighborhood. It started when he and Helen were newly-weds. It was supposed to be a drink or two before everyone walked over to St. Patrick's for Midnight Mass. It ended with the sun coming up and all the guys opening presents a few hours later with varying degrees of a hangover.

The party had evolved over the years. They dropped the pretense about going to Midnight Mass after a few years and by the fifth edition of the party it had grown to the point that Mike shut down the bar at midnight for all his friends.

The lead up to this Christmas had been subdued because of Donal's passing. The guys tried to get in the Christmas spirit by putting up extra lights and decorations. The weather did its part, it had snowed almost every day since Thanksgiving. Quinn's looked like a scene straight out of a holiday special, with adult beverages. The buffet was picked over and the punch bowl was half empty by the time Seamus arrived wearing a new tweed jacket and a tie.

Roxanne was in a black velvet dress with lace trim. She looked like Mary Bailey's hot sister.

After getting two pints at the bar they joined Vince and Kate at the table under the newly hung picture of Donal. The picture was from Donal's last night in the bar. He was sitting at his regular stool and held a fresh pint in his hand, with the smile of a man who had years ahead of him.

"So, you're very well-dressed tonight," Vince said to Seamus.

Seamus gave him a scowl to shut up and don't give anything away.

"And Roxanne, you look exceptionally beautiful tonight," Vince continued, earning a scowl from Kate and a punch in the arm.

"We are starting a new Christmas tradition," Roxanne said. "I think Seamus looks so distinguished all dressed up."

"There you see, 'distinguished,'" Seamus said, straightening his tie.

"You could wear something other than a reindeer sweat- shirt, Mr. Di Pietro," Kate said in support. "And I don't remember you telling me I was beautiful tonight."

"I look bad because there's nothing I can do to come close to looking good enough to be your date," Vince said leaning in to kiss Kate but she pushed him away.

"Nice try, but you already lost your chance of any present tonight."

"Don't get any corned beef dip on your new tie then," Vince said to Seamus trying to change the subject before Kate could continue to berate him.

"I don't think I can eat anything," Seamus said.

"What's the matter, honey, you not feeling well?" Roxanne asked.

"No, no I'm fine," Seamus said, catching himself almost giving away the surprise himself.

"You look a little peaked," Vince said and winked. "Actually, I am hungry," Seamus said, trying to seem normal. "Why don't we hit the buffet."

"Okay," Roxanne said as Seamus stood up and offered his hand.

When they left the table, Kate looked over at Vince and glared.

"What's going on?" she asked.

"Who said anything was going on?" he said failing to look innocent.

"You guys better not do anything to ruin Christmas Eve."

"Well, that's possible, but you'll have to trust me for a little while."

"I'll wait, but I don't trust you," Kate said as she poked him in the side.

The couples ate, drank and mingled with the biggest turnout that Mike had seen in years. Vince finally got Seamus alone.

"Well, what's your plan?" Vince asked.

"I don't have one, that's the problem," Seamus said looking around the bar to make sure Roxanne wasn't in earshot.

"Maybe you should give Pete a heads up. He's been okay with you and Roxanne but asking her to marry you might put him over the edge."

"Good idea. He's over in the back corner. Can you keep Roxanne occupied while I take him out back and tell him?"

"Sure, but if he freaks out, he may give it away," Vince warned.

"I'll have to take the chance. Wish me luck," Seamus said and headed to grab Pete.

Fifteen minutes passed until Seamus and Pete came back into the bar from the kitchen door. Seamus gave Vince the thumbs up.

Vince got up and met Seamus at the bar before he got back to their table.

"So, he's okay?"

"Yeah," Seamus said. "He was a little squirrelly with it at first, but he's happy that his mom has settled down and now that she has her business, he thinks she really has changed. The bugger actually thanked me and wished me good luck at the end."

"That's great, so let's do this before Kate kills me. She thinks we are cooking up some kind of incident."

"This is what we'll do" Seamus leaned in and gave Vince the plan.

A few minutes later Vince took an empty pint glass and a knife and started clinking to quiet the crowd.

"Can I have everyone's attention? I want to make a toast. Everyone get a drink please." Vince said.

Vince grabbed a fresh pint and stood at the center of the bar.

"It has been quite a year and I just wanted to say that it is great that everyone is here and that we are together. I want to thank our hosts Mike and Helen Lee, you two are the glue that holds this neighborhood together. And I want to thank my wife Katie for putting up with me over all these years, and raising three great kids, that are all out of the house by the way. She really showed what an angel she is here on earth the way she took care of Donal in his last days. And Donal. Donal, I know you are up in heaven looking down on us and we miss you. Put in a good word for us with the big guy and thank you again for showing us how to be a neighborhood. And finally, to my best friend Seamus."

"Are you going to let us drink?" Pete yelled from the back of the bar, drawing a good round of laughs.

"I said 'finally' Pete, didn't I? Anyway, my best friend Seamus. Mike and Helen are the glue and Seamus is the heart of the neighborhood. You have changed this year, all for the better. I thought you were a good friend, but I was wrong. You are a great brother. I'm so happy that you and Roxanne are together, you both deserve all the happiness in the world. So, everyone raise your glasses, may you all have a very Merry Christmas and may we all grow in friendship and as a neighborhood for many years to come. CIN DON!"

The bar drank to Vince's heartfelt toast with cheers and clapping. As the approval of the toast died down a little, he picked up the pint glass and knife and started clinking again.

"What now, Vince?" Pete yelled from the back of the bar to laughs again.

"I want to turn the floor over to my brother, Seamus, come on up here."

Seamus walked up front to applause. When he got up next to Vince he whispered in his ear.

"That's right, Seamus, thanks for reminding me.

Roxanne can you come up here too?

Roxanne was surprised by the request, but she was urged forward by the crowd.

"Okay, Seamus the floor is yours," Vince said. He walked over and put his arm around Kate and she gave him a kiss.

"Is this what I think it is, tell me it isn't?" she said into his ear.

"Quiet, you'll ruin it," he said pointing up to where Seamus stood next to Roxanne.

Seamus took a long drink from his pint and cleared his throat.

"I want to thank Vince for that brilliant toast and I couldn't agree with him more. I want to add that the best thing that ever happened to me was back in September when Roxanne walked through that door and changed my life forever. So, Vince gave me the floor, but I only need a small part of it for my knee."

Seamus knelt down in front of Roxanne and clumsily dug the ring box out of his pocket. The crowd reacted with one shared breath.

"Roxanne Johnston, thank you for entering my life. You have given me the love I never thought I would be able to find."

He opened the box and showed the ring to the crowd. "Roxanne, would you do me the honor of being my wife?"

Roxanne had both hands over her mouth and she was shaking. She didn't say anything right away. Kate grabbed

Vince's hand and squeezed. It seemed like hours had passed since Seamus asked.

"Well, Mom, what's your answer?" Pete yelled from the back.

That broke her spell.

"Yes, yes, yes," she cried as she jumped forward and hugged Seamus, pulling him to his feet. They kissed to the cheers of the crowd.

CHAPTER 44
SECTION 8

"PIERSKY CALLED ME LAST NIGHT," Mike said as he sat down next to Seamus who was drinking coffee and reading the morning paper.

"It sure is exciting around here, what happened to the friendly neighborhood bar we used to have?" Seamus asked. "Well this time I'm sure it is personal. She's going after part of my livelihood with this one. This I'll have to take action on, running for mayor or not. She's proposing that all city landlords take Section 8 vouchers."

"Jaysus, what is going on with her?"

Mike looked over his reading glasses as he tapped the number he finally found and waited while it rang.

"Tracy and Tartaro how may I help you?"

"Tom Tracy please. This is Mike Lee."

"Just a moment."

"Your lawyer already?" Seamus asked.

"I'm tired of this crap. She's willing to kill the neighborhood just because of me, I won't stand for it," Mike said.

He heard the hold music end and he held up a finger to tell Seamus to wait.

"Mikey what can I do for you?" asked Tom Tracy, a kid from the neighborhood that Mike had known all his life and was now Mike's lawyer.

"The mayor's at it again, she's going to have a news conference today announcing that she is going to introduce a bill into the city council to force landlords to take Section 8 renters. We need to do everything we can to stop that."

"That's interesting. I have heard of other cities in New York that are trying it. Let me do a little research to see what the property owners have done. Don't worry yet, Mike. We can take this lady on. I've been itching to go at her since she went after one of my other clients."

"Thanks, Tommy, and don't worry about watching all your billable hours for now. I don't care, I'm not going to let her win this time. Because I'm unofficially running for mayor you better have this go through the landlord's association, but I'll pay for everything."

Mike hung up and looked at Seamus. "It's tough enough trying to keep your head above water in New York with all the regulations and taxes and now we have to worry about the local government making it impossible to just be a businessman?"

"You still sure about running?"

"No, but I still think I have to. She's baiting me. I know it sounds crazy, but I still think she wants me to run. I'll be easy to tear apart. I don't have the money, the organization, the name recognition, everything says I don't have a chance. But she needed someone."

"So what are you going to do?" Mike got up and heaved a deep sigh.

"Run, I don't know how we can turn this into a negative for the mayor, but we have to make this an issue we can use without looking like evil landlords."

CHAPTER 45

WEDDING PLANNER

SEAMUS AND ROXANNE set the date of the wedding for Valentine's Day. Seamus was a little scared about how quickly she wanted to get married. He was thinking about a longer engagement but at his age he agreed that there was no reason to wait. They were going to have a small ceremony and since Roxanne had been divorced, they didn't want to go through all the trouble of trying to get married in the church. That didn't bother Seamus, although he thought he would have to make up a pretty good excuse to tell his mother back in Ireland about that fact.

"If you aren't getting married at St. Patrick's, where were you thinking of doing it?" Mike asked after Seamus told the guys about the wedding plans.

"How about halftime at a Seneca University basketball game, right at center court?" Murph joked.

"I don't think Roxanne is a basketball fan," Seamus replied.

"What about one of the old mansions on James Street. I think they rent out a few of them," Mike said.

"Now you're talking," Seamus said. "And of course, we'll come back here for the real party after a reception."

"Of course you will," Mike said.

"What about the honeymoon?" Vince asked.

"I think I'm going to set something up somewhere warm. I know Roxanne misses Florida and she is suffering in her first winter back in Genesee. She'll go nuts if we go somewhere with a beach and fruity drinks."

"Remember that you're Irish, Seamus," Vince warned. "If one ray of tropical sunshine hits your pasty white Irish skin, you'll burst into flames."

Seamus laughed. "Yeah, unfortunately I think that's true. But she really wants someplace warm."

"Don't go on a cruise, it'll end of being one of those e.coli cruises and you'll spend the entire time in the can," Pete added.

"Just go to one of those all-inclusives down in the Bahamas, that way you don't have to worry about paying for every little thing," Mike suggested.

"Think of that. Me, Seamus Corrigan, confirmed bachelor, finally getting married and talking about all-inclusive honeymoons."

"I think it's the first sign of the apocalypse," Vince joked.

"I made the mistake of telling her I would take care of the place, the party and the honeymoon."

"Well, she's doing everything else. Has she showed you pictures of dresses yet?" Mike asked.

"Ah Jaysus yes. That reminds me, Vince, we need to go get tuxedos Mr. Best Man," Seamus said, slapping him on the back.

"Seamus, I know it gets cold in Genesee but I didn't think it would get so cold that hell would freeze over, but it must have because a woman is getting you to the altar." Vince laughed.

"Just one best man?" Murph asked.

"Yes, it's going to be a small wedding party. What? Were you looking forward to putting on a tux and dancing with a bridesmaid, Murph?" Seamus asked.

"Me and Pete are the only single guys left now," Murph lamented.

"Ah great, now I'm like Murph?" Pete moaned.

"Maybe you need to find a nice girl," Seamus said. "Okay, Dad," Pete said.

"I keep forgetting that part." Seamus laughed. "Come here son and have a drink with your dear old da."

This caused the group to laugh and after a few seconds Pete actually joined in.

"Hey, Davey, I'll take another pint, put it on my dad's tab," Pete joked.

CHAPTER 46

OVERSEAS ARRIVALS

VINCE STOOD outside the security area at the Genesee Airport waiting for the surprise wedding guests. The twelve-passenger van he rented was in the parking garage and everyone else was back getting ready for the big surprise for Seamus at Quinn's. He checked the board when he arrived and saw that the flight from JFK was on time, so he texted Mike to set the plan in motion.

There were ten people in total coming in for the wedding from various parts of Ireland. They had raised the money by passing the hat and doing a couple 50-50 raffles without Seamus knowing that the real reason for the raffle was to buy the airline tickets.

Seamus' family did the same over in Ireland, most of the money coming from people that lost bets that Seamus was finally getting married.

The ten included Seamus' parents, his two sisters and their husbands with four kids to round out the group. Seamus' sisters had married two brothers, twins, Kevin and Kieran Roddy. There had been more than one story about drunken nights at a pub and the confusion between the sisters on which twin was theirs. Seamus had also said of the twins that they made him look "like a teetotaler." Since Vince knew Seamus could go drink for drink with anyone who had ever graced the bar at Quinn's, he was very curious to meet these famous twin brothers.

Seamus had not seen his family since he left Ireland and Vince couldn't wait to see the look on Seamus' face when he saw them walk through the door. There was already heavy betting that he would cry.

Vince knew it was them as soon as he saw the first of Seamus' family come around the corner from the terminal into security. He held up his sign that said, "Corrigan Wedding" and started to wave.

They were easy to spot because out in front of the group, were the Roddy twins. They wore matching Ireland National Rugby jerseys. They had mops of curly hair on top of their massive heads that were supported by what should be a neck, but Vince couldn't see where their shoulders ended and their heads began. Side by side they took up almost the entire ramp coming from the gates. Even the TSA agents noticed and had to lean around the metal detectors to get a look at these giants.

Seamus's parents were straight out of an Irish tourism commercial and his sisters were redhaired Irish goddesses that belonged in the same tourism commercials serving pints to rich Americans. Vince's eyes stayed on the sisters for a beat too long, which put the thought in his head that he was raising the telepathic protection radar of the Roddy twins. For a second, Vince thought he heard a simultaneous growl, with a brogue.

Vince moved over to the group and shook hands and went through all the introductions before leading the Corrigan-Roddy clan down to the baggage claim. All the luggage made it from Dublin to Genesee and after some creative packing in the rental van he had all of them and their bags loaded up and they were heading for Quinn's.

When he arrived, he texted Mike they were outside and the plan was put into action. Mike asked Seamus to help him in the office to get him out of the bar. The family came in and were arranged in a line in the center of the floor.

Mike's phone buzzed, letting him know they were ready and it was time to bring Seamus into the bar.

When Seamus came out of Mike's office, his family was standing there, all with pints in hand.

Seamus stood stunned. Roxanne came out of the group and kissed him.

"Aren't you going to introduce me to everyone?"

Seamus wiped a tear and walked up to his parents and gathered both of them in his arms.

"Were you surprised?" Vince asked him when the reunion finally waned.

"I can't believe you guys did that for me. I never thought I'd get married and I never thought I would see me Ma and Da again and they are both happening at once. So, all that stuff about live streaming the wedding to Ireland was just a ruse to get the information you needed to get them over here?"

"No, we are still going to do the live stream. There's more family that want to see you when you stand at the altar so they can believe it really happened." Vince laughed. "Thank you, this is brilliant, I hope Mikey has extra kegs," he said pointing to the Roddy twins.

"Just show up for the wedding, so they didn't fly across the ocean for nothing," Vince said, grabbing Seamus's collar.

CHAPTER 47
BACHELOR PARTY RULES

MIKE, knowing the potential for disaster, had given a list of rules for Seamus' bachelor party:

1. The party couldn't be at Quinn's
2. No strippers
3. No cameras
4. Nothing that could end up on the news
5. Make sure our cop friends are there so no one gets arrested
6. Don't leave the city
7. Confiscate all phones and recording equipment at the door
8. No fighting

"That's it?" Vince asked.

"That's not enough? What are you planning?" Mike said, now more concerned than ever.

"Well I really only had one rule, no goats."

"Add that to my list, that's a good one. Just remember that I am going to be running for mayor. I'll be announcing soon and we don't need any bad press," Mike said calming down a little.

"I wouldn't worry so much about our Genesee crew. You should be scared shitless by those Irish twins. They don't have enough cops in the city to arrest those two if they get out of control and decide they don't want to go to jail."

"That's very true, so let's hope they don't do anything that would get them in trouble. What are you going to do about them?"

"Seamus says he can control them, he says he has something, some good dirt, that he can tell his sisters if they get out of line."

"That's as good as anything you can have. So, what establishment did you trick into hosting this potential international disaster?" Mike asked.

"The only place that knows us, but doesn't care if the place gets burned down," Vince confessed.

"The Hibernian Club? You were able to trick them into this?"

"Yes, The Hibernian Club," Vince confirmed.

"And what are going to be the activities, since strippers are not allowed?"

"Darts, a pitch tournament, a singalong with the band..."

"What band were you able to get to play this gig?" Mike asked, surprised that Vince was able to get a band.

"Some old guys, not important, what time do you think you can get there," Vince asked.

"Not them, tell me you didn't hire the cardiac Celts?" Mike laughed.

"Okay, yes, I hired the Irish Setters for the party," Vince confessed.

"Do the Hibernians have a defibrillator?"

"Yes, they are a little old, but they can still carry a tune.

I hear that the flute player has rigged his oxygen mask so he can wear it and play at the same time."

"I'm sorry that I won't be able to join the soiree until after the dinner rush."

"You'll be there for the 'tell your favorite Seamus story' contest?"

"Of course, I wrote it all down, so I don't forget any details. Does he know about the contest?"

"Absolutely," he paused, "not."

CHAPTER 48

SEAMUS STORIES

THE PARTY WAS off to a roaring start, with the drinks flowing freely and the band doing their best to create a festive mood by playing all the well-known Irish songs. Vince had Frankie from Caroma's cater the food, with large trays of baked ziti and all the fixings.

Seamus had been fitted with a large dunce hat with the words "Don't Do It" written across the front. He also had an old bowling ball that had a chain attached to it, locked around his ankle.

By the time Mike showed up the boys were lubricated enough to be singing along with the band, although not always with the lyrics of the song they were playing. They had broken out the cigars, breaking all the New York State indoor smoking laws and Seamus had cut off the top of his dunce cap and was using it as a megaphone to either sing or yell greetings to one of the party goers.

The band took a much-needed break, handing the microphone over to Vince.

"Gentlemen and the rest of you species of undetermined origin, it is time for the best Seamus story contest," Vince slurred a little into the microphone.

"Our first contestant is none other than Quinn's own, the next mayor of Genesee, Mike Lee."

The room filled with applause and whistles as Vince handed the microphone to Mike.

"Thank you, thank you. And don't talk about me running for mayor yet. These guys are probably all felons and can't vote anyway."

Vince bowed an apology and put his index finger to his lips showing that he was going to be quiet.

Mike smiled and changed his tone after admonishing Vince.

"How many of you know that Seamus is a little bit dyslexic?"

Smattering of applause.

"Well Seamus met this one girl about twenty years ago, she had come into Quinn's with some of her friends from the east side. Seamus sweet talked her all night and pretty soon had her out in his car for a little extracurricular activity. She had such a good time that she told Seamus she wanted round two the next night. The only problem was that she had to work. So, she told Seamus her address, which he wrote down, and she said she would leave the door unlocked so he could get settled in because she wasn't exactly sure what time she would be home.

Seamus found the apartment and it was unlocked just as she said. He settled in on the couch and started to watch TV. He noticed some tapes next to the TV and saw one was an adult movie. He pops in the tape and starts to get warmed up. He's sitting there with a raging pup tent when he hears someone walking up to the door. He starts to take off his pants to show his date his eagerness to get things started when a guy walks in, sees Seamus and drops the bag of groceries he's carrying. Seamus pulls up his pants as he jumps off the couch, knocks the guy over on his way out the door.

The next day the girl shows up at Quinn's furious that Seamus stood her up. "I was there" Seamus protested, "but some guy walked in and I ran before he tried to beat the shyte out of me."

"I live alone, there's no guy in my apartment," she declared. "You're lying."

Seamus reached into his pocket and pulled out her address that he had written down two nights before. She grabbed it out his hand and started laughing.

"I live at 736 Comstock Ave, not 763."

The room roared with laughter. Mike took a bow and exited the stage. Seamus covered his face with the dunce cap.

Vince retook the stage.

"I've heard that story a thousand times and it is funny every time. Who wants to be next?"

A parade of guys followed, each with a funny story about Seamus' antics or shortcomings. The judges were about to name Mike the winner when the Roddy twins walked up to the stage.

"We have one, that none of ye's have heard," the twins said in unison.

"It was right before Seamus left for the States."

"Aye, it may have been one of the reasons he left."

No one really knew which twin was talking, not that it

really mattered. They either finished each other sentences or took turns talking.

"Seamus had taken a holiday to visit his cousin Rory, who was away at boarding school. He had gone up there for

a big party the school was having, end of year craic, complete with a U2 cover band. Rory had snuck three bottles of whiskey into his dorm and Seamus was still just a wee drinker, barely used to more than a pint or two at the pub."

"The band is playing and Seamus is drinking whiskey out of a Mountain Dew bottle to fool the nuns. He's up at the stage dancing by himself when this brilliant bird sidles up to him and starts dancing with him. Next thing ya know, they are out in the car park rolling in the grass, groping and tearing at clothes and such."

"Seamus sneaks her into Rory's dorm room and they start to get serious. Seamus downs the rest of the whiskey in his glass and stands to take off his pants. When he gets his shorts down to his ankles he passes out, right there on the bed. The bird tries to wake him up, but Seamus is dead to the world."

"She's poking and poking, shaking and yelling to get him up. Seamus proceeds to roll over and he barfs all over her chest. She is right pissed and takes off her shirt and puts on one of Rory's. She's standing thinking of how to get revenge on Seamus."

At this point the room is shaking with laughter and Seamus is trying to get under the table to get away from the story.

The twins continued.

"So, the bird sees Seamus' suitcase in the corner, complete with his name and address and probably a love note from his Ma. She opens the suitcase and drops her pants and proceeds to take a pisser into the bag. Rory gets back to the room and it stinks of vomit and piss and there's Seamus, naked from the waist down. Rory calls to his mates and soon they are all standing at the door, laughing and taking pictures."

One of the twins digs into his pocket and pulls out a picture.

"Holy mother," Seamus yells out.

The room suddenly rushes the stage to get a glimpse of a teenage Seamus with his trousers around his ankles.

Vince grabbed the microphone. "The winners!" he yelled.

CHAPTER 49

NUPTIALS NO SHOW?

SEAMUS STOOD with Vince in a small side room, just outside of the ballroom where they had put up a makeshift altar and all the guests sat patiently waiting. Even though it was mid-February and five degrees outside, Seamus' forehead glistened with sweat.

Vince stood next to his best friend saying "take it easy" over and over as he watched Seamus swaying a few degrees north and south as they waited for the bride to be to arrive so they could start the ceremony.

"Is she going to show?" Seamus whispered over to his best man.

"Don't worry, big guy. Women are always late. Get used to it."

"If I could lift my arms, I'd look at my watch," Seamus said in more of an exhale than a statement.

Pete appeared at the door as Vince was trying to keep Seamus conscious. He poked his head in and gave them the signal that his mom was here and that they were ready.

"Jaysus, Joseph and wee Paddy O'Malley," Seamus croaked.

"This is it, big guy, your last moments of bachelorhood," Vince said before he walked over and opened the door. He got behind Seamus and with a slight push, nudged him to the door. He stayed closely behind to catch him in case Seamus tumbled over.

"Bend your knees so you won't pass out," Vince warned as they made it to their positions and the music started.

The double doors opened and Angela stepped forward in a low-cut red dress. Vince saw the Roddy twins gasp and get hit by Seamus' sisters at the same time. She sauntered down the aisle in teasing steps.

Then Roxanne stepped forward and offered her arm to Pete so he could walk her down the aisle.

Pete was almost unrecognizable in a suit, his face shaved and hair combed.

Roxanne was an angel. Seamus felt his knees go weak and felt Vince's hand on his shoulder holding him up.

When she finally made it up to the altar, Pete kissed her on the cheek and took his seat.

Seamus took her hand and saw stars, then the power went out or at least he thought it did.

Vince caught him before he hit the ground. Seamus came to almost right away, but his pasty white face was now beat red.

"He just locked his knees, he's okay," Vince assured the crowd.

The Roddy twins volunteered to stand next to their

brother-in-law although Vince was sure it was just so they could get a better view of Angela in her bridesmaid dress.

Seamus recovered and made it through the "I do's" and his long kiss after he was directed to kiss his bride, visibly reinvigorated him.

"You did it, bud," Vince said as Seamus and Roxanne prepared to walk back down the aisle as husband and wife.

"I am so glad that part is over," Seamus whispered back to Vince.

"Time to drink?" the Roddy twins asked in unison.

"The bar is open," Vince replied.

The wedding party moved into the main ballroom for the reception. Mike brought Seamus and Vince each a beer.

"You did it," Mike cheered as he gave Seamus a bear hug. "Vince, distract Helen so I can get my kiss from the bride."

"Easy now, that's my wife you are talking about," Seamus said, feigning anger.

The reception was very subdued compared to most functions that involved the crowd from Quinn's and free alcohol with one exception.

Pete had taken a shine to one of Seamus' nieces from Ireland. They were slow dancing to a fast song.

"Look at our boy," Roxanne said as she kissed her new husband.

"That's my niece Aoife and I think if his hands go any lower on her back Kevin is going to plant him in a snowbank."

"Don't worry, in a week she'll be back in Ireland and

he'll be heartbroken," Roxanne said, disappointed at the prospect of Pete with another reason to sulk.

"You never know," Seamus replied. "She could get sponsored by a relative and get a job here. That's something we could probably arrange."

"Let's not get ahead of ourselves," she said as the band switched to a slow song to match Pete and his newfound love interest.

"Shall we?" Seamus extended his hand.

Roxanne took it and they went out onto the dance floor to the cheers of the guests.

CHAPTER 50

AFTER PARTIES

AFTER THE FORMAL reception was over, dinner served and the open bar closed, the wedding party moved back to Quinn's to finish off the night.

"So, what do I get for holding down the fort while you guys were out having the time of your lives?" Davey asked from behind the bar as Mike and Vince led the group inside.

"We could only invite either you or your ex-wife, so we invited her," Vince shot back.

"That bitch," Davey growled.

"He's just kidding," Mike interjected quickly. "Why don't you join the party and I'll handle the drinks."

"You don't have to ask me twice," Davey said. He took off his apron and tossed it to Mike.

Mike poured a tray of pints and Vince played barmaid delivering them to the tables.

"Your parents go back to the hotel?" Vince asked as he handed out the drinks.

"Yeah, they had their fill at the reception. We'll meet them for breakfast tomorrow," Seamus replied.

"And your sisters and the Roddy twins too?"

"They're on their way here."

"So how does it feel to be married?" Kate asked joining the conversation.

"Well, it's been a couple hours now, so far so good," Seamus replied and kissed Roxanne on the cheek.

"You'll be an old married couple in no time." Kate laughed.

"Well at least you have the old part already," Vince said cutting into the conversation after his server duties were done.

"He's old, not me. There isn't a man alive that would say I look old in this dress," Roxanne objected. She pushed out her ample bust, that the dress struggled to contain, as proof.

Kate covered Vince's eyes.

"I hope he went and bought extra little blue pills for the honeymoon," Vince laughed.

Kate moved her hand over her husband's mouth.

"I'm a stout Irishman in my prime, I have no need for any of that nonsense," Seamus bragged.

"That's true." Roxanne giggled.

"How long before we hear the patter of little feet?" Vince joked.

"There's Pete and Angela, that's enough, and it's been a long time since their feet pattered," Seamus said, giving Vince a look for asking that question.

"Speaking of Pete, where is he?" Roxanne asked.

"Probably at the end of a shotgun, getting married." Seamus laughed.

"Oh, that would be nice," Roxanne said.

"That's where the patter of little feet will come from," Vince added.

"What about Angela? She's so pretty, why is she single?" Kate asked.

"She scares guys, but there is one man that kissed her, but I got him," Roxanne said poking Seamus in the ribs.

"Now that was under duress," Seamus protested. "There was an attempted robbery, broken arms and an exploding goat. I had to save the party and take everyone's mind off the troubles."

"Don't worry about it honey, I'll only bring that up every once and a while, when I'm mad at you," Roxanne said, kissing him on the cheek again.

"Welcome to married life," Vince said, raising his beer.

"Can I join the party?" Mike said and took a seat at the table.

"Have a seat Mikey," Seamus said offering the chair next to him.

"That was a great wedding, I'm so happy for the two of you?" Mike said putting his arm around Seamus.

"Has the mayor done anything lately?" Kate asked, too nicely for Mike to protest.

"No, Kate, but it might get worse when the campaign starts. Too many people have paid good money for her to be mayor and she doesn't like it when anyone rocks the boat."

"Let's not let that witch sully this fine day," Seamus winked across the table.

"Well she'll have plenty of reasons to go after us with both barrels pretty soon," Mike sighed.

"When is that going to start, Mike?" Kate asked.

"Soon, Kate, way too soon."

Seamus looked over at Vince and raised his eyebrow.

Vince understood and nodded.

"Soon," Mike said again.

PART III: SPRING

CHAPTER 51

THREATENING STATEMENTS

MIKE WAS in his office looking over the list of temp workers for St. Patrick's Day when his office phone rang.

"Mike Lee."

"Mr. Lee, hello, it's Mayor Lerner. I am glad that I could track you down. I wanted to chat for a second."

Mike was stunned and at first thought Seamus or Vince had put someone up to pranking him, but he looked at the caller ID and it read "Genesee City Hall."

"Good evening madam mayor, to what do I owe the honor?"

"Mr. Lee, I am glad you jumped into the mayor's race."

"I haven't officially entered the race," Mike interrupted.

The mayor continued like Mike hadn't spoken.

"Now, I applaud your civic spirit but saying a few bad things about me and the city on the news and in the paper hardly makes you a politician. I just wanted to let you know that I'm not going to hold back. I'm going to run my campaign like I'm behind in the polls."

He hesitated, not sure how to answer her statement.

"Mr. Lee are you still there? If you want to come close to challenging me you are going to have to be a lot faster on your feet than that."

"I'm surprised by your call. If I was going to be a candidate, I would make sure everybody in the city was aware of your real track record and how poorly the city has fared under your administration."

Mayor Lerner laughed. Mike could feel his anger rise.

"Mr. Lee, you don't understand the playing field you aren't ready for. This is the big leagues. Why don't you start off small, maybe the school board or the county legislature? But if you want a fight, then that's what I'm here for. I just wanted to let you know what you are in for. But at the end of the day I welcome an opponent, even if it's only you."

"Anything else or are you done threatening me?" Mike asked.

"Mr. Lee, I'm not threatening you. If I was, you would know it. And if I was you, I would know that running for mayor would be one of the most regrettable decisions you would ever make. But again, I think you should run. I know it must make your blood boil that I'm running unopposed."

"I'll take that under advisement, thank you. Was there anything worthwhile you wanted to say?" Mike said, resisting the urge to slam down the phone.

"No, Mr. Lee, I'm sure you'll run a good race. Just don't disappoint all those friends of yours into thinking you have a chance. Good night."

The mayor hung up before Mike could, but he still slammed the phone down. He got up to tell the guys what had just happened but he decided to keep this to himself for now. Everything was in motion and in a way, he was glad that she had called.

CHAPTER 52

ERIN GO BRAGH

QUINN'S WAS "THE" place in the city for St. Patrick's Day. The crowd started to build at 8 a.m. and went strong all the way to last call. For Mike and the guys, it was anything but a holiday. With the bar full of people they didn't know and the fact that almost everyone was drinking heavily, it made the day a procession of potential problems. There was the problem of underage kids trying to take advantage of the confusion of the crowds, the problem of drunk young men feeling their beer muscles and wanting to fight, and finally the problem of trying to weed out the people that had had enough and another drink might mean a lawsuit or another excuse for the mayor to exploit an incident.

All of the guys had their roles. Seamus and Vince controlled the extra security. Davey monitored all the temporary bartenders. Murph was in charge of the cash, making sure the excess went into a safe and that all the bar stations had enough change. Pete was given the task of walking around and eavesdropping on groups that looked like they may start trouble, it was a job initially created to make him feel included and to keep him out of the way, but he proved to be a savant at spotting trouble before it started. The kitchen was closed and the waitresses had the day off because there was no way they would be able to make it through the crowd with a tray of beer or food.

Mike's job was to be worried about all of it, bouncing around where he was needed, overseeing everything.

"I used to love St. Patrick's Day when I was a kid," Mike said in the planning meeting on March 16th.

"One of these years I'm going to go to the north side and drink at Caroma's," Vince said. "I don't know why I don't hang out with my own kind."

"You have a kind?" Seamus asked.

Vince laughed, "Yes, it seems to be crazy, middle-aged Irishmen that are always a pain in my ass."

"So Kate and Roxanne are going to have a spa day tomorrow?" Seamus asked, changing the subject.

"Yeah, Kate hates being in the neighborhood on St. Patrick's Day and she figures that she needs to start to bond with Roxanne since as she says you and I 'share one brain' sometimes, so she figures she is almost a sister."

"That's great, Roxanne has been feeling a little under the weather the last week or so and a spa day will cheer her up. She has had about enough of the winter and I'm glad it's over, she's not used to it and she definitely needs some pampering."

"Ladies," Mike interrupted, "We are still meeting here. Remember, I want this to be just about St. Patrick's Day."

"Okay," the group answered.

"Now, Seamus, how many off-duty cops were you able to bring in for tomorrow?"

"I had to pay extra, but I was able to get twelve, twice as many as last year. I also got some more security for the temporary fence around the back patio to make sure no one sneaks in."

"That's great, good thinking," Mike said, rubbing his hands together.

"Mikey, we've got this thing covered, stop worrying," Vince said.

"I know, but there is just so much that could go wrong," Mike said looking over the list of assignments.

"You worry like this every year and we take care of it," Seamus reassured him, although he shot a side glance to Vince to show him that he too was worried.

Vince acknowledged Seamus with a small nod.

"Maybe I should just shut down on St. Patrick's Day, I really don't need the money, it's not worth all the trouble."

"Mikey," Vince started, "St. Patrick's Day is ten percent of all the bar brings in for the year and you are an institution. St. Patrick's Day without Quinn's in the city would be a tragedy. No one would know what to do. What are they going to go have warm beer down the street at McCarthy's? Or, God forbid, go to Bennigan's?"

Davey walked into the office.

"Mikey, the beer distributor is here," he said. "You want to check the order?"

"Yeah, thanks," Mike said. "Okay I think we are ready. I want everyone here at 6:30 a.m., we'll have one last planning meeting before we open."

"Okay, Mike, we've got this thing. How many of these have we been through together?" Seamus said.

"You got them?" Vince asked when Mike was out of the room.

"Yeah, I had five thousand made, what do you think?" Seamus said handing a button to Vince.

"Perfect, we'll hand these out at all the entrances as people are being proofed. When the news crews show up to do their St. Patrick's Day stories, we'll make sure that the people in the background are all wearing these. What do we do when Mike finds out?"

"He'll be so busy he'll never notice because they're green and have a shamrock on them," Seamus replied.

"Mike Lee for Mayor, Driving the Snakes out of Gene-see," Vince said, reading the button.

"He's going to kill us but there's no better place or day to kickstart a campaign, half the city will be here and all of the TV stations."

"Okay, I have to get home, Vince said. "See you in the morning."

"Yep, tomorrow is going to be quite a day," Seamus said with a wink.

CHAPTER 53

BUTTON MEN

IT WAS noon before Mike actually read the first campaign button. He had seen them all day but with the shamrock he thought it was just a St. Patrick's Day button, just as Vince and Seamus had hoped.

"Seamus!" Mike screamed over the music and the crowd noise, "I thought I told you that I didn't want any campaigning today. That's all I need is an extra thing to worry about."

"Mikey, you'll never get a bigger crowd to get the message out, the response has been really good so far, everyone I talked to is going to vote for you. Besides that, we knew that all the TV stations would be here today and your campaign funds certainly can't afford all that press right now," Seamus replied with a mischievous smile.

"Well, we should have talked about this. I know I've been hesitant about starting and I thought we had a plan for the announcement. But I don't think the chaos of St. Patrick's Day is the right time and place."

"Okay then, I understand. I have something for you,"

Seamus said, taking a button out of his pocket and pinning it on Mike's vest.

"If I wasn't so busy I'd kick your ass," Mike said, now looking at the button and smiling. "Mike Lee, Mayor, what the hell was I thinking? At least it might be a good joke in a couple years. Is Piersky here?"

"Yeah, he showed up early and I told him what we were up to. He's already interviewing people for his story for tomorrow's paper."

"Well, at least you got that right," Mike said, now calmed down.

"We have this under control, Mikey. Now go shake some hands and kiss a baby or two."

An hour later the first news truck showed up for their live shot of the St. Patrick's Day party. It was Seamus' job to talk to them because he was such a natural in front of the camera and especially because he laid on his Irish accent thick when he talked to the reporters. It was all part of the show of St. Patrick's Day and gave Quinn's an air of authenticity.

Mike inspected him before he went over to the first truck.

"Okay, make sure you mention the bar's name at least three times before you are done. Leave the stuff about running for mayor alone, let's do the regular St. Patrick's Day news story first. Thank God for such a nice day," Mike said. He looked up at the bright blue sky which was a miracle for mid-March in Genesee. "And say something about how the Irish built Genesee and that on St. Patrick's Day everyone can feel like they are Irish."

"I know the drill; how many times have I done this before?"

"I know, I just want to make sure everything is good this year and you have me worried about doing something crazy, so don't. When they ask about me running for mayor, please don't say anything negative about Lerner."

Seamus started to walk to the interview, but Mike called him back.

"Let me give you one last inspection," Mike said, straightening Seamus' collar then holding him by the shoulders and giving him a good once over.

What he really called Seamus back for was to make sure he was wearing a campaign button.

"I've got this, Mikey."

"Okay, good luck." Mike watched Seamus walk over to the first news truck.

As Seamus waved to the reporter he reached into his pocket and made sure he had a couple extra buttons for anyone in the camera shot that wasn't wearing one.

The questions were the usual. How did St. Patrick's Day here compare to St. Patrick's Day in Ireland? How long had he lived in the States?

Seamus mentioned Quinn's in his first three responses, but he also mentioned Mike as the owner, which he hadn't done in any previous year.

"Mike Lee, can we get him out here?" the reporter asked.

"Yes," Seamus replied, pulling out the button and holding it out for the camera so they would be forced to do a close up. "Mike Lee, the owner of Quinn's. Mike Lee, candidate for mayor. He's lived in the neighborhood all his life. He led St. Patrick's High School to a county championship, he's the glue that holds Liberty Hill together and he's the candidate that can make Genesee a decent place to live again."

"When will we get to talk to Mr. Lee?

Seamus ignored the question and continued with his prepared remarks.

The reporter turned to the camera to finish off her report.

"There you have it Genesee. Green beer, shamrocks, a raucous St. Patrick's Day celebration and the first shot in the campaign for mayor of our city. Kelly Kelley, Channel 4 News, reporting."

The lights on the camera went out and Seamus put on an extra button and headed to the next live shot.

CHAPTER 54

TWO LINES?

ROXANNE AND KATE stopped for coffee after their day at the spa. They were in no hurry to get back home. Many of the streets in Liberty Hill were blocked off as the crowds overwhelmed the neighborhood for St. Patrick's Day.

"So how long have you been feeling sick?" Kate asked once they got their drinks and sat down.

"About a week, just feeling tired and a little sick to my stomach. A lot of the customers have been sick, it's the change in the weather," Roxanne replied, stirring in more sugar after her first sip.

"How is business at the salon?"

"It's been great, I never dreamed of owning my own place, but Seamus and Mike helped me make it happen. I'm having the time of my life."

"That's because you're a newlywed. How is married life anyway? I never thought I would see Seamus Corrigan walk down the aisle, but he looks like a kid in love."

"He's acting like it too," Roxanne admitted. "He's been

very, um, frisky, since the wedding, not that I'm complaining."

Kate laughed, "What are you feeding him? So I can make sure Vince doesn't eat the same thing."

Roxanne laughed, "How long have you been married, Kate?"

"We got married thirty years ago this July. We were so young, but we made it through. Three kids, all out of the house thank goodness. Now I'm waiting for a house full of grandkids, although I don't feel old enough to be a grandmother.

"Well, my one kid has finally come around. I thought Pete would never forgive me for running away to Florida, but he seems to be having a good time kidding Seamus about being his stepfather. He's also writing and calling Seamus' niece in Ireland. I'm almost afraid he's going to jump on a plane and go over there. And Angela is so sweet and so pretty, it's only a matter of time for her."

Roxanne took another sip and grabbed a couple more packets of sugar and emptied them into her cup.

"I haven't had a sweet tooth like this since I was..."

Roxanne stopped stirring her cup and looked at Kate, her eyes were wide and unblinking.

"What's wrong?" Kate asked.

"Since I was pregnant with Angela."

"No," Kate said trying to hold in a laugh. "You think?"

"It wasn't something I was worried about at my age, but again Seamus and I haven't been particularly careful either..."

"Oh my goodness, drink that and get another cup. I'm

going to run across the street to Walgreens. I'll be right back."

Kate grabbed her coat and went over to the drugstore while Roxanne drank her coffee and then went and got a refill. When Kate got back, they went into the ladies' room.

Kate handed her the pregnancy test. Roxanne stood there staring at the white plastic stick.

"You can't take the test telepathically, you have to pee on it!" Kate laughed.

"I know, I know. I'm just scared and I don't know if I want to find out. What will I tell Seamus?"

"You'll say 'congratulations, Dad, surprise!' Just like I did with Vince when I found out I was pregnant with Dominic."

"Okay, I think I'm ready, here I go," Roxanne said without moving.

"You'll find out eventually. It might as well be now." Kate said, grabbing Roxanne by the shoulders and turning her toward the stall.

"Okay, here I go," Roxanne said without much confidence. She took a deep breath and walked into the stall and closed the door.

"Everything good in there?" Kate asked after a few minutes of not hearing anything.

"I'm almost there," Roxanne said with a waver in her voice.

Kate turned on all the faucets and started singing 'Don't Start Chasing Waterfalls.' By the time she reached the chorus she heard the toilet flush. Roxanne came out of the stall holding the test at arm's length like it was an explosive device.

"How long until we know?" Roxanne asked. Kate grabbed the box and read the back.

"Three minutes," she said after finding the instructions.

A woman about their age walked into the bathroom and saw the pair staring at the pregnancy test.

"Better you than me," she said as she went into the stall.

"It's turning color!" Roxanne screamed.

"Okay!" Kate screamed back, "One line is not pregnant, two lines is pregnant, what is it?"

"I can't tell, yet, oh my God it's, it's..."

"What?" Kate shouted bouncing up and down. "What is it?" came from the stall.

"It's two lines, what is that again?"

"Pregnant!" Kate and the lady in the stall said in unison.

CHAPTER 55

PRESS CONFERENCE SURPRISES

BY SEAMUS' second interview the buzz about Mike running for mayor was building and the day had turned into a huge campaign event. The remote trucks usually left after they did their obligatory Liberty Hill St. Patrick's Day live shot, but the crews stayed and were still ready to broadcast if anything happened. The reporters were fighting with Seamus to get him to talk to Mike and convince him to do an interview. It was almost 5 p.m. and the reporters wanted to start their evening broadcast out with the first speech Mike would give in the race.

Mike popped his head out of the front door causing the reporters to yell to him to come over to the cameras, but he shouted back that Seamus was his spokesman.

Seamus held up his arm and pointed to his watch, the signal to Vince that it was time to hang the banner from the second floor.

Vince went upstairs with Murph and unrolled the banner, a larger version of the campaign buttons, so it was in full view for the cameras because of the strategic position that Seamus had taken in front of Quinn's.

Lacy Turnstone grabbed Seamus by the arm and pulled him away from the crowd.

"Okay, Mr. Corrigan, Seamus," she softened. "This all started when I showed up to do a story about the meth heads that tried to rob this place, I think you owe me an exclusive, especially since you let that nothing intern hack from Channel 4 have the story first."

"No, sorry, Miss Turnstone, Lacy, you'll have to join the crowd. I want Mike on camera to go out on all the channels at the same time so that the message is the same and you guys don't have time to monkey around with the editing."

"Then get me the first interview with Mr. Lee," she pushed.

"That." Seamus paused. "That I'll think about."

"Good, do me this favor and you'll be happy you did so. You want us to be your friends now that you've gotten into this race all the way."

"I'll talk to Mike after the live shot," Seamus said, chuckling to himself as he thought about using the phrase "Live shot."

Seamus positioned himself in his spot with the banner right behind him. He cleared his throat and smiled broadly, waiting for the lights to come on.

As the next live shot started, the lights blinded him for a second. As he was getting hit with the first question, he saw Roxanne and Kate across the street. Kate was jumping up and down and waving to him. Roxanne stood quietly next to her with a strange look on her face.

More questions brought Seamus back to his task.

"I want to thank St. Patrick for such a glorious day. It's always dicey in the middle of March but today was sunny and warm. St. Patrick's Day at Quinn's is a city institution and we are proud to keep tradition going. Just as Quinn's is an inseparable part of the city, so is Mike Lee. He is Genesee and I want all the people of the city to know that they'll never get a person in city hall who cares more about them and their lives, not what the people in Albany think."

Kate was still bouncing and pointing to Roxanne. Seamus saw that Roxanne was holding something white in her hand, but he didn't know what it was. He held up a "wait a minute" finger to the ladies as he took another question. Lacy noticed that Seamus was distracted and turned to see what he was looking at. She saw Kate and Roxanne and she recognized what Roxanne was holding.

"Mr. Corrigan, who is the woman you are looking at across the street? The one that is holding the pregnancy test?" Lacy asked pushing herself in front of the other reporters.

"The what?" Seamus asked, looking back over at Roxanne.

The cameras turned to Kate and Roxanne then back to Seamus.

"I'm pregnant!" Roxanne yelled, "You're going to be a father."

"She's pregnant!" Kate seconded.

Seamus ran over to Roxanne and took the pregnancy test out of her hand. She stood there nodding her head "yes" while Seamus stared at the test.

Lacy Turnstone grabbed her camera man and pulled him across the street to where Seamus stood.

"Mr. Corrigan, who is this that you are talking to?" she said sticking the microphone in Seamus' face.

Seamus looked at the microphone and then back at the test.

"I'm going to be a dad?" he said to Roxanne, ignoring Lacy's question.

"Yes," Roxanne said. She hugged and kissed him.

Lacy persisted, "Mr. Corrigan, can you let everyone in on the news?"

"This is my wife! I'm going to be a father!" Seamus picked up Roxanne and twirled her around.

"So, there you have it, Genesee, quite a day up here on Liberty Hill, St. Patrick's Day celebrations. Mike Lee, owner of Quinn's, officially starting his campaign for mayor and Mr. and Mrs. Corrigan are going to have a baby. This is Lacy Turnstone, Channel 9 News."

Lacy lowered the microphone. "You have my cell, Seamus, call me when Mike's ready, I'll be in the truck."

CHAPTER 56

NO TURNING BACK

VINCE WENT BACK to the office where Mike had hidden out for the last half hour, having turned off his cell phone, that had been buzzing constantly and even unplugging the dinosaur land line so he could get prepared for what he knew was going to be a hectic seven months until the election.

Vince knocked, then tested the doorknob which was locked.

"Mikey, it's almost six o'clock, time for the next live news broadcast. Seamus warmed them up at five. The reporters are foaming at the mouth waiting to talk to you. The crowd is primed to cheer behind you. So far, the campaign is off to a great start."

Mike opened the door and sat back down. Vince went in and sat across from him.

"Thanks. You guys have done a great job setting all this up. If I am going to do this thing then I need to get to work. Time to jump into the fray," Mike said as he massaged his temples.

"Okay, I think you should do some interviews after the announcement, tell the city why you decided to run and what your message is. Just say what you have been talking about since you decided to enter the race."

"Okay, I'm ready, can you get the reporters assembled?"

"Already done. Lacy Turnstone is clamoring for a chance to get at you for an exclusive. She'll be first."

"I can do that. I talk all the time. I'm talking right now."

Vince looked at Mike for a second and then planted his hand on Mike's shoulder.

"That's the Mike I know and love. And that pretty young thing is ready to introduce you to the world. We can trust her about as much as we can trust anyone from the stations. Think about it, they love to have a real mayor's race. They didn't want to cover a coronation of that shrew running unopposed. You've given them a real campaign to report on. Now go out there and charm her."

"Thanks for the motivation. You're right, we need to promote a horse race. I'm a choice. A choice the voters should consider. That'll be my message. Get the press excited about all the extra news stories this can generate. Play this to win. Where's Seamus by the way? I thought he handled the press?"

"Ah, he's a little worn out from all the cameras. I think he may be a little shellshocked by all the lights and the news, I guess you could say."

"Vince, what the hell are you talking about?"

"Nothing that can't wait till later."

"What?"

"Nothing, you need to concentrate. Why don't you check out the crowd and shake some hands for the cameras like a lousy politician?"

"Yeah, right. Me, Mike Lee, a politician."

CHAPTER 57

WHY WE FIGHT

MIKE WALKED UP to the reporters and said hello to each one on the line. Vince made sure he was positioned with the banner in the background.

"Let's get this started," Mike said to the group.

The lights turned on the cameras and Mike heard someone say, "we are live."

"Hello everyone, I'm Mike Lee, candidate for mayor of Genesee. I hope everyone is having a great St. Patrick's Day and that you are celebrating responsibly. I didn't want to turn the day into a campaign event, but my friends wanted to take advantage of the crowds to get the word out that we are here to take Genesee in a different direction. I don't represent any party or ideology other than common sense. I don't want to work as the mayor for lobbyists or interests, just for the people of Genesee. I think if we get the politicians out of the way then maybe we can get the city back to work, clean up their damage, make our neigh-borhoods safe and make the schools a place where you don't dread sending your kids. We are working on ways to do that so stay tuned to our campaign. If you don't like the decline of the city over the past thirty, forty years, we are simply a choice. Thank you."

Mike walked away and headed back to the bar, but Vince grabbed him and whispered in his ear and pointed to Lacy Turnstone who had moved and set up away from the other news crews.

"All of them? Okay, let's get this over with," he said as Vince again positioned him in front Lacy, making sure the "Mike Lee for Mayor" banner was in the shot.

The camera lights came on again as Mike exhaled. "This is Lacy Turnstone live at Quinn's Bar on Liberty Hill where I have an exclusive interview with Mike Lee, who has just announced that he is a candidate for mayor. Mr. Lee, thank you for talking to us before any other news outlet," she said as she turned slightly toward the camera.

"My pleasure," Mike said, remembering to look at the camera.

"Mr. Lee, can you tell us why you have entered the mayor's race?"

"I think the primary reason is that I love the city of Genesee and it is very sad to see how much the city has declined, especially over the last four years."

"The last four years under Mayor Lerner," Lacy said, obviously trying to bait Mike.

"She is the mayor. If I may continue with the original question?" Mike said. "As I was saying, I love this city and I think it is important that the people of Genesee have a choice. I know I don't stand a chance against an incumbent mayor with a huge war chest. I'm running as an independent because I want to be beholden only to the people and not to a party. Our campaign is currently being funded by a jar they just put on the bar here at Quinn's. My main goal is I want the people to have a choice."

"So, what do you plan to do, if, by a miracle you do win?"

"Miracle, yes it would take a miracle. But I would focus most on the people that work hard to make a living here in the city. Right now, the attention is on all the wrong things. Crime is up, it's supposedly the police that are at fault. The schools are a mess, it's supposedly the teacher's fault. The city is out of money, it's the business and home-owners that aren't paying their fair share in taxes. Well as a business owner and homeowner I can tell you I am being bled dry from taxes. I would love to expand and hire more people or make improvements to my businesses by remod-eling or putting on a new roof, but I don't have anything left to invest after I pay all my taxes. And you were here a few months ago when we were the victims of crime. We have to let the police do their jobs and protect the people of the city. And finally, that ridiculous school policy of codling students who disrupt, who assault teachers, they aren't there to learn. We need to clear them out for the kids who want to learn and the teachers who want to teach."

"Pretty tough words for the mayor, Mr. Lee," Lacy said. "Just the truth that everyone is afraid to say these days."

"Anything else you would like to say to the people of Genesee?" she asked

"Yes, as I said I think it's important for people to have a choice. I don't think there is anything more dangerous to the pursuit of happiness than a politician who thinks they can do whatever they want because they won't be challenged. A politician that feels they don't have to answer to the voters because no matter what they do, they will be re-elected. I am here to be that challenge."

"Tough words from a man who seems to know why he is in the race. This is Lacy Turnstone reporting from Liberty Hill, Channel 9 News."

Mike made the rounds with the other three stations, facing more pointed questions because the reporters had the benefit of listening to Mike with Lacy. He handled each one better than the other, sticking to his message and not falling for any of the trick questions or traps that they set for him. He never once mentioned the mayor by name or directly criticized her.

Vince and Murph were waiting for him as he finished. "You were magnificent," Murph gushed.

"You were a natural, the mayor is shaking in her boots right now," Vince added.

"I'm sure she is, Mikey, you did great," Murph said. "Yeah, I was good? Well, if she's shaking, that means she's mad and that might not be very good news for us. We need to be twice as careful with everything, checking IDs at the bar, jumping on any complaint from a renter. We follow every city code down to the smallest detail. Most importantly, we need to talk to everyone we know that works for the city and every cop and make sure we get ahead of what- ever she is going to do. Because as sure as I'm standing here, she is going to come after us," Mike said and looked at his friends one at a time to make sure they understood. He then walked slowly into the bar, leaving them to think about what he said.

As Mike was about to open the door, he turned, "Well it's still St. Patrick's Day, c'mon guys, I think we all need a drink."

CHAPTER 58

BUMPS

EVERY SEAT in the conference room was occupied except the executive chair at the head of the table. The assembled members of the mayor's staff talked amongst themselves as they waited for the mayor to storm in late, as she always did when she was angry, which was pretty much all the time.

Nancy Elliot was wavering back and forth between terror and joy, because Mike Lee was in the race officially and he was all over the news yesterday, every station and on the front page of the *Herald*.

Person after person that was interviewed at Quinn's said how nice it would be to have a choice in November.

The door slammed open, causing an immediate stop to the murmur in the room.

Mayor Lerner walked in without looking at anyone and waited for her assistant to hold her chair for her before sitting down on the stack of cushions that had her towering over the table.

"Talk," she yelled.

"Our initial polls show that he still doesn't have a chance, even with all the positive press yesterday."

"He has very low name recognition but almost everyone polled has heard of Quinn's and we'll have to redo this poll after yesterday. Half the city was at Quinn's for St. Patrick's Day."

"And how do we stop that?" she yelled, this time slamming her hand on the table.

"We really can't change that, Madam Mayor," a brave soul finally said after a moment of awkward silence. "Quinn's is a city institution, with the St. Patrick's Day party and the Irish Music Fest."

The mayor glared at the speaker, her head shaking slightly as she pursed her lips ready to speak or scream.

"But," the brave soul continued, "it doesn't really bring any gravitas to Mr. Lee himself."

The mayor turned her chair and spoke to the wall. "Okay Ms. Elliot, your turn. You are the one that got this guy into the race. You were supposed to get someone that we could easily beat but all the buzz today is about how great it is to see a fresh face. A fresh face! Did I ask you to get me a fresh face?"

Nancy swallowed hard before speaking.

"A bump like we've seen is normal for the campaign kickoff, unfortunately he had St. Patrick's Day and thousands of people at his bar. But he admitted he's not a politician and now we have the opening to show everyone how true that is."

"Okay, I won't fire you right now, but I better see that bump dissolve and very soon, Ms. Elliot."

"I've already started our people in the local press on that job."

Nancy closed her eyes and waited for the mayor to scream her next question.

The mayor turned back to the table and glared at Nancy, then took a deep breath and leaned back in her chair.

"What about dirt, what have we dug up? Anyone?" The mayor said just above a whisper.

The group all looked at Carter. Dirt was Carter's department. He had no choice other than to deliver the news.

"Nothing at all. I'm sure there is dirt there but almost every cop in the city knows him and half of the cops that know him also drink at his bar. That's how they found out about the sting. That is a disadvantage we have to be cognizant of – we can't trust our own police. His liquor license is clean, nothing all the way back to the first license in 1946. His rentals all have clean inspections although we have more scheduled where the inspectors have been told that if they want to keep their jobs, they'll find something."

"Great, that is just great. Carter, put the police chief on my calendar for tomorrow. Keep digging, there has to be something. And if we can't use it in the election, then you know what to do with the information, Carter."

"Yes, I will turn it over to the proper authorities, either local, State or Federal so that Mr. Lee will know that he shouldn't have challenged you Madam Mayor."

"Exactly Carter. What else? Anyone? And somebody better have something."

The room was silent.

"Everybody out of here except Carter and Elliot. I want the rest of you to come back with something we can use."

After everyone left and the door had closed behind them, the mayor put her hands on the table and lowered her voice.

"This conversation never took place."

"Yes, madam mayor," Carter and Nancy confirmed.

"Our friends in the Federal building, Homeland Security and IRS. I want them approached. I know you already cleared that one man to see if his immigration status was legal but go back for more. And the IRS, I want more action like the Cincinnati office did to those conservative groups. The usual fee plus a double bonus if they have something good. And remind those Federal idiots that this can never get back to us."

"Yes, madam mayor."

Nancy blinked, she thought she saw Carter's stone-faced expression crack for just a second out of the corner of her eye. She shook her head, she had to have been seeing things.

CHAPTER 59

SPIES LIKE US

NANCY WAS ROTATING her Quinn's surveillance team in two-week intervals but she was becoming increasingly worried about being discovered. Luckily, Quinn's popularity meant that there was a steady flow of regular patrons that acted as camouflage for her team. But she had to increase the coverage of the bar since Mike Lee had formally announced and she was getting reports of some of her team being recognized as regulars.

Nancy settled into an empty table by the bar for her shift. She always tried to be within earshot of either Seamus or Vince or both. A new waitress that she had seen a few times came over to take her order.

"Hi, my name's Alison, what can I get you today?" Nancy looked up from her menu, "I'll have the Dublin Salad and an iced tea, please."

Alison locked eyes with Nancy for a second and then started writing on her pad.

"Great, anything from the bar or an appetizer?"

"No thanks, just the salad."

Alison took one more look at Nancy before going back to the kitchen window to place the order. She walked over to Seamus and whispered in his ear.

"Can I see you out back for a second?"

Seamus was surprised by Alison's request, but he got up from his stool and joined her by the back door.

"The brunette at table twelve works for the mayor, I recognize her from when I was working the undercover team at City Hall. Go out and look for yourself."

Seamus walked back into the bar and looked at the table Alison pointed out and then went back to where Alison waited.

"I've seen her before. I think I actually had a conversation with her. Are you sure she's with the mayor?"

"Let's meet in Mike's office after the shift and I know how we can check. Call Mike and see if he can come up."

Alison brought Nancy her food and then took a seat at the bar and started to text on her phone. In between texts, she took a few pictures of Nancy.

Nancy paid with her credit card and left Alison a nice tip as a way to stand out, with the hope that the staff may become chatty in the future. As the lunch crowd thinned and Alison finished her last table, she motioned to Seamus to join her again.

Once inside the office she got on the computer and pulled up the web page for City Hall just as Mike walked in.

"What's going on?" Mike asked.

"Espionage," Alison answered without turning her head from the screen.

Alison pulled up the City Hall employee directory and saved it to a spreadsheet.

"Mike, how do I get to the credit card transactions for the last few months?"

Mike leaned in taking over the computer and pulled up the bar's ledger. Alison copied the credit card transactions to the same spreadsheet. Mike and Seamus watched as she clicked and typed for a few minutes until she pushed her chair away from the computer.

"There you go," she said smiling.

"You're very proud of yourself. What am I looking at?" Mike replied.

"I matched the credit card names to the City Hall directory, I got nine matches, but I'd bet there's more. You have spies Mike."

CHAPTER 60

GETTING ON THE BALLOT

MURPH RETURNED from his reconnaissance mission at the City Board of Elections with a stack of papers about a foot high in both hands.

"I see you made some progress," Mike said, folding the newspaper he'd been reading when Murph put all the paperwork on the table.

"This is going to be a lot easier than we thought. Since you aren't seeking the nomination of a party and you are running as an independent, all you need is fifteen hundred signatures from city residents that are registered voters. I got enough pages of the petition for almost five thousand just in case," Murph said slapping his hand on the first stack of papers.

"What's the other stack for?" Mike asked.

"It's a list of all the registered voters in the city, name and address, phone number, everything we need."

"Great job, Murph, you really outdid yourself. If we only need fifteen hundred, why get five thousand?"

"Well," Murph said, opening the folder, "Any of the

candidates that have qualified for the ballot already can challenge your signatures. They can go so far as filing lawsuits, line by line in the petition."

"I'm hoping at this point Mayor Lerner won't challenge the petitions. She needs me as her whipping boy."

"Great. Okay, all we need to do is divide the list up and start knocking on doors," Murph said, flipping through the list of registered voters. "We have to follow all the rules to a tee. Check IDs, make sure the address on the ID matches the voter registration and the house that they are standing in front of. If there is any doubt whatsoever they need to pass and thank them for their time. I think we can get to over five-hundred signatures with just the people that we know in the neighborhood. No one is to be left out, I even want you to hit the Somali refugees on the northside."

"'That's true, but we need to have equal coverage all over the city, every neighborhood needs to be represented. I don't want the mayor going after us on the premise that we only represent Liberty Hill and that the other neighborhoods won't have a voice."

"Mikey," Murph said as he shook his head and smiled. "You're right, you are getting really good at this."

"Thanks. Anything against offering a free beer to any voter who signs the petition?" Mike asked.

"Probably."

"I gave it a shot," Mike said. "Call the guys you want to do this. I can offer free beer to the people that walk around getting signatures?"

"Sure, how about starting with one for me?"

Mike laughed. "This thing is going to cost me a fortune in drinks before it is all over, but you deserve one for all this work. We have a long way to go, one step at a time. So, we need to get on the ballot, that's obvious. I think she'll squash us and keep us off the ballot if she wants, but I think we can hit her on 'what is she afraid of' if she does."

"She'll love the headlines showing she won by sixty points?"

"Right, beating someone by sixty makes her look like the overwhelming choice of the people. Almost national news maybe. Beating no one doesn't make any paper outside of Genesee."

"We have the council vote coming up on the Cleveland Middle School Project, so we can get a lot of airtime from that," Murph said.

"Yeah, I can ask why she wants to spend the money when there are empty spaces in existing public housing. I can have a good crowd of old ladies standing behind me with signs saying, 'Save our Neighborhood.'"

"And she'll hit you as anti-poor and racist for opposing public housing."

"I'm going to suggest to Piersky that he do an article, interviewing some of the people in the neighborhood, about how they'll move out to the suburbs if they build the project. Not just the projects themselves, but as the final straw in the declining city."

"Good idea, just make sure to add they are afraid of crime and they don't think the mayor is letting the police do their job," Murph replied.

"Well, let's get this thing started. The sooner the better."

"Consider it done," Murph said. He stood straightening the only tie he owned and headed out on his mission.

CHAPTER 61

ROCKING THE VOTE

THE MAYOR WAS all over the news talking about how the landlords in the city were practicing "one of the worst forms of discrimination" by refusing to rent to Section 8 renters. She purposely held a news conference in front of one of Mike's rentals with his "Liberty Hill Properties – For Rent" sign prominently in view of the cameras. She touted the bill that she had before the City Council, that would force the landlords to end this abhorrent policy of excluding the poor from the nicer parts of the city.

She announced that for the first time in the history of the city, that cameras would be allowed into the City Council meeting, for a live airing of the debate and vote on the bill. She encouraged everyone to watch "social justice" in action.

Mike and his lawyer Tom Tracy were prepared for the bill passing since they were filled in about the details by Piersky earlier in the month. Piersky was sure that the mayor had enough votes on the council to easily get it passed.

Mike had contacted the current leadership of the Genesee Landlords Association, which as a former president, it was easy for him to get their support and to get a lawsuit drawn up to challenge the bill. They would have it ready to file the same day of the vote on the measure. The suit wouldn't have Mike's name on it, although it was his attorney and his money behind the suit.

Every member of the association was told to say "no comment" if they were asked about the pending bill, to give more impact to the filing of the suit as their first public statement. Tom Tracy had his speech ready with Piersky and Lacy Turnstone given a heads up so they could bring the press to the news conference.

The mayor's choreographed Council meeting went off without a hitch. Six of the seven councilors gave impassioned speeches about the different forms of discrimination that had to be eradicated. The Council members didn't bother actually connecting the various grievance groups, that were supposedly being discriminated against, to actual cases of them not being able to rent in a specific neighborhood. Since there was no true opposition, they did not bring up a survey by the State Housing Authority which showed that properties in which landlords accepted Section 8 vouchers were only at fifty percent occupancy.

The mayor even arranged for one councilor to talk about the importance of an owner's property rights without once mentioning the bill itself or their opposition to the bill directly. The show was complete and even the councilor that gave the canned, feeble dissent, voted in favor of the measure.

When the triumphant mayor went out onto the steps

of City Hall to gloat in her news conference, she saw the cameras set up across the street at the County Courthouse. Tom Tracy was talking to the reporters about the suit he had filed the second the last "Aye" was recorded by the City Council.

Tom talked about real property rights, the fact that there was an overabundance of rentals accepting Section 8 vouchers, most of them empty and that the mayor should focus on listening to the complaints of the tenants in the current rentals and force the landlords to fix the issues that existed. He also hit on the fact that the mayor and city council failed to produce a single Section 8 tenant that had a story of discrimination.

"Focus on the real problems, not the imaginary ones, Madam Mayor," Tom thundered into the microphones, then paused for dramatic effect before dismissing them to walk across the street and ask the mayor to stop focusing on perceived discrimination when real problems were rampant amongst the absentee, uncaring Section 8 landlords.

The reporters ran across the street to where the mayor was waiting at the podium. They all noticed that she was fuming on having to wait to talk to the cameras.

"What was that all about?" she screamed to the press as they set up to go live.

An aide stepped up to her and whispered in her ear.

She screamed again and then turned to see the cameras focused on her.

"Madam Mayor!" came the queries from the reporters.

Mayor Lerner straightened up and fixed her suitcoat

and returned to the podium. The cameras caught her stepping up onto her platform for the first time in public.

CHAPTER 62

SIGN ME UP

THE CREWS that Mike sent out for signatures outpaced every expectation that the team had when Murph first came back with the guidelines for the petitions. They had filled out every page that Murph brought back from the Board of Elections and another fifty pages when Murph returned for more forms. They gathered 5,223 signatures.

"I think we have enough that they won't think about mounting a challenge with the Board of Elections," Murph said, proudly looking over the stacks of forms.

"I think you're right," Mike said. "Dan Halligan confirmed that she did say that she actually wants us to run so that she gets headlines and can gloat over a big win, then use it as a springboard to start her campaign for governor or senator."

"What's left to do, Mike?" Seamus asked.

"Murph and I talked it over. We think we should have Tom Tracy deliver the signatures. We think having a lawyer do it will lend credibility to our petition. It will also show them that we aren't afraid of legal action, even though we are," Mike conceded.

"Okay, I'll pack all this up and bring it over to Tom's office," Murph said getting the boxes ready.

"I'll go with him, just to be safe," Seamus offered.

"This is a big step, how long does the board have to give us an answer?" Mike asked.

"Thirty days. This paperwork is in perfect order and I even cross-referenced each person's registration number on the voter rolls. In reality, they could approve this in a week, ten days, tops."

"Did I say you did a great job, Murph?" Mike put his hand on Murph's shoulder.

"You did, but that doesn't mean you have to stop. I can hear it all day."

"Okay, stop the love fest and let's bring this to Tom so he can deliver them today," Seamus said.

CHAPTER 63

THE DAY THE MUSIC DIED?

AFTER THE DEBACLE for the mayor at the Section 8 vote, Mike and the guys waited for the mayor to hit back. They knew her biggest opportunity to cause trouble was to do something to disrupt the music festival.

The annual Irish music festival was Mike's second biggest moneymaker after St. Patrick's Day. Held over Memorial Day weekend, Mike had a big tent put up in the back-parking lot with a stage. There were acts all day, each day of the three-day weekend, with the headliners on Monday. Bands came all the way from Ireland for the fest and vendors selling t-shirts and Irish goods, set up along the street. Since this was just Mike's event and did not involve all the bars on Liberty Hill, he was the one that had to apply for the permits to have the city block off the streets for the vendors, the waiver for the noise ordinance and the waiver for open containers in the blocked off streets.

A week before the festival was supposed to start, the permit to block off the street, the one permit that every-thing about the festival hinged on, had not been approved.

"It's very obvious why, it is the mayor's doing," Vince said as they started the meeting to discuss what to do about the permits.

"I have a million things to do for the festival and this is the last thing I need," Mike said, exasperated, but not surprised, with all the trouble the mayor was causing.

"She's just showing you who is in charge," Vince said. "Yeah, I know that. Who do we know in the permit office?" Mike asked the group.

"No one right in the office, Mikey, we'll have to call in a favor or go a little harder," Vince said.

"Define 'harder,' please," Mike said.

"We block the streets off ourselves?" Seamus asked.

Mike ran a hand through his hair and sighed. "We can't do that."

"We do have enough cops lined up for security, they probably can block the streets themselves without a permit, make up some excuse, you know, challenge the mayor to do something," Seamus suggested.

"No, I'm tired of these games. You know I'm a taxpaying citizen, what law says I can't go right to the source?" Mike said, getting out his phone.

Seamus and Vince leaned across the table, so they could try to hear who Mike was calling.

"Mayor's office, please hold."

"I'm calling the mayor; who do you think I was calling?" Seamus and Vince gave Mike a thumbs up.

"Almost there, on hold, now I have to figure out what to say if I actually get to talk to her." Mike grabbed the permit applications out of a folder.

"Mayor's office, how may I help you?"

"Good morning, this is Mike Lee, I'm the owner of Quinn's on Liberty Hill. I would like to speak to the mayor please."

"Please hold."

"I actually have something I can do if I get elected, I can change this god-awful hold music."

"Mr. Lee this is Mayor Lerner, what can I do for you?" Mayor Lerner said in a syrupy, condescending tone.

Mike gestured to the guys to quiet down because they were dancing around him once they realized he had gotten through.

"Mayor, it's great to talk to you again. I hope it isn't inappropriate for one candidate to call another one?"

"Again?" Vince and Seamus said to each other at the same time.

Mike waved them off and turned back to his phone conversation.

"No, not at all. What's going on, Mr. Lee?" the mayor replied.

"Mike please, call me Mike. As you know, we have the Irish music festival this weekend, it's kind of a city tradition. The festival is in danger of being cancelled because our permit to have the streets around the bar closed off and the others that we need haven't been approved yet. I have my applications right here; they were submitted on April twentieth."

"Is that so, well I know how much the people of the area enjoy the music festival. Let me see what I can do. Do you mind if I put you on hold?"

"Not at all, Mayor, I appreciate your help." Mike hit mute on the phone.

"Holy cow, I can't believe this might work," Vince said, slapping Mike on the back.

"I'm surprised. No threats to call the media, nothing. Just ask, brilliant." Seamus laughed.

After a minute on hold the group stopped laughing. At two minutes, Seamus began to rub his chin as he always did when he was worried. At three minutes, Mike had to find his phone charger.

At ten minutes, Vince went and got three pints. At fifteen minutes, Mike sat back in his chair and started to drum his fingers on the table.

"Should I hang up?" Mike asked the guys.

"No, show her you can wait her out," Vince said.

"At this point we could have driven down to city hall and knocked on her door," Seamus said, checking his watch. At thirty-minutes the hold music stopped with a click, then silence.

"Did she hang up?"

"Mr. Lee are you still there?" the mayor said without a trace of apology.

"I'm still here," Mike said before realizing he was still on mute. "I'm here, sorry, had you on mute, we were waiting quite a while."

"Yes, I called the permit office, they'll email over the approval today."

"Thank you for your help," Mike said. "Yes, Mr. Lee."

Mike didn't know what to say next. "Well, thank you again. Have a good day."

"Yes, Mr. Lee."

Mike waited a second and then hung up. They all stood, looking at each other trying to read into what had just happened. Was there something else they should do? Was she setting them up for a big surprise? Could she have possibly backed off?

"I guess she was a little surprised that you actually called her directly," Seamus finally said, breaking the silence.

"Maybe, but I still have a bad feeling about this," Mike chimed in.

"She probably thought about the backlash from the people and the bad press she would get if she did something to cause the festival to be cancelled," Vince added.

"Well, either way, we have a lot to do to get ready still. Let's forget about the mayor for now and do what we normally do to get ready. We have a lot of work left," Mike said and closed the folder with the applications.

PART IV: SUMMER

CHAPTER 64

RAINBOWS AND COFFEE

MIKE COULDN'T STOP WORRYING about the festival. In a normal year, he worried himself into over-preparing and this year had him worried even more. He and Seamus met with all the off duty cops they had hired and asked them to be ready for anything. Mike tried to think of the potential disturbances that couldn't be traced back to City Hall. A fight? More underage drinkers? A gang of kids stealing from the vendors?

The morning of the first day of the festival started as an ominous sign for the entire weekend, with a windy downpour rolling through the city. Mike, Seamus and Vince were up before sunrise and in Quinn's having coffee when the deluge started.

"Ah, Jaysus, listen to that," Seamus said when he heard the first rumbles of thunder.

"Get your raingear on," Mike directed. "We'll need to make sure that nothing happens to the stage or the vendor tents."

"Look at what's about to hit us," Vince said as he directed everyone's attention to the weather radar on the television.

The entire Genesee area was in the path of a mean storm, highlighted in red and orange by the Doppler radar. They were under a severe thunderstorm warning with wind gusts up to sixty miles per hour.

"Just what we need. Bring hammers and extra tent stakes. I also have lengths of rope on the patio, get those too," Mike ordered but he could see that Seamus and Vince were already in action.

"I'll take the main stage," Seamus called out as they went to work.

Vince and Mike checked the rows of vendors' tents.

The wind started to test the limits of the stakes and ropes holding down the tents. The lightning and thunder were getting closer.

They ran around pounding in stakes and adding tiedowns to tents that were starting to lose the battle with the wind. Lightning cracked around them and the wind was stripping leaves from the trees.

Just as the sun started to rise, Pete and Murph showed up and joined in the battle as the storm continued to rage through the city. When the skies finally cleared and the sun began to filter through an hour later than it was supposed to shine, the guys settled down on the front steps of Quinn's. Murph brought out a pot of coffee as they stripped them- selves of rain suits and wet boots.

The sky was awash in color as the rising sun hit the remnants of the storm. Hues of orange and red colored the eastern sky.

"Look at that," Seamus said, pointing up.

A shining rainbow had formed in the morning sky and seemed to end right at the front steps of Quinn's.

"I really need to get up and look for the pot of gold but I'm too tired," Mike said, sipping from his cup.

"Yeah, that would be nice with a kid on the way," Seamus seconded.

They didn't see the photographer from the *Genesee Herald* who had showed up hoping to get shots of a destroyed festival area. He snapped a few pictures of them as they rested and chatted.

The festival got off to a slow start because of the weather, but as the afternoon began, the last of the clouds gave way to perfectly blue skies. The crowds soon started to build, drawn by the clearing of the weather. The music and the crowds hummed as everyone settled in to enjoy the bands, food and Irish goods for sale.

To try to get the newspaper on his good side, Mike had given them a free tent to sell newspapers and sign up people for subscriptions. He asked Piersky to make sure that the tent was staffed with people that wouldn't feel the urge to call a reporter with something bad about the festival to make some points at the paper.

Around three o'clock in the afternoon, the evening edition was delivered to the tent. On the front page, in full color, was the picture of the guys sitting on the steps, the sky painted with the rainbow ending at Quinn's, and the "Mike Lee for Mayor" banner that hung from the second floor of the bar. You couldn't have paid a photographer to set up a better picture for the campaign or the festival.

Seamus was the first to see the front page and grabbed

a copy off the *Herald's* table. He called to Mike and Vince on the walkie-talkies that they used to coordinate what was going on and to give instructions to the staff.

"Mike, Vince, front doors as soon as you can," Seamus sent out.

"What's wrong?" Mike asked. "You have to see this."

A few minutes later Mike and Vince hurried up to the front doors where they had been photographed earlier in the morning. Seamus was standing there holding up the newspaper smiling like Harry Truman holding up the famous "Dewey Defeats Truman" headline. He handed a copy to each of them.

"Oh, my goodness, this is beautiful," Mike said as he held the picture close, studying the details.

"We need to get more of these." Vince slapped the paper as proof of its potential.

"Right, we do," Mike said, grabbing his walkie-talkie. "Pete, Murph, grab a couple guys and meet at the front doors."

"Roger," echoed back on the handset.

Once the team was assembled, Mike handed out cash and sent each guy out to hit the grocery and drug stores to buy every copy they could find.

"Be back in thirty minutes," Mike instructed. "What about Piersky?" Vince asked.

"Yeah, I'll ask him too," Mike said hitting Piersky's number on his phone.

"Murder at the festival?" Piersky asked without saying hello.

"Have you seen your newspaper this afternoon?"

"Not yet, I'm not on the front page, they killed my story on City-County consolidation."

"Well, I did and I'm on the front page instead of you."

"Oh no, what did they do?"

"I like the way you assume the worst about your employer. No, there is a picture of us on the steps of Quinn's and it's amazing. I wanted to see if you could get as many copies as possible, I want to hand them out to the people at the festival."

"Let me look at it online, just a sec," Piersky said.

Mike's phone buzzed with a text Helen had sent: *"THE PAPER!"*

"Holy cow," Piersky said once he had seen the picture. "I'll be there as soon as I can with all the copies I can get."

"Thanks, Piersky," Mike said. He hung up and texted Helen back: *"I KNOW!!"*

The stacks of papers started to arrive from all the people tasked to retrieve them. As soon as the papers arrived, Mike sent people out with them, to hand copies to the festival- goers along with "Mike Lee for Mayor" bumper stickers.

Lacy Turnstone showed up to do a story on the festival, but as much as she hated to do a story about the newspaper, she ended up talking to Mike on camera about the great photo.

The picture turned out to be so popular that the paper ran it again the next day. Attendance at the festival soared. Before the last night of music, Mike ran out of campaign materials to hand out. Everything was gone, yard signs, bumper stickers and buttons.

"I think we really built some momentum," Mike said over celebratory drinks after the last act finished.

"We are on a roll," Seamus seconded.

"Still a long way to go, but it could be happening. We could at least get my forty percent." Mike swirled his whiskey as he leaned back in his chair.

CHAPTER 65

DOUBLE ANXIETY

SEAMUS HAD NEVER FELT MORE uncomfortable in his life than he did in the waiting room of Roxanne's OB-GYN. The room was filled with pregnant women and kids crawling all over everything. The noise combined with the anxiety attack that he felt building ever since he saw Roxanne waving the pregnancy test. He was about to hyperventilate. Everything at home, since St. Patrick's Day, had been all about the baby. Which would be the baby's room? Where would they put the kid in daycare, or should they get a nanny? Which were the best diapers? And lists and lists of potential names.

Kate pulled a few strings and got Roxanne into Dr. Aimee Desimone, the best OB-GYN in the city. She was booked up for years, but Kate knew her from the hospital and threw in a month's worth of free help at her office to get Roxanne an appointment.

Seamus was numb, completely out of his element with all the baby business and wracked with the paralyzing thoughts of himself as an old man with a teenager running roughshod all over him. The noise of the waiting room built into a chorus of screams for mom and muzak versions of the Rolling Stones. Roxanne was filling out a book worth of forms. Seamus held all the relevant cards like a poker hand, his health insurance, driver's license, credit card, all ready for Roxanne to pick when she needed the information.

He nearly jumped out of his chair when Roxanne tapped him on his shoulder.

"Seamus, they're calling us," she said with a glowing smile that made him forget for a moment all his anxiety.

They followed the nurse through a labyrinth of hallways to an examination room.

"The doctor will be right in," the nurse said as she left the room.

Roxanne was sitting, going over all the things she wanted to ask the doctor while Seamus paced back and forth. He jumped again when there was a knock at the door. Dr. Desimone came into the room with Roxanne's chart. She looked like she was still in college Seamus thought, not old enough to be the best doctor in the city.

"Mr. and Mrs. Corrigan, so nice to meet you," she said before going into a long list of questions that Roxanne answered easily.

"Okay then, here's a gown, everything off and up on the table. I'll be back in a minute with the sonogram technician and we'll do the internal exam and check on how everything is progressing."

Seamus actually turned his head while Roxanne got undressed, feeling like this wasn't a place to see his wife naked.

The doctor came back in with the technician pushing the sonogram machine.

"Okay, let's do a quick check before we do the sonogram," Dr. Desimone instructed as she set up the stirrups.

The sight of Roxanne with her legs up and the doctor looking at all the important parts pushed Seamus back against the wall without him realizing he was backing up.

"Okay, everything looks good here, Mrs. Corrigan. Let's see how far along you are and we'll take some measure- ments. Now this is going to be cold," the doctor said as she squirted the gel onto Roxanne's abdomen.

As much as the sight of the stirrups pushed him away into a corner, the black and white fuzzy images drew Seamus in. He leaned over, looking at the screen. He couldn't make out anything that actually looked like a baby, but the doctor obviously knew what she was doing as she moved the sensor around, stopped and then clicked on the image which froze it for a second and printed a picture.

"Very interesting," Dr. Desimone said as she moved the sensor back and forth a few more times.

"Is something wrong?" Roxanne asked, sitting up a little to look at the doctor.

"Everything is great, don't worry," she said placing her free hand on Roxanne's belly.

"Okay, everything looks good, let's hear the heartbeat."

"The heartbeat?" Seamus asked stunned.

"Sure," Dr. Desimone said as she flipped a switch and the rapid heartbeat of a baby filled the room.

"Unbelievable," Seamus said as he peered closer to the screen.

"Wait a minute, I thought so," the doctor said as she

started moving the probe around like she was going through the gears of a tractor trailer.

"There you are!" she exclaimed, "Wow, congratulations Mr. and Mrs. Corrigan, I thought I heard something and there it is, a second heartbeat."

"A second?" both Seamus and Roxanne said at the same time.

"Yes, twins, congratulations" she said, "two for the price of one."

Seamus fell into the nearest chair. "Twins?" he said trying to believe it.

"Twins! Seamus! Can you believe it?" Roxanne asked clapping her hands together and laughing.

"Not at all, not at all," Seamus whispered.

CHAPTER 66

AUTOMATIC TRANSMISSION

SEAMUS' life had changed drastically since Roxanne walked into Quinn's. He was now married and the expectant father of twins. He was also realizing that his unfettered life of retirement checks supplemented by odd jobs for Mike wasn't going to be enough.

"I need to go back to work," Seamus sighed as he discussed his situation with Mike and Vince.

"You have the pension invested, we still have our union healthcare and Mike can afford to give us a raise now that he's an important political candidate. You don't think that's enough?" Vince asked.

"I don't think it'll be enough with twins on the way. They'll need to go to St. Patrick's for grade school and then Bishop McCarthy after that. Have you seen what the tuition at Bishop McCarthy is right now? Ten grand a year and by the time they get there it'll be twenty. I have to take all those kid expenses and multiply them by two. Everything is doubled."

"Are you thinking about getting a job then?" Mike asked.

"Naw, I can't be tied down with a regular schedule, I like the flexibility of what I'm doing now."

"Why don't you open something up, maybe buy something established," Mike suggested.

"Do you think I could afford to take that chance?" Seamus replied.

"If not a startup then it would need to be something solid, with a good record of profitability," Vince offered.

"What's solid these days in the city? Mike isn't going anywhere but look what happens when something stupid happens, like the mayor thinking she can ruin him," Seamus said.

"What are we talking about?" Murph said, joining the conversation.

"Where have you been?" Mike asked.

"Doing work for you. Remember, I am your official campaign manager. I was going around to the businesses in the neighborhood asking for donations to the campaign, thank you."

"Any luck?" Vince asked.

"As a matter of fact, yes," Murph said puffing out his chest. "I have checks from Marty at the Liberty Hill Diner, old man Barone wrote me a check for a grand."

"A campaign financed by a funeral home," Mike laughed.

"I have commitments from almost everyone else in the area, I even got a check from Brian. And he's retiring and wants to sell, and I still got him to contribute."

Mike, Seamus and Vince stared at Murph.

"What? I'm doing all that I can," Murph apologized. "Brian, as in Brian Gridley, as in Westside Transmission?" Seamus asked.

"What other Brian do you know that owns a business around here?" Murph said still on the defensive.

Seamus and Vince grabbed their coats and headed for the door.

"Boy... sometimes I don't understand those guys," Murph said looking at Mike.

Mike got up and went behind the bar and poured a pint. He came back and handed it to a still confused John Murphy.

"Great work Murph, here's a pint on the house," Mike said slapping him on the shoulder and then proceeded to tell Murph just how good he had been.

CHAPTER 67

GROWING UP

SEAMUS REVIEWED Brian Gridley's books, tracking every penny that had moved through the business in the last thirty years and then had Mike go through them to confirm that the numbers were solid. He had a steady customer base and easily beat the dealerships on price and trust. He also wasn't earning as much as he could because he only had two mechanics and did most of the work himself. The location was perfect and the only problem was, for Brian only, that no one in his family wanted to run it. Instead he decided that he would find a buyer as soon as possible so that he could start snow birding down to Florida.

Mike bought into the shop as well as Vince. Roxanne's salon was doing well, so Seamus felt comfortable digging into his savings for the rest of the price. Brian had been very generous with the asking price because he knew the chances of getting another buyer were pretty slim and he was happy that he was selling to people from the neighborhood.

Pete put in his notice at Sears and brought in a couple guys that he knew and trusted. Seamus kept on Brian's mechanics. He had the paint booth reopened and bought new equipment so they could start doing body work, paint and rustproofing.

Seamus called his family in Dublin and told them there was a job waiting for anyone if they wanted to come over, especially Aoife, she could run the front counter and keep Pete from hopping a plane and heading overseas.

The grand opening was set for July 15th and Brian had agreed to stay on and help in the transition until it started to get cold and he'd head south. They even made it through all the city licensing and inspections without any trouble from the mayor. Maybe she had finally given up with the harassment. But Seamus knew that if he made even the smallest mistake there was a chance that the mayor would make sure he was fined or closed.

To make sure this didn't happen he followed every rule, set aside extra money to pay sales taxes and paid extra for the best Worker's Comp insurance so that there was no opening for any government inspector to make up something.

"It is a thing of beauty," Seamus said to Vince as they prepared to open for the first time under Seamus' ownership.

"Look at you, Seamus Corrigan, business owner. This is sure a long way from the two of us gophering on the assembly line at Chrysler."

"Yeah, married, about to be a father, starting a business. Tell me why we just didn't leave well enough alone and stayed spending most of our time at Quinn's drinking?"

"We turned fifty and it was time to grow up," Vince responded, putting his arm around his best friend.

CHAPTER 68

DEEP THROAT?

CARTER PARKED his car in his assigned spot at the downtown condo he rented. It was well past midnight after he spent another long day at City Hall working for a woman he disliked more each day. He reminded himself that as she rose, so would he. It was the only way he could stomach some of her requests.

As he approached the entrance to the building, he saw a man and a woman standing in the shadows. He was tall and smoking a cigarette. She was half his size and stood a few feet from him with her arms crossed over her chest. Carter was instantly worried because the pair seemed so out of place.

He pulled out his phone and pretended to flip through screens, but he was really preparing to call 9-1-1 even though he knew calling the police would make it into the papers. He saw the headline, "Even the Mayor's Staff is Afraid of Crime".

"Mr. Carter, do you have a minute?" the woman said.

"No thank you, it is very late" Carter replied, still

trying to figure out who these people were that were accosting him.

"That wasn't a request Mr. Carter," she said without emotion.

"Who are you? I'm about to call the police."

"Mr. Carter I'm Special Agent Balsam, FBI. This is my partner, Special Agent Kamholz. Why don't we go to my car and chat for a few minutes."

"What is this all about?"

"We'll discuss that in the car please."

Carter followed the two agents to a rental car that was parked in an unlit corner of the parking lot. Agent Kamholz opened the passenger door for him. Carter noticed that the overhead light in the car had been turned off.

Agent Balsam sat in the driver's seat. She turned and looked at her partner to make sure he was settled in the backseat before she turned and faced Carter.

"Mr. Carter, we would like to talk to you about your work at City Hall," Agent Balsam started.

"We hear you are in charge of digging up dirt," Agent Kamholz said. Carter didn't know if he was trying to sound menacing, but Carter felt his legs begin to shake.

"Yes, the dirt Mr. Carter," Agent Balsam seconded in a kinder tone. "We want you to tell us about the dirt."

CHAPTER 69

IN OR OUT?

MIKE LOOKED at his buzzing phone. It was his lawyer. He took a deep breath before he answered.

"Hey, Tommy, please tell me you have good news."

"Don't know yet, I have a registered letter from the Board of Elections that was just delivered to the office. Do you want me to open it?"

"Does it feel like good news?"

"I'm a great lawyer, not a clairvoyant. Tell you what, I'll be there in five minutes."

"How much is that going to cost me?"

"A Reuben and fries."

"I like those rates, councilor. See you in five."

Mike sent out a group text to everyone important and told them that the letter from the Board was on its way and to get to Quinn's as soon as possible. Half the people on the text beat Tom Tracy to the bar. Within a few minutes everyone was there except Helen.

Mike hit his home number.

"Hey, honey, what's going on?"

"Did you see my text?"

"No, I was reading, had my cell turned off, what's going on?"

"Letter from the Board of Elections, everyone's here to see what it says, except the most important person, you."

"I'm on my way," Helen said.

"Why do I bother paying for her cell? Okay everyone, Helen will be here in a minute."

"Can we take bets on what the letter says?" Vince asked.

Mike answered by hitting him in the face with a bar towel.

Helen rushed in the door and was greeted by the sight of everyone hovering over Mike and Tom at the table with the envelope. Mike held it up and smiled.

"Here goes nothing," he said, tearing into the envelope.

Mike read the letter and then handed it to Tom.

"Well?" came a half dozen voices.

Mike smiled and stood up.

"We're in, on the ballot, no challenges."

Cheers and clapping echoed in the bar. Mike sat back down. Helen hugged him from behind and kissed the side of his face.

"It's real now, I'm an official candidate for mayor."

CHAPTER 70

PLAN OF ATTACK

MIKE ASSEMBLED ALL the people that would work on the campaign again at his house, including former mayor, Dan Halligan.

"Well, I looked on Amazon and they didn't have a book on 'Running for Mayor for Dummies' so I thought we would get together to get an initial game plan on how we are going to attack this. I wanted Dan here to give us some overall guidance and then we can start assigning different responsibilities. I also wanted to thank Dan for pulling the strings to get us the meeting with the political consultants in Albany. We couldn't afford their services but because of Dan they gave us their assessment for a great price and we will use that as a jumping off point."

"The overall theme of the campaign will be that we want to bring common sense back to City Hall and that we will work for everyone in the city, not just the politically connected people."

"Well said Mike, and thank you for letting me help out," Dan chimed in.

"We'll skip the budget report because I don't want anyone to give up before we start," Mike joked. "So unless there are any questions, I'll turn the floor over to Dan."

Dan proceeded to talk for over a half hour on how they should run the campaign. They posted a map of the city that had been broken into the voting precincts with the number of registered voters in each. There was another city map divided into the city council districts. The Council map resurrected old wounds. Liberty Hill was split into two districts twenty years ago to reduce the political influence of the neighborhood.

The last map was for working out the timeline for Mike to visit all of the precincts, to try to knock on every door he could. They looked at the maps of registered voters and came up with the areas that needed a voter registration push, which was limited because unfortunately there weren't a lot of potential voters for Mike who were unregistered.

They worked throughout the day before Mike and Dan felt comfortable with the plan.

"Is there anything else we need to do today?" Mike asked as they reviewed the work they had accomplished.

"Yes, we all need a pint," Seamus said to everyone's agreement.

CHAPTER 71

PRESUMPTION OF INNOCENCE

MIKE WAS in his office doing his weekly liquor order when he felt his phone vibrate and had a sinking feeling that it wasn't good news. He looked at the screen and he knew he could be right.

"What's going on, Piersky? Anything bad?"

"Hey," Piersky said in a tone that almost sounded apologetic.

"What's wrong? The mayor find out that I don't always recycle?"

"Worse," Piersky said, "I got wind of something the mayor has and that they are looking into to see if there is anything they can do with it. There have been all kinds of rumors about Feds poking around the city and this might be it."

"What do they have?" Mike asked, now genuinely worried about what Piersky was about to say

"It's information about one of your friends." Piersky hesitated.

"Who?" Mike asked not really wanting the answer.

"It's Seamus, it seems the mayor has some information about some possible damaging activity that he was engaged in in Ireland before he moved here. It could compromise his citizenship, get him deported possibly."

Mike swallowed hard, this was his worst fear, that once he got into the mayor's race that she would pull something like this. Would it be worth hurting his friends even though Mike had no chance of winning?

"What are you talking about, Piersky? Did he commit a crime or something in Ireland? He has talked about some- thing happening before he left, but I always thought he was just joking."

"Worse."

"What could be worse than a crime?" Mike asked as he felt his chest tighten.

"Worse, as in being involved with a bombing. The IRA, Mike."

"That can't be true. There's no way Seamus would be involved with anything like that."

"It seems the mayor's team has something that they are asking around about. They talked to Homeland Security at the Federal Building and gave them whatever they had come across."

"Even if that is true, what does that have to do with me running for mayor? Seamus is my friend; he is not running."

"A candidate for mayor associating with a known terrorist?"

"Damn," Mike said, lowering the phone and shaking his head. He could hear Piersky talking and brought the phone back up to his ear. "What were you saying?"

"I asked you if you know whether there is any validity to Seamus being involved with the IRA."

"I don't believe a word of it." Mike said.

"Okay. Well let's see if they find out anything. If they do, I will give you a heads up because I want an exclusive on your reaction and what your campaign does if it is true."

"Thanks, Piersky. I really appreciate you giving me a heads up, so I didn't have to find out by turning on the news."

"Or opening the paper," Piersky said. "We are still a relevant news source."

"If you say so," Mike said, regretting immediately the dig. "Sorry, Piersky. Let me know what you find out."

"Will do," he said, and hung up.

Mike put his phone on the desk and covered his face with his hands. He cursed to himself the decision to enter the mayor's race. He questioned himself if his decision to run was really out of spite toward the mayor more than any real sense of civic duty.

Mike picked up the phone and called Seamus. "Mikey!" Seamus answered in his usual jovial tone.

"Hey, Seamus, what are you doing right now?" Mike tried to sound normal.

"What's wrong, Mikey?"

"Can you come down to the bar?"

"Sure Mikey, what's wrong?"

"Not on the phone, Seamus?"

"Okay Mike, I'll be there in a few minutes."

"I'm in my office, see you in a few."

Mike went out to the bar and grabbed a bottle of Jameson's special edition and two glasses and returned to the office to wait for Seamus. He thought back to when Seamus first showed up off the boat from Ireland. He was exactly the same today. Mike couldn't recall one thing that would make him think Seamus had been running from something. His uncle had gotten him the job at Chrysler and had sponsored him. There was nothing sudden or urgent about his arrival. What Piersky had told him couldn't be true. Mike was sure of one thing, that when Seamus got here, he would tell him the truth and he would believe him without reservation.

Seamus filled the doorway to the office and knocked lightly on the doorframe causing Mike to look up and smile a little.

"Come on in and have a seat." Mike grabbed the bottle and poured a good glass for Seamus and himself. Seamus sat down and picked up the glass and then turned the bottle around to see that Mike had brought in the best whiskey in the bar.

"How bad is what you're about to tell me, Mikey?" Seamus asked as he left the whiskey glass sitting on the desk.

"Piersky called me and told me that the mayor might have some information that is really, really bad," Mike said. He took a sip, as if the words he was about to speak needed a drink more than he did.

"And it's bad enough that you needed the best bottle in the bar to tell me?"

"Maybe," Mike said. "But once you give me your answer, I'll know whether it is something we need to be worried about."

"What is it?"

"Piersky said they have information that you were involved in an IRA bombing before you left Ireland."

Seamus looked at Mike without any reaction. He picked up his glass and finally took a sip and then another.

"And the mayor is thinking about releasing that information to scuttle your campaign then?"

"That's what he told me. They are floating it around to see if there's something there."

"Well, Mike, I was involved with the investigation of a bombing, but I was not in the IRA."

Mike let out a sigh. "What happened?"

"There was a bombing at a market in Dublin. People were hurt. The police thought I knew something about it and they brought me in for questioning. I knew some guys that may have been involved in the IRA, but I did not have anything for the police. That didn't stop them from questioning me for two days, without letting me sleep or eat. When they let me finally leave, they let it leak out that I had cooperated and as you know if certain people had thought I talked I would be in trouble."

"Jesus," Mike said, shaking his head.

"Yes, it was bad. I tried to tell people that I hadn't said anything, that I really didn't know anything worth knowing, that I couldn't have told the police anything, but that didn't matter. That's when people stopped talking when I came into the Pub and other people that knew me my entire life stopped talking to me altogether. Then the police grabbed me again and put me in the back seat of their car in plain view for everyone to see. That's when my dad called my uncle here in Genesee and I started the process of coming over. I had no choice, Mikey."

"I can't even imagine what that could be like," Mike said. He finished his glass and refilled his and topped off Seamus'.

"So, whatever the mayor has is shyte. If they say I was in the IRA, it's bullshit."

Mike reached across the desk and shook Seamus' hand. "I can't believe I wasted the good stuff on a piece of crap story."

Seamus laughed, "It wasn't a waste. Can we break this out again tomorrow if I tell you the story about when I was an altar boy nipping at the altar wine?"

"Now I know that's a total lie. You? An altar boy? I could have believed terrorist but never an altar boy."

"Now what do we do, Mikey? I have nothing to hide. There's no way they can ruin me. It will be a pain in my arse but let them try."

"I'll call Piersky and tell him whatever they have is bull- shit and let them do whatever they want to do. Let her try. I'll tell the people that it shows the character of the mayor, or her lack of character. That they would stoop to such a level against an average guy bar owner, who is prac- tically running his campaign from a tip jar on the bar, speaks volumes of what a low life she and her band of soul- less lackeys would do."

"Is that all you'll do? I would have just said they could bloody piss off."

"I could do that too," Mike said laughing as he picked up his phone to call Piersky.

CHAPTER 72

LIBERAL LOGIC WEAPONIZED

PIERSKY WAS STARTING to show his value to Mike but had also expressed concern that his boss was going to find out how much interaction he was having with Mike's campaign.

"I have an idea," Piersky told Mike across the table. They had met for lunch an hour outside of Genesee in Delphi, a little farming crossroads.

"What is it?"

"I can do a story on people who immigrated to the United States and settled in Genesee. My editor will eat it up because he'll think it is a positive immigrant story that they'll use to offset opposition to immigration."

"And you'll interview Seamus?"

"Yeah, I'll get him to tell the whole story from his perspective. I'll throw in some background on how the government over there, both in the north and south, used and ruined people. It'll make Seamus look like a refugee who found happiness and security in America."

"That's brilliant. Are you sure you aren't sticking your neck out too far this time?"

"I probably am, but at this point, I can't go back."

"Let's go for it. She'll know we found out, but I don't think she can pin the leak on you," Mike assured him.

"She can pin it on me, so we'll see what happens. If I get canned, you'll have to find me a job."

"No problem, Piersky. We'll teach you how to put together a transmission."

CHAPTER 73

A-O-IF-EE

THE DAY before Piersky's immigration story was going to run, two men in a Chevy with US Government plates pulled into the parking lot of the transmission shop. Seamus watched through the office windows.

"Pete," Seamus yelled out into the garage. "Text Mike and let him know that the Feds are here and to be on standby in case I need him."

Pete went out back and sent Mike the text.

Seamus stood at the counter and waited for his guests to come inside. The man on the passenger side was rifling through some files, the driver was on the phone. They finally got out and walked into the shop.

Seamus was expecting badges and guns on their hips but they had neither.

"We are looking for a Mr. Seamus Corrigan," the man with the folder said.

"I'm him."

"Right, my name is Agent Heitzman and this is my

partner Agent Johnson. We are here to do a site inspection of this business."

"What is this all about?" Seamus asked, confused since he was expecting Homeland Security or the FBI.

"You are Seamus Corrigan? Right?"

"Yes."

The second agent stepped up to the counter. "This is about your application to sponsor the green card for your niece, an Aoife Roddy," he said, checking the folder.

He pronounced her name as it is spelled, A-o-if-ee.

It took Seamus a second to process all of this.

"Yes, my niece, of course. What can I do to help you gentlemen? Would you like some coffee? Lunch maybe? Pete, get in here."

"That's okay, Mr. Corrigan, we just want to do the inspection."

Piersky's story ran the next day.

"SO, ALISON WHAT ARE YOU STUDYING?" Mike asked his favorite new waitress. Alison and Mike had grown close since she started working at Quinn's. Mike missed his daughter and he enjoyed Alison's wit and strength. She could go toe to toe with anyone in the bar.

"I'm in the Stein School, Radio and Television. I want to be a reporter."

"A reporter?" Seamus said in disgust. "Not all reporters are bad," Alison said.

"Just ninety-eight percent of them." Mike laughed. "That's what was so great about my job with the city, it was undercover work, it would have looked great on my resume. Until you guys got me fired."

"You can help on the campaign," Mike said, trying to cheer her up.

"That's the wrong side of the fence, ninety percent of the people in my field are liberals. Sorry Mike, you're as white as a white male can get," Alison responded.

"I'm pasty white thank you. I can still talk to some of

the news contacts I have now, Piersky or Lacy Turnstone. They may be able to get you something, maybe an internship."

"Thank you, but the school is working to get me an internship in the city. Stein carries a lot of weight in the industry and there are Stein grads at every major network and production company."

"Well, good luck with that," Mike conceded, knowing that Seneca's Stein School could open much bigger doors than most schools because of their reputation and alumni base.

"We're supposed to find out any day about where we are being placed. I'm so nervous, I'll probably end up spilling beer all over someone tonight, so be prepared to pay for someone's dry cleaning."

"I know something that'd help with your nerves," Mike said with a big smile.

"Drinking?"

"No," Mike scoffed.

"I thought you prescribed drinking for most ailments given your profession and the profit margin."

"Yes, that's true most of the time, but in this instance, I think you've practiced enough and it is time for you to get up on the stage with the band tonight."

"So, to get over my nerves, you want me to get up on the stage and sing in front of a crowded bar?"

Mike had heard Alison singing along with the music a few times and he told her she had a beautiful voice. He convinced her to go over to see Matt Mayo. Matt's band were the regular Wednesday night act. Matt reported back to Mike after the first rehearsal that Alison should quit school and go to New York to start a career as a singer. He could hook her up with a few bands. Alison had declined the offer, saying she would use it as a backup in case she didn't become a famous network television personality.

"You know everyone in the crowd and it'll be good practice for being in front of the camera," Mike said taking her by the shoulders and looking straight at her.

Alison looked down on the ground, Mike lifted her chin.

"You are very talented; you need to show everyone. I believe in you. I'll even pay you a full share of what I pay the band."

"Okay," Alison said, rolling her eyes. "Just to get you off of my back."

"Great, I'll call Matt and let him know so he can change the set for your vocals."

"Then let me go home and get changed. I'll be back in a little while," she said, obviously trying to hide her smile from Mike.

"Sure, you're going to be great, Alison. Thank you for taking this chance."

CHAPTER 75

RED IS THE ROSE

ALISON CAME BACK an hour and a half later, dressed in a stylish green dress and her hair was curled and bounced on her shoulders. With the dress and make up she looked years older and Mike could see that she would sparkle in front of the camera if she ever got her chance.

"I'm so nervous," she confessed to Mike when he waved her over to the bar.

"You'll do great, just start with the one song you've been rehearsing and if you feel comfortable, just keep going."

"How long do I have before we go on?"

"The boys will be here in a few minutes and they'll go on at seven. I think you should let them do a few songs and then I'll have Matt invite you up."

"Okay," Alison said. She twirled her hair with one hand and drummed her fingers on the bar with her other.

"You will be great, you have a beautiful voice," Mike reassured her.

"Thanks, I'm going to do it."

"Tell you what, I'll pour you one beer to help with your nerves, but nothing else until after you're done," Mike said grabbing a glass.

"Thanks, that'll help." Alison said as she looked at the stage and exhaled a long, nervous breath.

The boys showed up on time and started setting up. Mike went over the plan with Matt and whispered to him what to do if Alison froze. He stopped when he saw Alison walking over to them.

"You ready, Alison?" Matt asked.

"Yes, I can do it," she replied.

"Okay, I'll introduce you. It's a slow song so take your time. Just follow the music. They'll love you," Matt said.

The band played a few reels as the crowd built to a respectable level for a Wednesday night. Alison sat at the bar, trying not to look at the crowd.

When the music stopped, Alison got off the bar stool.

"We have a special treat for you this evening," Matt said. "Joining us this evening for a song and maybe a few more, is the lovely Miss Alison Bradbury. Alison, come on up please."

Alison made her way through the polite applause. She stepped up and took the microphone and gave the crowd a meek "hi" before she nodded to Matt and the band started to play.

Alison turned to the audience and waited for her place to begin. When she began to sing it was pure magic, a slow and hauntingly beautiful version of Red is the Rose.

Come over the hills my handsome Irish lad
Come over the hills to your darling
You choose the road love, and I'll make a vow

That I'll be your true love forever....

She finished without looking up. It took the stunned crowd a second to begin their applause and when they did, they stood and cheered, clapping lustily, some of them only stopping to wipe tears out of their eyes, Mike included.

The applause didn't stop.

Matt took another microphone, "How about one more, Alison?"

The applause grew again.

Alison nodded.

The crowd did not stop until the music started again.

Alison floated through three more songs.

When she finished, she made her way over to Mike and hugged him. Mike twirled her around and set her down.

"I am so proud of you Alison. I am going to miss you when you're famous, you better come in and visit every time you are back in Genesee."

"Thank you, Mike," Alison said, her voice breaking with emotion. She looked at him as her tears began to well up and she hugged him again.

CHAPTER 76

KALE SALAD

MIKE WAS RETURNING to work after spending all morning and the early afternoon knocking on doors with Murph, campaigning. They had been going neighborhood to neighborhood for weeks. He was looking forward to a busy Friday happy hour and evening at the bar to try to feel normal.

About a block away from Quinn's, he saw what looked like a big cotton ball sitting on the bench outside the bar. As he got closer, he could swear it was a guy in a sheep costume, but why would there be someone in a sheep costume outside the bar?

He checked his phone to see if anyone had texted him about something strange going on while he had been gone, but he didn't have any messages. Crossing the last side street, he could see that it really was a young man in a sheep costume.

Mike walked up to his visitor and stood there looking at him, trying to think about what he would ask him. The sheepman was busy checking his phone and did not see Mike approach.

"May I help you?" Mike finally asked, after ruling out asking what the hell he was doing.

The sheepman looked up from his phone and slowly blinked his eyes. Mike couldn't tell if the kid was stupid or just staying in character. After considering Mike's question for a few more seconds he answered.

"Do you know what time the protest is, dude?" the sheepman asked, proving to Mike that he should have chosen stupid.

"And what protest might that be?" Mike asked, now worrying that this was going to be something he was going to regret.

"The PETA protest, it was supposed to start at one, wait, is today Tuesday or Wednesday?" he said looking back at his phone before Mike could answer.

"Actually, it's Friday. Okay, sheepman, this is my place of business, I want you to tell me who you are and why you are here. And what's this about a protest?" Mike asked, feeling he was losing his patience.

"I'm Kale with a 'K.' I'm the other green leafy substance. We're going to protest the dude that owns this place, because he killed a goat," Kale said sounding annoyed.

"I'm Mike Lee, I own Quinn's, so you will be protesting me. But if you are here to protest what happened to the goat, why are you in a sheep costume?"

Kale looked at his costume, holding up his arms for a closer inspection and then down at the sheep head that sat next to him on the bench.

"Oh, because they didn't have a goat costume, dude."

Before Mike could ask another question, a Lexus hybrid pulled up to the curb and two young women with close cropped hair and two young men with ponytails piled out and opened the trunk. They unloaded signs as another three cars pulled up and stopped.

"There they are," a relieved Kale said, getting up and putting on his head.

Mike watched while the group assembled, distributed signs and put on their PETA t-shirts. He got out his phone and called Seamus.

"Hey, what are you doing?" Mike asked when Seamus answered.

"Just looking at a parts catalog a salesman dropped off at the shop. Why, what's going on?"

"Can you come down to the bar, you have to see this."

"Okay," Seamus said. "Is something wrong?"

"Not yet, but I'd rather be safe than sorry. See if Vince is free and bring him with you if he is."

"Will do, be right up."

"Okay, see you in a few minutes." Mike turned his attention back to the protesters.

"Is someone in charge here?" Mike asked the assembling protesters trying to sound congenial.

One of the young women stormed toward him. "We don't believe in patriarchal hierarchies, so no one is in charge," she said through clenched teeth, trying to get in Mike's face but failing to come close because she was barely five feet tall.

"Come again?" Mike asked.

"We are a collective group that operates without any

phony, stereotypical, societal labels," she said, still trying very hard to reach Mike's face, losing her balance as she strained on her tiptoes.

"Is there anyone else I can talk to?" Mike asked the group.

A less angry young woman walked up.

"It's okay, Pat, I'll take care of this," she said, gently prodding the angry young woman back to the group.

She turned back to Mike, "Hi, I'm Wyoming, I'm from the regional chapter of PETA and we were informed of an incident that took place at this bar, where an innocent animal was maliciously killed and we are here to peacefully protest your treatment of that precious animal."

"Goat killer!" Pat the angry young woman yelled, trying to get back into Mike's face before Wyoming stepped in front of her.

Mike smiled, "We did not kill the goat. We were being robbed by strung out meth heads and the meth heads killed the goat. By the way, I'm Mike Lee and I own Quinn's. I would appreciate it if you would cancel this protest because, I'm sorry, but you were misinformed."

"You're right, you'll be sorry," Pat yelled from behind Wyoming.

"Be that as it may, this is the site of the killing and what was a goat doing inside of the bar anyway?" Wyoming said unfazed by Mike's logic.

"He was attending my birthday party as an honored guest. What else would he be doing in a bar? Anyway, that was months ago, why are you here now?"

"Our regional chapter of PETA was just informed of

the murder," she said her tone showing a bit more impatience.

"And who may I ask informed you of the incident where the robbers killed the goat?" Mike asked although he had a good feeling he already knew the answer.

Wyoming pulled out her phone and scrolled through her email.

"We were informed by Harmony Woods," she held up her phone.

Mike looked closer at the email and saw the address, hwoods@Genesee.gov, she was from the mayor's office.

"Well if it is any consolation, we were very sad about what happened to the goat. We have a memorial service planned for him on the anniversary of his passing and you are very welcome to join us for that solemn occasion," Mike said trying to remain serious.

"We are here and we have already arranged for the news stations to show up. The press releases were sent out this morning. So, I'm afraid the protest will go on," Wyoming told Mike.

"Okay, just don't block any of my customers from getting into the bar, keep it quiet and we won't bother you."

"But, we are here to bother you, we are the protesters, that's what protesting means," Wyoming said, pointing to her group and the signs as proof.

Mike saw Seamus and Vince walking up the hill from the transmission shop. By the time they reached Mike, the protesters had formed a circle and had begun their chanting. Kale-Sheepman was walking as if he was being tortured and every few minutes, he would dramatically die writhing in pain.

"The mayor?" Seamus asked when he reached Mike. "Of course, it was her. The news trucks will be here short-ly," Mike informed his friends.

"News trucks? Jaysus, what are we going to do?" Seamus asked.

"I have an idea," Vince said. "Get some of the hand-held campaign signs and round up about a dozen people."

"What's your idea?" Mike asked.

"Counter protest," Vince said as he ran into the bar.

CHAPTER 77

METH KILLS GOATS

TEN MINUTES LATER, Vince had taken the campaign signs and written "Down with Crime" and "No Drugs in our Neighborhood" and other anti-crime slogans on the blank side of the cardboard and handed them out to the people that Seamus had rounded up. They formed their own circle and began shouting the slogans from their signs, drowning out the PETA protesters.

Seamus saw Pete walking up the hill from the transmission shop.

"What are you doing here?" Seamus asked Pete when he joined them.

"I put a 'Back in 1 Hour' sign in the window and came up here to help when I saw your text."

"Well, make yourself useful and get a sign and join the protest," Seamus said. He directed Pete toward the signs and the markers.

Pete grabbed a sign and started writing after thinking for a second.

"Meth Kills Goats?" Seamus asked looking at Pete's sign.

"It's all I could think of, I was in a hurry," Pete apologized.

"Well, get out there and make some noise then," Seamus said, shaking his head.

The first news crew to show up was from Channel 9 and none other than Lacy Turnstone jumped out of the van's passenger seat. Seamus saw her and cut her off before she could reach the PETA protesters.

"I'm calling in my favor for getting you that first interview with Mike," Seamus said to her as he pulled her aside.

"Maybe, what is it?" Lacy said eyeing Seamus.

Seamus explained the plan, finishing up just as the other three channels showed up. Lacy went over to her colleagues.

"She said she would do it, but we owe her double now," Seamus said when he returned to Mike and Vince.

"Great, hope this works," Vince said as all the news stations started to set up their equipment.

Wyoming left her place in the protest circle and took out her note cards for her impending interview with the reporters. She went through her notes and then readied herself for her rehearsed outrage. The reporters walked up to her, then right past her, and headed straight to Mike. She turned, stunned, and in the process dropped her note cards.

"Yoohoo, I'm here. I'm the PETA spokesperson. Hello, reporters, over here," Wyoming called out to no avail.

The reporters surrounded Mike as they exchanged

pleasantries. Mike said hello to each one by their first name.

The cameras came on and Mike stepped up to the bank of microphones. Wyoming was still off to the side, waving her arms, trying to get the attention of the reporters.

"Mr. Lee," Lacy started, "What prompted you to organize this rally against crime today?"

Mike smiled like the politician he was becoming and looked straight into the cameras.

"As you know, we were the victims of crime a few months ago and we wanted to join with our good friends at PETA and honor the victim of that horrid crime, our beloved mascot, Bart the goat, by trying to bring awareness to the rampant crime in the city."

The news stations got their story after a few more questions for Mike, about crime in the city and what he would do as mayor to reduce the crime rate.

Their work complete, the counter protesters filed into Quinn's for a free round, as promised for their efforts.

The PETA protesters were completely deflated after failing to get on the news with their condemnation of Quinn's and the murder of the goat. Wyoming followed the reporters to their trucks continuing to let them know that she was the PETA spokesperson without any success.

They finally skulked away and got back in their hybrids and left. Everyone except Kale. He went inside Quinn's, took a seat under Bart's portrait and proceeded to drink until he left on all fours, either from all the drinks he had had or from his commitment to stay in character until the bitter end.

CHAPTER 78

GIVE THE INTERN A CIGAR

ALISON WAS the only waitress left after the Friday lunch rush. She was still riding the high of her appearance on stage and had fielded questions all during lunch about when she was going to sing again.

It had been over an hour since she checked her email and she had a feeling that today might be the day she would hear something about her internship. She delivered her last order and then took a seat at one of the booths by the kitchen door and started to look at her phone.

"Still on the clock?" Mike asked her.

"Yep," she responded without looking up from her phone.

"I'm glad I'm paying you then," Mike said, realizing that his attempt to motivate her was doomed.

Mike went over to chat with the group of retirees that came in every Friday for the corned beef special. He had just started to say hello when they heard a scream and everyone turned towards the kitchen door.

"I got it!" Alison screamed again.

She began to dance around the bar saying "I got it" over and over.

Mike walked over to her and crossed his arms as he waited for an explanation.

"Okay Alison, what did you get? Is it the internship you wanted?" he asked when she finally settled down and it was safe to get close enough without being hit by a dancing elbow.

"Yes, yes, yes! The internship I applied for, the one I really, really wanted," she said setting off a new round of dancing.

Mike didn't wait for her to settle down this time. "Which internship, Alison?" Mike asked, finding himself smiling from her contagious joy.

"I am going to be an intern for *The Stone Saunders Show* on HBO starting in a few weeks in New York City," she screamed again while shoving her phone into Mike's face to show him the email she had just received from her school.

"Well, congratulations sweetheart," Mike said.

Stone Saunders was the hottest show on the talk show circuit. Saunders ignored all political correctness and skewered all sides of the political spectrum with relentless confrontations until he usually had his target whimpering for mercy. It didn't matter who you were, a politician, business leader, or a sports star. All felt his wrath. Although after the beating a strange thing happened, if you were able to withstand being pummeled without crawling into a corner, as if it was a badge of honor, the politician gained in the polls, the business leader saw their stocks rise and the athlete landed a new endorsement deal.

Those that sought the shelter of the corner became trivia questions or the fodder for "what ever happened to" stories on the news.

"Remember that you knew us once you're famous and go clear table three," Mike said trying to bring Alison back to earth.

CHAPTER 79

WELCOME TO THE HAREM

ALISON and the other dozen interns for *The Stone Saunders Show* sat in a conference room on the 80th floor over- looking midtown Manhattan. This was her third day and everyone was excited because now they were going to meet Stone. The first two days had been a blur, moving into the apartment that she shared with three other interns, getting the orientation presentations from all the departments and finally the unofficial orientation on how to stay out of trouble when Stone tried to get you in bed.

Alison knew something was up on the first day when the interns had their welcome meeting and everyone in the room was female and beautiful. They were a rainbow of hair and skin colors, including a few with British and French accents. She texted her friend at school and told her that they weren't interns, they were a harem.

The unofficial orientation contained a list of do's and don'ts when you were working with Stone and especially what not to do if he was able to get you alone.

Unlike all the other presentations this one didn't have a PowerPoint or a hand-out. They were told not to write anything down and to commit the rules to memory. They obviously wanted complete deniability that this meeting ever took place.

The producer checked her watch and then looked around the room.

"Any questions?" she asked.

Alison wanted to raise her hand but when everyone else remained silent she decided not to ask.

"Good then, I'll go get Stone."

The interns waited in silence. Alison watched the planes leaving LaGuardia and started to wish that she was on one of them.

Stone knocked at the door, peeked in and then slowly walked to the head of the table, followed closely by a team of producers. Alison thought he didn't look anything like what she had imagined given his over-the-top, on-air persona. He was dressed casually instead of the perfectly tailored suits he wore on air. He seemed shorter than his oversized personality.

He looked around the room and then cleared his throat before speaking.

"Good morning, ladies, welcome to *The Stone Saunders Show*. I am sure that you will learn more this summer about production and show management then you will learn in the four years at your college or university. I look forward to working with you. Thank you in advance for your effort and dedication. See you around."

He then looked at the producers and nodded. He took

one last look around the room and left as slowly as he came in.

The interns sat stunned, all except Alison. She had an idea of what game he was playing.

CHAPTER 80

RIGHT ON TARGET

ALISON WAS ALONE in the conference room setting up for the final production and script walk through, on the day before taping the weekly show. She had all the name plates in place and a fresh copy of the script with red pens and yellow highlighters. She checked the refrigerator to make sure there was enough diet soda that Stone was paid to drink on camera. While walking down the hall, she started to text her boss to tell her that everything was ready when she was grabbed by the arm and pulled into an empty office. It was Stone.

"Well if it isn't my favorite intern," Stone said, looking over Alison.

Alison thumbed her phone and started the video recording. She noticed that Stone was too busy looking at her assets to see she had her phone.

"Hello, Mr. Saunders, what can I do for you?"

"You can help me get ready for the read through." Stone ran his hand up and down Alison's arm.

"I need to get back to the conference room to make sure everything is ready."

"Not so fast, stay here and talk to me for a little while. The meeting can't start without me. We won't be late."

"But Mr. Saunders, we shouldn't be in here alone."

"I want to be alone with you," he said and moved his hand to the small of her back, pulling her closer.

"No, let me go Mr. Saunders."

"Just relax, honey. You are about to get Stoned."

"Let go of me now," Alison said, feeling her anger rise.

Stone pulled her into his arms and started to kiss her neck. Alison twisted to her left giving her enough room to kick her knee up and drive it into Stone's stones.

She looked at her phone which thankfully was still recording and left the room, leaving Stone in the fetal position on the floor.

CHAPTER 81

PAYING THE PRICE

STONE SAUNDERS really didn't have a choice, at least according to the corporate lawyers. Alison was the twelfth intern to bring sexual harassment charges against him. They just couldn't keep sweeping all these young women under the rug or buying them off with jobs or money. They had tried in vain to keep Stone from bringing in all-female interns but Stone always got his way.

Alison had the entire incident on video on her phone. She had kicked Stone in the stones and caught his agonizing facial expression as he grabbed his crotch and fell to the floor. It was the perfect video she could sell for millions and still sue Stone for even more. But she had terms and they advised Stone that he had no choice other than to give her what she wanted and more.

Alison wanted a job after graduation, with HBO corporate in Los Angeles, something on air, with a salary of $500,000 per year, a Mercedes and an apartment. She also wanted the job to be guaranteed for five years and that at the three-year mark she had the option of moving to another role within HBO of her choosing. There was one more thing she wanted and this part was what Stone had balked about the most. He had paid a lot more to an intern that he had wronged, but he was completely against her final demand.

"Didn't Clinton make it acceptable for powerful, important men like me to have my way with interns with just a slap on the wrist?" he asked the lawyers and his boss Dennis Scott.

"Don't be crazy, Stone. If you weren't bringing over a hundred million into this company, I'd market her video myself to the highest bidder," Dennis said throwing the legal paperwork in front of Stone for his signature.

"But why would I do a story about a mayoral election in a place that no one gives a shit about other than the unfortunate people that have chosen to live in a godforsaken place like Genesee, New York?" Stone complained as he turned over the paperwork to show his objection.

"I don't care if you want to do the story or not, she wants you to do it as part of the settlement. It's not that bad, a bar owner running against a machine-type politician. The little guy against Goliath. You can choose which side you want to skewer. She's smart but she isn't that smart," Dennis said trying to placate his star.

"Sir," one of the lawyers that neither Stone or Dennis knew his name nor did they care, chimed in. "Actually, on page seven, section three, subparagraph eight, she stipulated that it has to be a positive story about the challenger, a Mr. Michael Lee. Make Mr. Lee a hero of the people. She also stipulates, and I quote, 'Stone Saunders must use his unique talents to humiliate, ruin or show as a fool, the incumbent mayor, a Ms. Leona Lerner. Whatever it takes, she must be made to beg for mercy.'"

"Balls," Stone cursed.

"Yes, she kicked you in them and now holds yours in her hands and she's squeezing," Dennis advised.

"Well, Mr. Saunders, what is your decision?" another lawyer asked.

"Looks like I'm visiting the rustbelt wasteland of the lovely burg of Genesee, New York, population, frozen, drunk and ignorant," he said turning over the document and holding out his hand as three lawyers simultaneously handed him a pen.

"Drunk wasteland?" Dennis asked, "Then you'll fit right in."

CHAPTER 82

STONE FECKING SAUNDERS

ALISON WASN'T due back from her internship for another week, so everyone except Mike was surprised when she walked in during happy hour, parading with her new outfit she had charged to Stone's account at Prada in SoHo.

"Will you look at that," Seamus declared as Alison did a twirl. "She's back from the big city to rub our noses in her success."

"Quiet," Mike admonished as he came out from behind the bar and gave Alison a big hug. "I got your text, why are you back early and what's your surprise?"

"Did you bring us some autographs of all the famous people you met?" Murph inquired because he had been keeping a list of every guest on the show while she was there.

"I want to tell you, but me throat is so dry, I'm sure I can't speak a word," she said in an Irish accent as she winked at Seamus.

"Pour the famous lady a pint and put it on my tab," Seamus instructed.

"Why don't we have a seat, are you hungry, Alison? I can get you a sandwich," Mike said reaching out and taking Alison's hand. "You look so successful, we're all so proud of you."

"Well, you'll love my news. How's the campaign going anyway?"

"Still slugging it out, trying to get out to the neighborhoods and meeting people. Murph has done a good job raising some money and we are going to have a mailer going out next week," Mike said.

Davey handed them their pints as Mike invited her over to the table where Seamus waited so they could continue their conversation and hear the great news.

"So, what is the news?" Seamus asked.

"I was able to convince Stone Saunders to come up to Genesee and do a story about Mike and the campaign," she beamed.

The guys sat quietly without reacting.

"What's wrong? This is great news. You'll get tons of exposure, more than you could ever afford. Everyone in the city will know who you are. Everyone in the country actually. Just the fact that he's coming is going to generate tons of news." She reassured them.

"But he's going to come up here and make fun of us, a simple bartender in over his head," Mike replied.

"No, it's in the contract. It has to be a positive story. And, this is the best part, it's in the contract that he has to bash Lerner, I took care of everything," she said enunciating each syllable of "everything".

"How did you do that?" Seamus asked. "I charmed the pants off him."

"Ah, Alison, what did you do?" Mike asked.

"I just made a proposal and kicked it around with him for a while. He told me I was his favorite intern, practically got down on the floor and begged me," she said, smiling.

"When is he coming then?" Seamus asked.

"Next week, the show will air in the middle of August. Plenty of time to build some momentum before the election," she said and raised her pint.

Mike looked at Seamus. Seamus shrugged his shoulders and nodded. They each picked up their own pints.

"To Alison," Seamus toasted.

"And to Stone fecking Saunders," Alison said back in her Irish accent.

CHAPTER 83

HERDS OF HIPSTERS

THE ADVANCE PRODUCTION team for *The Stone Saunders Show* descended on Quinn's in a manner that would make a biblical swarm of locusts feel like chasing fire- flies on a warm summer night.

Brooklyn hipsters were everywhere. Associate producers walked around Quinn's forming imaginary screen frames with their index fingers and thumbs, looking for the perfect shot, closely followed by junior producers with light meters and note pads.

The regulars tried to ignore the swarm until they started rating them for their background appeal as "scenery" in their shots.

"The camera will love this one, he screams blue collar, white ethnic," one producer said as they framed a regular as he tried to enjoy his pint in peace.

Mike watched all of this from behind the bar.

"I hope I have customers left by the time this is all over," he said to Seamus who also eyed all of the activity.

"Remember all of the exposure that you are going to

get from this. We just have to make sure he doesn't try to make you look like an Upstate hick," Seamus warned.

"Alison has assured me that this will be a positive story. She really must have something on this guy or he has fallen head over heels in love with her."

"If he touches that sweet girl, I'll break him in two," Seamus said, loud enough for at least three associate producers to hear and turn their heads.

The producers finally settled for moving a table on the right of the corner of the bar that had four stools and a booth in the background. Finding customers to serve as backdrop proved to be much harder when the producers asked the people they had chosen. Mike had to step in and offer free drinks while they were filming and that *The Stone Saunders Show* was buying.

Mike picked out what to wear, his best Harris Tweed jacket, jeans, and a plaid shirt that Helen had ordered for him from L.L. Bean. Everything was ready, they just needed Stone, who was arriving on a private plane in an hour.

"Okay, Mike," one of the producers said, sitting Mike down at the interview table, "Stone is going to ask you some funny questions first and then will follow up with some serious ones. We want you to play along with the funny questions. You can play it any way you want; you can get angry or joke back, whatever feels right for you."

"I just want to make sure he doesn't try to make me look like a fool."

"Don't worry, that's not going to happen. He's going to make you a star," the producer said.

"Yeah, okay, I'll settle for him making me a viable candidate."

CHAPTER 84

MAYOR OF THIS?

JUST WHEN MIKE thought the Stone Saunders entourage couldn't get any bigger, a caravan of six limos pulled up in front of Quinn's. The security team that the show had hired, moved the barricades so they could park.

The streets were filled with onlookers as the news teams caught all the action for the biggest event to hit Genesee in years.

Stone exited the last limo and was surrounded by security, so that all you could see was his wave to the bystanders above their heads.

Mike waited at the table as the lights were turned on and the makeup girl put more gunk on his face to adjust for the lights.

Seamus came over with a pint, "You'll need this I think."

"Thanks, it'll make a nice prop," Mike joked as he watched Stone in the makeup chair.

"We're going to roll in three," someone yelled over the din of the crowd.

Stone emerged from the gaggle of producers and came up to the table where Mike sipped his beer.

"Stone Saunders," he said extending his hand. "Mike Lee, nice to meet you."

"They told you all about what we're going to do here?"

"Yeah, I'm ready. I appreciate you coming up here. I need something to kickstart my campaign and this is more than I could have ever expected."

"Well, I am the most watched weekly show on cable," Stone bragged.

Mike nodded. He didn't want to say that he had never seen his show until he found out Stone was coming. He had to go to Vince's, since he had HBO, and watch a few episodes so he could get an idea of what to expect.

"We aren't going to rehearse or go over the questions. I like the natural reaction of the person I'm interviewing."

"Sounds good, let's do it."

"I like your style Mike Lee," Stone said with a wink.

The lights got a final adjustment and producers surrounded them in a pile of hipsters for the final prep.

"We are rolling, quiet everyone," the producer's voice boomed.

Stone turned to the camera with the red light on.

"Stone here with Mike Lee, independent candidate for the mayor of Genesee. For those of you that don't know, Genesee is in upstate New York. It is a small city known for snow, Seneca University hockey, empty factories, and snow. Mike let's get started. Mike Lee if you were ice cream, what flavor would you be?"

"Well, Stone, first I want to thank you for coming up to Genesee. I hope you get to enjoy some of the great things that Genesee has to offer before you head back to the other New York. As for your question. I would definitely be chocolate chip."

Seamus wiped his brow with relief as he peered over the heads of producers. As with the local news, Mike was a natural on camera.

"Can you do an Irish step dance, Mike?"

"I do enjoy step dancing and I really enjoyed Riverdance until it became an overplayed, bouncing circus. As for me, I have never worn tights or sequins."

"Tell me something you've lied about since you announced your candidacy?" Stone said leaning forward a little and putting his index finger on his chin.

"To be honest, I lied about watching *The Stone Saunders Show*. I don't even subscribe to HBO."

"I see," Stone said, now tapping his index finger on his chin.

"Mike Lee let's get serious about Mike Lee. Where do you see yourself in five years?"

"I hope that I am just starting my second term as mayor of Genesee. That crime has gone down, businesses and people are moving back into the city and the Department of Education is here to see how we really turned the schools around."

"And you have a plan to do all this?"

"I'm not going to do anything different than what has worked in other cities. I'm going to treat crime just like Rudy Giuliani did. I'm going to cut taxes and regulations like I was Ronald Reagan's barber. And I'm going to send my own third-grade teacher, Sister Robert Rita, into the city schools to clean them up. She's ninety-three, but I'm sure she can still command a classroom of forty kids with just a ruler and her malevolent stare."

Stone nodded thoughtfully during Mike's responses.

"Mike are you an animal lover?"

"Of course. I love horses. Seamus, Vince and I go to OTB every Tuesday."

"Would you prefer to be the tortoise or the hare?"

"If that is an analogy for the election, then I am the tortoise. I think I polled at 5% in the first one the local paper did. But I'm in the race for the long haul and I'm going to keep plugging along," Mike looked straight into the camera and not at Stone. He then picked up the beer and took a long drink before giving the lens a wink.

Stone laughed.

"As we were flying into Genesee, once we got under the clouds, I looked down and thought, 'why would anyone want to be mayor of that?' Why do you want to be mayor, Mike?"

"Stone, I was born and raised here in Genesee. It is my home and I consider the good and hard-working people who live here my friends. I think if the city has a mayor that wants the city to have better days ahead, then they need someone who wants the job for reasons other than they want to suck up to the governor or a political party, a mayor that is more interested in working their way into being a candidate for the next level up the ladder."

"Are you talking about the current mayor? Leona Lerner?"

"I didn't say that. I disagree with a lot of what Mayor Lerner has done with the city. She has handcuffed the police, there isn't a regulation she hasn't said 'no' to and the schools are a disgrace. Now she didn't do all the damage, it's just her policies have continued the failed policies of a succession of mayors. But she has put these same failed policies on steroids. The results of these policies are what you saw as you flew in. Did your plane happen to take any gunfire as you were landing?"

"No, Mike, we were lucky. Keep going on that theme, what do you believe Mike?"

"I know it sounds too boilerplate and progressives would say naïve, but I believe in the ideas that America was founded on. I believe especially in equality. A good guy is a good guy, no matter what religion, color or ethnicity. I believe in equality of opportunity not equality of outcome. Most the damage you see in the city is from the government and progressives trying to use policies to create equality of outcome. They will always fail because they are not based on free choice."

"Preach, Mike preach."

"Look at the cities that are in the most trouble, the common denominator is one-party government. It doesn't matter which party. That's one reason after approaching a party, only to be rebuffed, I have chosen to run as an independent. I want to represent a different way to approach government. One that worked up until the 1960s. Reduce the size of government to the essentials."

"Well, I might not agree with everything you said but I believe in your conviction Mike Lee. One last question, Mike. Can I have one of those?" Stone said pointing to Mike's beer.

Seamus had pints ready for when the interview was over. He hurried to the table and put two down.

"Thanks," Stone said without taking his eyes off Mike. "The Irish are good at toasts Mike, why don't you give my audience a toast?"

"Sure thing, Stone. May those who love us love us. And those that don't love us, may God turn their hearts. And if He doesn't turn their hearts, May He turn their ankles, so we'll know them by their limping."

"Good one, Mike," Stone said. He took a drink and looked back into the camera. "Here in Genesee, New York they have a candidate for mayor who really loves this backwater, rustbelt, hell hole of a city. Why? I can't for the life of me tell you. But I know that he is sincere and that he is not a politician and look what the politicians have done. Any man who serves an honest pint, looks me in the eye and gives it back to me as good as I can give it, has earned my vote. Good night America, you have time to move to Genesee, if you have a strong stomach, register to vote and vote for Mike Lee."

STONE KEPT his word on making the mayor look ridiculous. They didn't interview her, she refused, they just cut together clips of her talking and interspersed them with shots they took around the city of the squalor and poverty. The boarded-up buildings and the drug corners.

"She's going to be fuming," Mike said to Helen when the show finished.

The morning after *The Stone Saunders Show* aired was the best day of the campaign so far. Murph texted Mike that donations on the website were through the roof, money coming in from all around the country. There were also emails from national organizations such as Politics without Politicians and Common Sense America. Murph also said that he was going to make the rounds before lunch to hit up the local businesses that were on the fence about donating, maybe the show changed their minds.

At breakfast, Mike was swamped by well-wishers to the point where he asked the waitress to box up his frittata so he could take it to his office and finish. Vince paid the check and waited for another fifteen minutes before Mike could tear himself away from the crowd.

When they walked down the street to Quinn's to open up, there were trucks from all the news stations hoping to get a live interview for their morning news. Mike obliged, knowing he had to take advantage of this momentum.

Seamus showed up shortly after with boxes of campaign buttons and bumper stickers, yard signs and t-shirts. Piersky was also there taking notes about all the commotion for the article he was writing and getting quotes from people in the crowd on their reaction to Mike's appearance.

By lunchtime the bar was packed to the point that Mike had to open the back patio and call Davey to see if he could come in on his day off. Vince had emptied the donation jar three times already and for the first time, there were unsolicited checks and bills larger than a ten spot.

Lacy Turnstone showed up looking like she just came from a salon makeover and was wearing a dress instead of her station polo.

"What's with the look?" Seamus asked when she made her way through the crowd to Mike's table.

Lacy tried to stay professional but her giddiness bubbled out like a shaken-up soda.

"The network wants me to do a report for the national news. They can't get a crew up here in time, so they asked the station and they sent me!"

"Congratulations," Seamus said, shaking her hand. "You've come a long way from covering exploding goats."

"I know, Seamus, you have to make sure Mike will do an interview."

"Don't worry, he's in full campaign mode now. He'll talk to everybody now that he sees an opportunity to cut into the mayor's lead."

"Great, the network wants this by two so they can edit. Is that too much to ask?"

"No problem, Lacy, you've been in the game from the beginning and we owe you one."

As Lacy got ready with her questions a real national network crew showed up to do an interview. Seamus greeted them as they set up.

"You work for Mike Lee?" the reporter asked Seamus.

"Yeah, who wants to know?"

Seamus could see the anger rise in the reporter's face, probably because Seamus did not seem to recognize him, even though Seamus knew exactly who he was.

"I'm Hudson Franklin from CNN, we are here to interview Mike Lee."

Seamus could see Lacy deflate as she realized she was about to be pre-empted by a network crew.

"I'll put your name on the list, there are people ahead of you," Seamus said as he looked over to Lacy and gave her a wink.

"But we're from C-N-N," Franklin protested.

"I heard you, I'll fit you in when I can."

Seamus went back to Mike and leaned through the people surrounding his table and whispered in his ear, "do you want me to get Pat Quilty and a couple uniforms up here to keep things in line?"

"No, that's okay, I want the cameras to catch all the enthusiasm. Can you believe all this?"

"It's great but I have a feeling we'll be hearing from the

mayor. Probably the health inspector so he can carry a rat out of the kitchen for all these cameras."

"If that happens, I want you to make sure he doesn't have a rat in his pocket when he shows up."

"Will do, Mike. Can I get you anything?"

"Yeah, ask Piersky to come over to the table." Piersky made his way to the table.

"Wow Mike, I knew your appearance would change the game, but this is amazing."

"Can you do me a favor?"

"Sure, what do you need?"

"Can you ask around at City Hall to see how they are handling this? Make sure she isn't sending the SWAT team to the bar to shoot us up?"

"Already done, I got that started before I came up here."

Mike smiled. "I take back anything bad I ever said about you Piersky."

"Typical politician, going back on your word. I thought you were different, Mike."

"Don't worry, I'm still swimming with sharks, just waiting for the 'Jaws' music to start."

CHAPTER 86

CRAWLING BACK

WAYNE GARRET WALKED into Quinn's and joined Mike, Seamus and Vince at the corner table. Murph came over with a pint for Wayne.

"Well I probably know why you're here Wayne," Mike said, starting the conversation.

"I am here, hat in hand, willing to jump on the Mike Lee bandwagon. I underestimated your chances when Murph came to me last year. You were exactly the kind of candidate we needed and I wasn't smart enough to recognize it. But, I'm here today to apologize and I am here today to offer you the support, both monetary and organization- ally, of the city Republican Party, for your campaign for mayor."

Mike took a long drink from his pint and looked around the table at his friends. They had been split on whether to accept the support when Wayne called and asked for this meeting. Mike had remained silent on his position.

"Wayne, I want to thank you for making this effort

today. I really do appreciate the offer but my answer has to be 'no.' We really could use your help, but we had no choice but to position the campaign as an anti-party campaign. We have blamed both parties for the problems in the city even though you and I know that's not entirely true."

"I was prepared for that answer," Wayne cut in. "I think we can support you without an official endorsement. We can give you access to donor lists, we can give you volunteers, we can do other things too, all unofficial. We'll make it look like the supporters on our team are joining you out of their own volition. To be honest Mike, this is happening without us even trying to make it happen. We don't have to really do anything other than put out the word that we don't mind if they join you."

Mike looked around the table at his guys for any looks of disagreement and found none. Murph had a wide smile. "I'm glad Murph doesn't play poker," Mike thought.

"Wayne, I can live with those terms. If the press asks, you tell them what you just told us, you did nothing to help but would not stand in the way of any city Republicans from putting their support behind our campaign."

"Done," Wayne said standing and extending his hand. "Good," Mike replied. "Feel free to stop by anytime, the door's always open."

CHAPTER 87

NANCY SACKED

NANCY KNEW IT WAS COMING. The mayor was going to blame her for bringing Mike Lee into the race even though she had no way to control all of the positive events that fell into Mike's lap. She couldn't believe that her team had stopped getting any intelligence from their surveillance of Quinn's. They must have found out they were coming in, that's all that she could figure. She didn't know about Alison's chart of Nancy's team, with their name and picture, that was hidden behind the Guinness calendar in the linen room of Quinn's. Each bartender and server had to memorize and alert everyone when the spies were spotted.

She underestimated Mike in every turn, especially his luck. Maybe he is destined to be mayor. Maybe she should join the other side after she gets fired.

She sat alone in the conference room waiting for the meeting. Carter walked in.

"Where's Lerner?" Nancy asked.

"The mayor is busy."

"So you get to have the pleasure of showing me the door?"

"It isn't a pleasure. We are just a middling rust belt city and we are acting like this is a Hollywood political thriller. Trying to trick a man into running for mayor with petty retaliation and half-assed intimidation. Either way I'm leaving after the election. Following you down to DC."

"What? Carter, I can't believe you are disillusioned."

"Well, if you knew some of the things..." he tailed off.

"What?"

"Nothing," Carter sighed. "Just trust me. You are getting out at a good time. Count this as a blessing actually."

"What's going on Carter? You know something. Something big."

"Just be glad you're out Nancy," he said offering his hand.

Nancy looked at him waiting for more of an explanation that she knew wouldn't come and finally took his hand.

CHAPTER 88

THE NEXT LEVEL

WITH MONEY COMING IN, the press paying attention to him, including articles about his candidacy in *National Review* and *The American Spectator*, Mike was on a remarkable roll.

"This thing is getting bigger than us," Mike said to open the meeting he called on where to go next.

"We could hire a professional," Murph offered.

"I don't think we could afford anyone that would make a difference. Besides, remember how much the guys in Albany were charging," Mike replied.

"Why don't you say something in the interview you have with Fox tomorrow morning," Vince suggested.

"Yeah, I'll do that. I'll find a way to bring it up during the interview. Maybe we can get a real consultant to come in for a couple days to just point us in the right direction," Mike said shaking his head.

"What's wrong Mikey?" Vince asked.

Mike picked up the list of campaign appearances. "We're spinning our wheels. I think we need to bite the bullet and hire someone, even if they're local. You guys are doing a great job, but we are gaining."

Mike showed up at the local Fox affiliate to do the satellite interview with the *Fox and Friends* morning show. The national spotlight was great and it was bringing in money, but was it getting them any votes within the city limits?

The questions were boilerplate and Mike handled the friendly interview with ease. He invited the morning crew up for the next St. Patrick's Day and maybe a show from City Hall. He was able to fit in that he wouldn't be surprised if a political consultant showed up to help them. Mike liked fishing.

As he drove back home, he knew something had to change. But how and what?

CHAPTER 89

SELLING BODY PARTS

MIKE'S PHONE buzzed with a text from Lacy Turnstone: *check your email.*

He went into his office and opened the email:

Mike, I have attached a copy of the ad that the mayor is going to run on all the local stations. She has bought a week's worth of time for the commercial to air at the beginning of each newscast. Thought you might like to see it before it airs. P.S. You owe me. Again.

Mike clicked on the link. The video started with a patient on an operating table. A child's voice is heard reading the instructions on how to perform an appendectomy. The child fumbles through the medical terms as two children in surgical garb look at the instruments and the beeping heart monitor. One asks to read the last part about how to cut with the scalpel again. The child narrator reads again as one of the children takes the scalpel and is about to cut into the patient when the screen freezes.

Mayor Lerner pops up in a screen with a fuzzy image of the child surgeon in the background.

"You wouldn't let an untrained child operate on one of your loved ones. The same goes with our city. Why would you let a rank amateur run the complexities of our city, run the schools, run the police force, gamble with a quarter billion-dollar city budget? I wouldn't either. You deserve the experience and proven leadership that I can bring to the city of Genesee."

The voice over then came on with the legal disclaimers as LERNER – MAYOR filled the screen.

Mike unplugged the laptop and brought it out to the bar. He called to Vince, Seamus and Murph to join him at the table. When everyone was seated, he clicked on the video again. They all sat silently watching. When it was over, they looked at each other around the table. Vince broke the silence when he started to laugh. Seamus joined him and their laughter intensified.

"Okay, what's so funny?" Mike asked.

Vince tried to compose himself, "What's so funny...is.... She's almost right."

"And why are you laughing?" Mike asked.

"Cause it's perfect," Vince said gathering himself. "That's all she has? No accomplishments? She starts by attacking amateurs?"

"He's right," Murph said, his voice cracking with excitement. "We can use this, it's a blind haymaker and we have a dozen ways to counter punch. She must really be scared of us to come out with an ad like this before any real campaigning has started."

Vince had stopped laughing. "We could counter with a snooty know-it-all type trying to sound overly intelligent with big words, talking about the little people as all the terrible stats flash across the screen: crime rate, graduation rate, tax rates."

"I like it, I really like it. There's just one problem," Mike said clicking on Lacy's email and zooming in on the last paragraph where she had included the cost of airing this spot just on her station. "That's just Channel 9, five airings. Where do you think we can get that kind of money?"

"Sell a kidney?" Vince offered.

"We need help," Seamus admitted.

"We can't spend that kind of TV money now. We have to save it for right before election day, when people actually start to pay attention. We'll have to ride the wave of *The Stone Saunders Show* for a little while longer," Mike said, shaking his head as he started the mayor's ad again.

CHAPTER 90

TEARS OF IRISH VIRGINS

AS SOON AS he walked in everyone could tell that he wasn't a local guy. His clothes looked like they cost more than the cars that most of them drove, he did not have a hair out of place and he had a Bluetooth phone in his ear and he was talking to someone. The leather of his briefcase was polished and perfect.

Mike watched him come in and thought to himself that twenty years ago, people talking to themselves like this guy were crazy. He hoped that he was just lost and not crazy.

He walked right up to Mike and stood in front of him finishing his call.

"Tell Senator Tremblay that I'll work on her re-election, but she has to come up with at least one mil up front and that if she gets re-elected my bonus will be three times that. She also has to stop that crazy, liberal grandstanding and move to the center or she'll lose half the counties in the rural districts before she announces. Those are my terms. Uh huh, uh huh. Does she want to win or not? You have my number."

He stopped talking and stood there looking at Mike.

Mike wasn't sure if he was still on the call or waiting for Mike to say something.

Mike finally relented.

"Can I help you?"

"You look better in person; Stone Saunders should fire his make-up people."

"Thank you, I guess."

He looked at Mike for a few more seconds then stuck out his hand.

"Brahm Barbour."

"Mike Lee," he said using his candidate combination of firm handshake, eye contact and confident smile that Stone Saunders had shown him.

"Good, good. Someone who knows what they are doing taught you that handshake? Was it Stone?"

"Yes, how did you know?" Mike asked as he realized this guy really was a pro.

"I've been watching you on all the national networks since you were on with Stone and I had to come meet you. Do you know who I am?"

"You're Brahm Barbour, you just told me." Mike laughed.

"Of course. I'm a political consultant," he said handing Mike his card.

Mike read the card. "What can I do for you, Mr. Barbour?"

"Brahm, please. I was completely intrigued by what you're trying to do. I haven't had a challenge like this in years. I want to help you."

"Thanks, Brahm. But I can tell that just by looking at

you that I can't afford your help." Mike pointed to the big jar on the bar with the sign "Campaign Donations."

"That's my campaign fund over there. I'm sure there isn't enough in there for the time you've already spent talking to me."

Brahm laughed and stood there looking Mike over again.

"No Mike, I want to help you, pro bono. I've been at the top for so long I don't know what it's like to be in the trenches anymore. I want to re-sharpen my teeth. Re-load my arsenal and I'm thinking that by getting you elected, I can accomplish that mission. What do you say, can I join the Mike Lee team?"

Seamus was sitting at the bar and had been listening to this exchange. He walked over and stood next to Mike.

"Have a seat, Brahm, I think we need a drink to talk this over," Seamus said as he offered Brahm a chair at the nearest table.

"Seamus Corrigan. I love the ethnicity and working-class verve that you add to the campaign. I want to use you in a big way," Brahm said extending his hand.

"You've done your homework and I'm thinking for now I'll say thank you," Seamus said shaking his hand.

"Of course," Brahm said.

"What'll you have, Brahm?" Mike asked.

"I'll have a pint and can you bring three whiskey glasses? I brought you a treat."

Brahm opened his briefcase and produced a bottle of Nun's Island Irish Whiskey.

"I bought this at an auction and I was waiting for the right occasion to open it up. It's over a hundred years old. I think it was distilled from the tears of broken-hearted Irish virgins."

"Holy cow," Mike said. Are you sure you want to waste that on two shlubs like me and Seamus?"

"Now, Mikey, if Brahm wants to share that with us, we shouldn't insult his generosity," Seamus said getting up to grab the three glasses from behind the bar.

Brahm poured two fingers for each of them. He smelled it, swirled it and held it up to the light.

"Well, Mike Lee, here's to your campaign, I hope you'll let me on board and help you get to the finish line."

"You're off to a great start," Seamus said as he lifted his glass.

They each took a sip. Brahm swirled it and took a few short breaths with the whiskey in his mouth.

"Of course," Brahm said as his whole body relaxed with the pleasure of the golden spirit.

"Wow," Mike said. "Too bad there aren't as many crying virgins anymore."

"So, do we have a deal Mike?" Brahm asked.

"Brahm, this is the greatest beverage that has ever passed these lips. How could I say no?"

"Great, here's what we are going to do." He pulled a folder out of the same briefcase that had held the whiskey of the gods. He handed Mike and Seamus a complete plan for the rest of the campaign, with dates, timelines and stump speeches for Mike.

Brahm went on for an hour without stopping. Seamus ordered food and Davey kept the pint glasses full. Brahm had everything you could imagine: talking points, graphics for signs, billboards, press releases, and a schedule for an action for every day up until the election. He even had an acceptance speech for Mike. Only when he finished did he refill the whiskey glasses.

"Now, Mike Lee, are you ready for me to mold you into a real politician, a laser-focused machine that can take Lerner on?"

"I'm all yours, do with me what you want," Mike replied.

"Don't worry, that's what I am here for. Besides, Groucho Marx said that politics is the art of looking for trouble, finding it everywhere, diagnosing it incorrectly, and applying the wrong remedies. I keep all that from happen- ing. At least during the campaign. How you govern is completely up to you."

"Groucho? I was hoping for Jefferson or Lincoln, but if that is what politics is then we have that and more here in Genesee," Mike laughed

"Groucho never said that, did he?" Seamus asked.

"Doesn't matter if he did, you guys are definitely looking for trouble by getting into politics because of an exploding goat. Anyway, I'm with you now. To success then gentlemen," Brahm toasted.

"Success," Seamus and Mike seconded.

PART V: FALL

CHAPTER 91

TOO CLOSE

AS MUCH AS Mike was trying to be a real candidate, he didn't feel like a real candidate, even after the Stone Saunders appearance and assurances from Brahm that things were going well. He didn't like that he was now spending more time campaigning than he spent running the bar. He missed just being in the neighborhood, feeling its pulse, and being a part of the daily life of his friends.

He couldn't sleep, even after staying at the bar until last call, because of the added anxiety and because of all the people he had spoken with on the unusually busy Saturday night. Being "on" as a candidate, with the right smile and answers was hard to turn off.

Since *The Stone Saunders Show* aired the business at the bar had picked up almost twenty percent over the last month. He decided that trying to sleep was a lost cause, so he got up and took a shower. He kissed Helen goodbye and headed to the 6:30 Mass.

The first Mass was his favorite since it was devoid of all the singing and waving hands and arms around. The first time he saw all the changes that were being incorporated into the Mass, he looked up to heaven and thanked God his father hadn't lived to see that the Mass had become more like a Protestant revival. Big Steve Lee left the church when they stopped the Latin Mass and didn't go back until they rolled his casket up to the center aisle at St. Patrick's.

During the prayers for your intentions, Mike asked that November 3rd get here as soon as possible so the election could be over and he could go back to his regular life. He felt as though he had proven his point, that at least some of the city had listened when he talked about bringing back jobs by getting the government out of the way, to let the police do their jobs, and lower taxes would help people stay in the city.

On the way back from Mass he stopped at his corner store to grab a Sunday paper. Vince's nephew Phil was just unlocking the door. Mike carried the papers in and put them in the stand and cut the plastic that was holding them together. He took the wrapper off and had caught just a glimpse of the headline when Phil asked him a question. He thought he saw his name, but it couldn't have been, what could he have done to be on the front page?

"Mike, can you take a look at this cooler? I don't think the compressor is working like it should," Phil said pointing to the soda cooler near the register.

"Yeah, I think that one is on its last legs. I'll call the Coke salesman and see if I can finagle a new one out of him," Mike said, checking the sales receipts from the night before since he was near the register.

He walked back over to get a paper to take home and

there was the headline, "Mayors Race Close – Lee Cuts into Lead."

He started to read the story; a Seneca University poll done by a professor that follows all local politics had Mike down by only seven points. The last poll right after the St. Patrick's Day bump had Mike down 69% to 31%, but that had evaporated within a month and went back to being down 80% to 20%. Murph had assured him and Brahm backed Murph up, that a poll that early in a race against an incumbent, was nothing but a poll of name recognition.

He took out his phone that he had silenced when he went into church. He had twenty missed calls and over fifty text messages, half of them from Brahm. He grabbed an extra paper and raced home.

Helen was already up and had made coffee. She was sitting at the kitchen table when she heard Mike come in. She thought she heard him run up the back stairs.

"Mike is that you?"

"Helen!"

"Kitchen," she replied.

"Helen, you'll never believe it," he said slapping the paper down in front of her.

"It's going to rain," she said looking at the front page.

"No, look at the headline!"

"Yes, I know, Murph already called and woke me up. Congratulations, hon, I knew people would come around."

"Now if I can get her to debate me, I think I can make up the difference. That or she'll chew me up because I'm a 'rank amateur,' because that's what I am. But I think she would turn off a lot of people because she really isn't likable."

"And you are," she said getting up from the table and fixing a cup of coffee for him and brought it to the table and kissed him on top of this head as he read through the article.

"Just promise me you won't run for governor if you win this."

Mike looked up from the paper. "That I can promise you."

CHAPTER 92

NUTS

IT WAS Mayor Lerner's office that reached out to Mike first about a debate, a week after the poll that showed Mike was catching up. It was a coordinated attack. She sent the invitation to Mike by FedEx and had the news stations on standby to let them know that she had thrown down the gauntlet and that she would wipe the floor with this "rank amateur."

When the newspaper called for Mike's comment, he said that for once the mayor had gotten something right, he was an amateur.

The debate was set for the beginning of October. Brahm's office sent over hundreds of pages of debate notes for Mike to study. They even sent prep questions and a mock script. Murph volunteered to play the role of the mayor.

All the prep was going smoothly and Mike's confidence was growing, that he would be able to take her on. That was until the mayor changed the playing field.

A messenger from the mayor's office came in person to Quinn's and handed the debate "rules" directly to Mike.

"I'm supposed to wait for a response," the nameless minion told Mike as he took a seat at the bar.

Mike flipped through the pages, reading as he walked over to Seamus and Vince at the corner of the bar.

"Wait till you hear this," Mike said as he showed the cover page to the guys.

"Mayor Lerner's Rules?" Vince asked reading the top of the list.

"These are her conditions she has added for the debate," Mike said. He cleared his throat and started to read.

"Condition one, the debate moderator will be chosen by Mayor Lerner's office. Two, Mayor Lerner has veto authority over the debate categories and the categories will be provided to her office at least a week before the debate. Three, Mayor Lerner will make the opening and closing statements. Four, Mr. Lee will have to provide all sources of any statistic, claim or statement of fact, that he makes during the debate at least one week prior to the debate date. It goes on, do you guys want to hear more?"

"Do you get a blindfold and a cigarette at least?" Vince asked.

"At least I don't have to refer to her as 'your majesty' and bow when she enters," Mike said. He continued to flip through the pages.

"What are you gonna do?" Seamus asked, "Do you want me to show that guy the door... and the sidewalk out front?"

"No, I know exactly what to do," Mike said after walking over to the register and grabbing a pen.

He put the rules document on the bar and wrote in all caps, "NUTS". He went back over to show the guys.

"Perfect," Vince said, giving Mike a huge smile.

"Fecking genius," Seamus seconded.

Mike nodded his agreement and brought his answer over to the mayor's messenger.

"Nuts? What the hell does that mean?" the perplexed young lackey asked.

"It's a historical reference, when the Germans demanded the surrender of Bastogne, the commanding General responded 'Nuts.' You did study World War II in school, didn't you?" Mike asked a little deflated by the messenger's lack of knowledge.

"Of course, Rosie the Riveter, the Japanese internment, the segregated armed forces," he rattled off.

"Oh, my God, do you even know who won?"

"Yes, we dropped an atomic bomb on innocent women and children and it was over," he huffed.

Mike stood looking at the messenger for a minute until he started to shift on the barstool.

"Just deliver the message, that's about all you seem good for," Mike said, turning and walking away.

"What are you going to do?" Vince asked when Mike came back to them.

"I'm going to call Brahm first. Then I'm going to get the TV cameras over here and call her out, tell the city that she is scared of a 'rank amateur' and she won't debate me without crazy rules that practically hand the debate right to her," Mike said.

After Mike explained the situation, Brahm agreed that he should call a press conference.

"Call her out, embarrass her, tell everyone she's scared," Brahm advised.

"What if she refuses?" Mike asked.

"Well then you keep calling her out until she agrees. Cite the polls, hold up the newspaper headline for the cameras that the race is close. Also, I want you to really start pushing. Have your friends on the police force call you when there's a crime bad enough for the news to show up. I want you on the scene and get in front of those cameras and hit her on crime".

"Got it, I'll have Seamus round up our friends," Mike said. "I'll keep pushing until she relents."

"Good, good. I'll be back in town in a week and we'll do an all-day debate prep because this will work."

CHAPTER 93

RACOON GIRL

MIKE WAS SITTING in a chair at the public television station rubbing his temples. A young girl with layers of makeup over her bad skin and enough black eyeliner to qualify as a human raccoon was trying to apply Mike's makeup for the cameras.

"Can ya hold still for a second?" she said with a slight lisp from her tongue piercing.

Just don't make me look like you, Mike was thinking, but he smiled and put his hands on his lap.

Seamus came into the dressing room to check on him and to go over some last-minute notes. He took one look at the make-up girl as she turned to see who had come into the room and he had to keep himself from jumping back.

"Jaysus, I'm nervous," he said, although he hadn't taken his eyes off the racoon girl.

"I'm glad you're nervous because I have no reason the be the least bit worried," Mike fired back.

"Sorry, you're right. You got this thing; she'll look like the shrew that she is."

"I hope so," Mike said as he pictured himself on the stage and the mayor screaming at him about something he hadn't thought to prepare for.

"When she hits you about your inexperience, shoot back with either the crime rate or the graduation rate. Or both, we know they're connected," Seamus advised.

"I know," Mike said closing his eyes as the girl patted on more powder.

Seamus started the same quiz they had been going over for the past week.

"Crime rate increase since she took office?"

"Twelve percent."

"Graduation rate decrease?"

"Six percent overall, but she'll harp on the increase in graduation rate for minorities. I hit back that it's all smoke and mirrors, no real learning, just social promotions."

"Good, very good. Property tax increase?"

"Fifteen percent per thousand dollar of assessed value."

"Population decrease?"

"Three percent just last year. Almost nineteen percent over the past ten years."

"You're ready, Mikey. You have the Saint Benedict medal I got you?"

"In my front pocket."

The girl stopped applying the make-up and looked at Mike in the mirror.

"Thanks," Mike said as she packed up her case and left the room.

"Ready," Seamus asked.

Mike got out of the chair for a closer inspection in the mirror, moving his head side to side.

"I'm ready for old man Barone to box me up and put me in the main room for the wake," he said as he finished his inspection.

"You think you are a big enough draw for the main room?" Seamus joked.

Mike took a deep breath, "I'm running for mayor, I certainly hope so."

"They're having a watch party back at the bar. They have to do a shot every time the mayor says 'amateur,' two shots if she says 'rank' with it," Seamus informed Mike.

"At least I'll make a lot of money tonight. But don't tell the mayor, she thinks making money is evil."

"That's a good line. You should add it to your opening statement," Seamus suggested.

There was a knock at the door. Mike took another deep breath and shook Seamus' hand.

"You were born for this. Mikey, you're better than her and you look more feminine than her with all that makeup packed on you, I'm tempted to ask you out, but I'm a married man."

Seamus opened the door. Instead of the stage manager they expected, it was Piersky. He came into the dressing room and locked the door behind him.

"Bad news. That asshole Rebecca Munson from Channel 5 gave the mayor the questions for the debate a week ago, you're being set up, Mike," Piersky informed them.

"Should we cancel, Mikey? All the press is here, we

could go outside and do a press conference, tell them what happened," Seamus asked.

Mike slumped back down in the chair.

"No, we go on. I don't think we have a choice. Are you one hundred percent sure Piersky?" Mike asked.

"Yes, I got it from two different sources. They are too afraid of getting shut out of any stories if they say something, so they won't go on the record."

"So why are they telling us then," Seamus asked.

"Because it's just wrong," Piersky replied.

"Now they found a conscience? Mikey, what can we do? Can we turn this back on her?" Seamus asked as he checked his watch to see how much time they had before they had to start.

There was another knock at the door.

"One minute!" the voice from the other side of the door screamed.

"So, what are you going to do?" Piersky asked.

"I'm pretty sure I'll have a chance to expose her. Maybe if she gives an answer that seems too rehearsed or something like that. Maybe I can shake her in front of the cameras. That'd be a big win," Mike said.

"It might work," Piersky added. "Wait for the right point. I'll try to give you a sign. I'll take my hat off and put it back on if I think it's the right moment."

"Thanks, I think we can turn this. I wish we had time to call Brahm, but it's way too late for that. We don't have anything to lose at this point," Mike said, straightening his tie one more time.

"Good luck. Don't look her right in the eye, you'll turn

to stone," Piersky said, and shook Mike's hand and then Seamus'.

"Actually, this is going to be the first time that I'm in the same room with her," Mike laughed. "We have been dealing with all her surrogates, I guess she's too good for a lowly bartender."

Mike and Seamus left first so Piersky could sneak out a minute later. They walked out on the set and Mike took his position behind the podium.

"That's my name on the card, right?" Mike asked.

"You don't know your own name?"

"I can't see anything right now, Seamus."

CHAPTER 94

AMIABLE DUNCE

THE PUBLIC TELEVISION station had gone all out for the debate. The stage had huge blow-up pictures of the city behind each of the podiums. There were multiple American flags and what Mike could only assume was the City's flag, because he couldn't remember ever seeing it before.

The platform for the mayor was already behind her podium, so that on camera, she would appear to be the same height as Mike. The mayor's people had already told Mike there would be no meeting at center stage before or after the debate. If he wanted to shake the mayor's hand, he would have to walk across to her podium and shake her hand there. Seamus immediately told them what they could do with those rules.

The audience consisted of invitation-only people, each side getting an equal number of tickets so that the applause, if any, would be balanced and would not influence the viewers.

Helen sat in the front row of the chairs that were arranged in a semi-circle. She gave Mike a big thumbs up and a smile. He wasn't supposed to leave the stage, but he walked over and gave her a kiss, much to the chagrin of the stage manager who shook his clipboard at Mike and motioned him back to his assigned podium.

The rules were only slightly altered from the initial ones that the mayor had demanded as a condition for her giving Mike the "privilege" of being able to debate her. She didn't get to make the opening and closing statement and Mike did not have to provide the sources for all the statistics he might cite to the mayor prior to the debate. Even with those changes, everyone agreed that Mike was at a disadvantage, but they knew that they had to have people see them face to face. He had to show the voters that he was a viable alternative if they weren't happy with how she had governed the city.

The moderator, Howard Robbins, was a professor at Seneca University. He taught both Political Science and Magazine, in the Bennett and Stein Schools respectively. He had a long list of protegees in all the liberal newspapers, networks and magazines across the country. Every other host on MSNBC had a Howard Robbins story of inspiration. It was quite a coup for the mayor to get him to moderate the debate. Brahm protested but to no avail. After *The Stone Saunders Show* had aired and the race caught the national attention, it was almost a given that the only city resident worthy of asking questions for the mayoral candidates was Professor Robbins. C-Span was also carrying the debate on tape delay solely because of Robbins' celebrity.

Robbins looked into the cameras as the first red light came on and launched into a soliloquy about how democracy was built from the local level, the tradition of the town hall meeting, the beauty of politicians beholden to the people. How the greatness of the Constitution gave the power to "We the People" and those we chose to serve owed their "sacred honor" to the people. Of course, if you judged a man by his creations, he didn't believe what he just said.

Mike didn't hear Robbins' words. He was trying to think through scenarios of how he could expose that the mayor had been given all the debate questions, while he had only been given the broad categories from which the questions would be drawn.

Robbins introduced the mayor first, citing highlights of her record, her fine pedigree and education and finally a quote from the governor about how she was the nucleus of Central New York government.

Mike was introduced as a scrappy local businessman. A neophyte to politics, with rustic appeal to the working class. All he left out was "amiable dunce."

Robbins reveled in the applause from the left side of the audience and reluctantly turned the spotlight over to the mayor.

The mayor's opening statement was full of the usual, the schools are so much better, the cops are to blame for the crime rate, the rich don't pay enough taxes, the county owes money to the city. Nothing new, nothing they hadn't prepared to take on.

Mike's turn came and he looked right into the camera and followed the script that Brahm had prepared. He hit the mayor on the points she had just used as strengths. He connected her to the failures of the other politicians of her party throughout the State and Country, and how their policies were producing nothing other than growing the size and power of the government, as it squeezed the middle class more and more in failed cities such as Detroit and Baltimore and that Genesee was close to joining that ignoble list.

The first question went to the mayor and it was about how to keep the improvement in the minority graduation rate going in the city schools. It was a total softball question and her answer was just as predictable, which gave Mike his first opening on rebuttal.

"Do you believe in bigfoot? Or maybe the Loch Ness Monster, madam mayor? Because those creatures are just as mythical as the improvement in graduation rates. They are just statistics used to make the schools look better when there is actually no improvement. How do we know this? Because the measurement of whether the graduates are ready for college has not moved at all, it is actually getting worse. These poor kids are pawns to prop up the people that run the city and the schools. They are no better prepared for their futures. They are being pushed through. The politicians running the schools have failed them."

The mayor maintained her painted-on smile throughout Mike's answer. Robbins nodded thoughtfully at first, then looked down at his script and started making notes.

When Mike finished Robbins looked up with an expression of disappointment, like he just found out his doctor didn't go to an Ivy League school.

"Thank you, Mr. Lee." He then turned to the mayor and smiled. "Rebuttal Mayor Lerner?"

"Yes, thank you, Professor. We are proud of what we have accomplished in the schools. In the face of the lack of funding, the wealthy that do all that they can to escape their responsibility to the tax base, and the institutional racism that we fight with all our breath every day. The wealthy, like Mr. Lee, also take their children out of the public schools which exacerbates the lack of funding and achievement that we are battling against. I am proud of all of what we have accomplished."

The questions continued in this vein for the next thirty minutes. Mike felt he was scoring points with anyone who could see through the mayor's non-answer answers. He was still waiting for the opening to bring up her having received the questions before the debate.

The next question was for Mike. Robbins cleared his throat.

"Mr. Lee, the ability of a city to raise capital, is vital to the long-term viability of any municipality. Which risk to the current city bond portfolio poses the greatest threat? The Call Risk, Credit Risk, Interest Rate Risk or Inflation Risk?"

Mike laughed to himself. This was it, his chance to strike. He saw Piersky take off his hat and put it back on. Mike nodded to him.

The question was written to make him look like he was not qualified to handle city finances. In fact, that was the general category of the question. He would stumble through an answer because the question was so specific that there was no way, even with a pro like Brahm preparing him, that he had an answer. The mayor, with the questions in advance would follow that up with a textbook, perfect answer worthy of a Wall Street Hedge Fund Manager.

"Thank you, Professor, that question is truly difficult, a question that is more suited for candidates running for City Auditor. It is a question that I would, as mayor, ask the City Auditor and seek their advice. I know that the city has run increasingly record deficits under three straight administrations and that Mayor Lerner has done nothing to change that disturbing trend. As mayor, I would look to experts at Seneca University and also national experts such as Stephen Moore or even Arthur Laffer as to the best way to reverse these dangerous trends. I yield the rest of my time to the mayor, so that she can give her well thought out, pre-prepared answer to this question."

"Pre-prepared?" the mayor scoffed from across the stage.

She took the bait.

"Yes," Mike replied. He looked right at the mayor. "Pre-prepared. As if you were reading a statement about the city's finances on *Voice of the City*, you know the show on Channel 5 with Rebecca Munson?"

The mayor stammered; she almost lost her balance on her elevated platform.

"Madam Mayor, your reply?" Robbins asked.

Mike thought he heard a glimmer of curiosity in his voice.

"Credit risk is ... ahhh... the risk that the bond issuer may experience problems financial, I mean financial problems, that make it difficult or impossible to pay interest and principal, although predictions of, no, in full a high rating...

ummm... does not reflect a prediction that the bond has no chance of defaulting."

Mike had her. Professor Robbins flipped through the questions while staring at the mayor, who in turn was giving him the circle motion with her hand trying to implore him to go on.

Seamus pumped his fist and gave Mike a long distance high five from the audience. The mayor recovered her composure within two more rounds of questions, but the damage was done.

CHAPTER 95

CLACKERS

ROXANNE'S PREGNANCY had been uneventful, but her doctor still kept a close eye on her because of her age and because she was carrying twins. They had started a couple pools at the bar on whether there were two boys, which Seamus was sure they were, or two girls and for one of each. There was also a pool on the date, time and birth weight of each twin and all the possible combinations had all the different pools combined totaling almost a thousand dollars.

The first pool was going to be decided on Friday because Roxanne had another checkup and they were scheduled to do another sonogram. She was far enough along that they would be able to tell the sex of each of the babies.

Seamus had pared down a long list of boy's names. In order, he settled on Declan (after his favorite uncle), Dermot, Kevin, and finally Thomas.

Roxanne had a list of girl's names, but her list had only two, Caedence and Cathleen.

Friday finally arrived after a long, drawn out week of anticipation. With a payoff in sight, the betting had intensified and the pot had doubled in just a few days. Several of the bettors were waiting at Quinn's for Seamus' text with the results, which he swore to his wife he wouldn't do because Roxanne told him he would sleep in the garage if he did.

Again, Seamus endured a waiting room full of pregnant women and children crawling over everything and every- one. When they were finally called back into an examining room he didn't hide in the corner during the internal exam, instead he skillfully rattled off questions from *What to Expect When You're Expecting.*

This time they took Roxanne into a room with a special color 3D sonogram machine. Seamus asked for his 3D glasses which made the technician laugh. "I hear that one all the time."

Seamus laughed along, but he had been serious.

He held Roxanne's hand as they applied the goo and started moving the sensor over her very pregnant belly. The little black and white screen was now a huge color screen worthy of watching the Super Bowl.

Dr. Desimone came in for all the festivities.

"Okay, Roxanne, let's see how those babies are doing," she said taking control of the sensor.

Seamus walked up next to the screen, waiting to see any sign of manhood.

"We'll start with some measurements," Dr. Desimone said as she measured and clicked and measured again.

She finished up and made some notes in Roxanne's file.

"Okay, have you two decided if you want to find out the sex of the babies today?"

"Yes," Seamus said louder than he intended.

"Yes, we have," Roxanne said. "I am sorry about my crazy husband, he's just very anxious to find out."

"Okay Seamus, here we go, baby number one," Dr. Desimone said as she moved the sensor to find the right view.

The screen flashed different colors that definitely looked like a baby, but not the important bits. The movement on the screen stopped as Dr. Desimone froze the screen.

"There's baby number one," she said smiling at the expectant parents.

"What am I looking at?" Seamus asked. "Are those clackers I'm seeing?"

"Clackers?" the doctor asked.

"Bollocks, balls, testicles, it that a boy?"

"Seamus, please settle down and Dr. Desimone please stop teasing my husband, I can barely handle his normal level of crazy."

"I'm sorry, I just like watching him when he gets all worked up. I can't wait to see him in the delivery room. Mr. and Mrs. Corrigan, I present baby number one, your daughter."

"A girl," Roxanne sighed.

"A girl," Seamus said with emotion that surprised Roxanne and the doctor.

"Disappointed?" Roxanne asked.

"Ah bollocks, or lack of them I guess. No, I'm as happy as happy gets," he said bending down and kissing Roxanne.

"Okay let's look at number two," Dr. Desimone said unlocking the screen and moving the sensor around.

"Number two is shy, tell your sister to get out of the way," she directed to Roxanne's belly.

Seamus squeezed Roxanne's hand and kissed her again.

"Okay, there's number two, looking, looking..." The screen froze again.

"Congratulations Mr. and Mrs. Corrigan, your daughter has a brother."

"A boy," Seamus said sinking into a chair. He leaned into Roxanne's belly. "Okay Declan, you take care of your sister in there. That's your job. That's a good boy now."

"One of each, Declan and Caedence," Roxanne said holding her belly as Dr. Desimone wiped the gel off.

"Okay, you're at 35 weeks. We start seeing you once a week from here on out. We'll do a sonogram at each visit and watch you like a hawk. I'm not letting anything happen to the three of you," she said patting Roxanne's arm.

Seamus helped Roxanne up off the table.

"My phone has been buzzing for an hour, everybody wants to know," he said as Roxanne got to her feet.

"Let them wait, I want to tell Angela and Pete first about their brother and sister, then you can tell the guys."

"Of course, anything you say," Seamus said as he deleted the text on his phone without sending it.

CHAPTER 96

AND THE WINNER IS

"ANGELA, call your brother and conference him in," Roxanne said as she tried to get comfortable in the front seat of Seamus' truck.

"Okay, Mom, just a sec."

Seamus drove back to Liberty Hill, taking the long way through the University section of the city, up through the suburb of Fredericksville and back down Seneca Turnpike into the city. The trees were at their peak color, as was his beautiful wife. He tried to keep his eyes on the road, but he had a hard time because he couldn't take his eyes off of her.

"We're here, Mom," Pete and Angela said together.

"What are we having!" Angela asked.

"One of each, a boy and a girl. They're both doing great. Five more weeks, if I can make it through." Roxanne laughed.

"I'm not going to make it," Seamus muttered.

Roxanne hit him on the arm.

"We are headed to the bar to tell everyone, why don't you meet us there. Your father is buying."

"Okay, Mom, see you there."

"Congratulations, both of you," Pete said.

Roxanne looked over at Seamus and gave him a happy smile.

"Love you, Mom," Angela said, "See you at Quinn's."

Roxanne texted Kate and Helen so they could be at the bar. She then sent a text to Mike to tell him they were on their way.

"Are you sure you want to do this?" Seamus asked after he parked.

"Sure, these are our friends and they are a part of this too."

Seamus opened the door for Roxanne. Everyone was standing and waiting for them. Kate ran up and hugged Roxanne followed closely by Angela. Even Pete was smiling.

"Well, what's the verdict?" Vince yelled.

"I can't make an announcement like this without a pint in me hand. And anybody else, freshen your drink, because if you've known me more than a minute, you know I have to make a toast," Seamus said, puffing out his chest.

"Get the expectant father a pint, Davey," Mike called over the bar.

Davey poured and then handed it to Seamus. Seamus took the pint and downed half. He then raised his glass.

"Join me, everyone, raise your pints, boys. I want to make a toast to my wife, the mother of my children. And I am pleased to publicly welcome first a daughter..."

People started clapping and cheering. Seamus had to quiet them and regain the floor.

"And welcome for my daughter, a brother, my son.

May they come into this world safe and healthy and into the arms of all their loved ones. To my son and daughter," he clinked glasses with Mike and then Vince and took a drink.

There were hugs and kisses all around, along with a lot more pints.

Pete stood up on a chair.

"What about the pool?" he yelled.

"Let me get the bets from the office, a boy and a girl" Mike said walking back and retrieving the boxes.

Mike located the right box labeled Boy-Girl.

"There are one hundred and forty-four bets in the boy-girl box. Roxanne, please do the honors and pick the winner," he said taking the top off the box and holding it out for Roxanne.

She reached her hand into the box and rummaged around for a minute, finally pulling out a slip of paper and handing it to Mike.

Mike unfolded the paper and cleared his throat.

"The winner of the first Seamus and Roxanne baby pool, with the winning bet of boy-girl is, ..." He hesitated and looked around the bar drawing jeers.

"The winner is," he continued, "Jimmy Schless. Schlesster are you here?"

A cheer came from the far corner as Schlesster came forward to claim his winnings. He accepted handshakes and requests that he buy a round as he made his way to Mike.

"How much did I win, Mikey?" Schlesster asked.

"The pool had a big run this morning because of the sonogram being today. The total pool is five hundred and fifty dollars," Mike said handing the wad of cash to Schlesster.

He waved the money to more calls for him to buy a round. Schlesster slapped a Ben Franklin on the bar to more cheers. He kept buying until all his winnings were gone.

CHAPTER 97

MAYOR OF ALL

THE WEEKLY STRATEGY meeting with Brahm was not going well. The entire first thirty minutes were spent on all the things that Mike was doing wrong or things he should be doing that he wasn't doing. Brahm was scolding them, pushing the team to work harder if they wanted to win.

"Since this meeting is going so smoothly, it's probably a good time to talk about something you have to do that is going to be very hard. The follow-up with the press after the event will be a huge minefield of tough questions, each of which has the potential to knock you out of the election," Brahm said in a tone more serious than Mike had ever heard him use.

"Just say it then, Brahm," Mike said.

Seamus and Vince looked at each other and then at the ground.

"We need to have you give a speech and answer questions at the Harriet Tubman Southside Community Center. This won't be like going through the neighborhood and knocking on doors. That was one on one. The mayor could use this event to set you up. But if we are going to have any chance of winning, this has to be done."

"But I'm only polling at about 10% on the southside, I'm not going to change any of their minds," Mike said, shaking his head. "It's not that I don't want to give a speech, it's that there is more potential for damage than potential votes."

"I agree wholeheartedly. But you have to show everyone that you are the candidate for the entire city. If you don't go, Lerner will hit you as an uncaring white male that is out of touch and frankly, she might go as far to combine that with your opposition to public housing and Section 8 renters and accuse you of being racist," Brahm said.

"She's just as white as me."

"Of course," Brahm said, moving closer to the screen. "But you are a white male, the source of all that is bad in the country. You are going to have to show the people on the southside that you'll be the mayor of all the people of the city. I can tell that you don't care about a person's race, but it's important that you show that to at least some of the voters on the southside."

"I've said from the beginning this was for everyone. You know there isn't a person that has ever known me that would accuse me of judging anyone on anything other than their character," Mike argued. "I'll do it, but I am not going to lie to any group I talk to. I'm not going to say what anyone might think they want to hear either. I am going to tell them what I think about the problems we are facing. They want a mayor that really wants to solve the problems,

problems that impact everyone in some way and I'm going to tell them how I would do it."

"Yes, you are," Brahm agreed. "But we are going to make sure that your message is airtight and there won't be anything the other side can use against you in the campaign.

This isn't going to be easy. We will have to practice and practice. We are going to throw all kinds of traps at you until you can recognize them and know how to answer. Who knows, Lerner might end up calling you a racist, but we don't want to give her a real reason to do it. She is going to have people there with planted questions to trap you. This is their best chance to take you out of the running."

Mike looked at Seamus and Vince. "What do you guys think?"

"I agree with Brahm," Vince said.

"Me too. Mikey, your heart is good. Everyone needs to see that." Seamus added.

"Okay, let's get started then," Mike said and got out his pen to take notes.

CHAPTER 98

JUST MIKE LEE

THEY HAD PRACTICED for two weeks with every possible scenario. Almost every answer Mike gave had a follow up question of "why are you a racist?" Mike was dreading going into the lion's den of the community center, not because of the people but because of the traps that the mayor could set. Especially with the chance that one slip-up could end his campaign.

He went alone, as Brahm had instructed. An entourage or even a lone handler would say that he was insincere. Mike kept reminding himself that the reason he wanted to be mayor was to make the city better for everyone. He had no hidden agenda or a donor constituency that he was beholden to if elected. He had a simple message of making the city safer, which would bring back people, business and jobs. His approach to crime included the schools, where he felt the teachers were inhibited by the approach that the mayor had taken under the moniker of "social justice." He felt it only benefitted the kids who did not want to learn at the expense of everyone else, students, teachers, and parents. He hoped that he could get this message out, without all the failures they had during the practices.

He wore a tweed jacket and jeans with his favorite pair of sneakers. He greeted the people as he passed them and shook hands with the people that recognized him, according to plan, he tried his best not to appear to be just a gladhanding politician.

When he walked into the community center he was greeted by Jackie Kellogg, the director who had arranged Mike's appearance. She explained the logistics of the town hall, the stage, sound system and capacity of the room. Mike saw that all four television stations were there, probably wanting to get a fight on camera. He waved to the reporters.

"I never got your email with your requirements for the format of the meeting," she stated.

"That's because I don't have any. I just want to talk to the neighborhood."

"Nothing?"

"No, I'm okay," he said with a smile.

She looked him over and waited a minute before she asked, "are you sure?"

"I'm good, just show me where I should stand, thanks."

"Okay, if you are sure. Are you going to do just a speech or are you going to take questions?"

"Both sound good, if that's okay."

"Okay, I will introduce you and tell everyone there will be questions after you talk. We'll try to get started on time, but I doubt that we'll have everyone here at eight. I'll wait until I think people have stopped coming in. We can have a podium with a microphone set up for the questions if you want?"

"Sure, that sounds great," Mike said as he waited for her to turn around before he took a deep breath and wiped the sweat off his forehead.

The people started to file in as Mike watched from behind the stage where he was studying all the notes that Brahm had sent him.

At 8:15 Jackie Kellogg took the stage and called for order a few times before everyone settled down.

"Thank you, everyone, for joining us this evening for the town hall meeting with mayoral candidate Mike Lee. Mr. Lee will give an opening speech and then he'll take questions. Anyone who wants to ask a question can line up at the podium we have set up here," she said pointing to the side of the room.

"Please join me in welcoming Mr. Lee to the Southside Community Center," she said as she clapped. A few people joined in, but the applause was over before Mike reached the center of the stage and took the microphone from his hostess.

Mike looked over the crowd and smiled.

"Thank you so much for inviting me to talk to you this evening. It is such an honor for me to have a chance to represent the city where I was born, grew up, and now have businesses in. I want to see all Geneseeans have a chance to prosper. I recognize a few of you from my door-to-door campaigning. Thank you for coming out for this speech. I am so happy that you have given me the chance to intro- duce myself and tell you what I believe and how those beliefs will shape my actions as your mayor. I don't repre- sent any party, any donors, or any causes other than the intense desire to have the years of decline that the city has seen, reversed. The role of city government is not to provide everything for the citizens but to create the environment where its citizens have the best chance to reach their potential. That means a city government that keeps the streets safe and provides schools where our children can get the best education possible. A government that doesn't impose unnecessary restrictions on businesses and people, with too many regulations and taxes that keep people from investing in their lives and businesses."

"The mayor has insinuated that I have hate in my heart because I don't believe in public housing or public assistance. She has it partially wrong. I believe we should absolutely help those who cannot help themselves. A hand up, not a handout. Ronald Reagan said that the best government program is a job and I believe that too. With a job you can own your own house and there are plenty of empty ones in the city that can be purchased for a song. How about we train young people in a trade: plumbing, carpentry, helping to fix up those houses. They can learn a trade and earn a living. A house you own, you can take pride in. A street full of cared-for houses is a neighborhood. I may be naïve, but I think that can still work."

Mike stopped and looked around the room.

"I am not a politician. I think you can look around any neighborhood in the city and see what the politicians have done. They like to blame the weather for people and businesses leaving. I think it is taxes, crime, and the poor city schools that have made all this happen. Now, I am realistic that the mayor can't fix all of this. A lot of the problems are at the state and national levels. The mismanagement in Albany makes the mistakes made in Genesee over the last forty years seem like kid stuff."

Mike had no idea what the people were thinking. Their faces hadn't changed since he started. He wasn't getting many nods of agreement or any smiles.

"Okay, enough about the political stuff, let me tell you about me, because I think once you hear about what made me, you'll understand why I love our city and why I think the ideas I am talking about can make a difference."

"I was born at St. Joseph's Hospital. I went to St. Patrick's School back when it was kindergarten all the way through 12th grade. My father died when I was in third grade and my mother was left to raise me. She worked two jobs to keep the house going. I got my first job when I was in fifth grade. I shoveled the snow for the rectory, convent and the main entrance to the school. Because of that job I got my own set of keys to the school, which was great because that was when I started going into the gym to practice my shoot- ing. I made the varsity basketball team as an 8th grader because they needed enough guys for scrimmages and because I was already six foot. By my senior year, we were pretty good and we won a county championship. That got me a partial scholarship to St. Benedict's College where I played basketball and got a degree. I met my wife in high school and started working at her father's bar which I now own. I own or am part owner of several businesses on Liberty Hill."

The crowd seemed to be warming up a little bit. Mike tried to make eye contact with everyone he could.

"So, let me tell you about what made me run for mayor.

My friends were throwing me a surprise birthday party at my bar, Quinn's. Two drug addicts came in with shotguns and tried to rob us. Thank God no one was hurt and they were arrested. That incident hurt my heart. How far had the neighborhood I grew up in and invested my whole life in, how far had it fallen for something like that to happen? I didn't think that enough was being done by the city to keep us safe."

This time he got a few more nods from the people.

"Then something bad happened that had nothing to do with politics or government but everything to do with what a community should be. My friend Donal Maroney got sick, he had cancer, and he ended up dying. But before he died, Donal showed us what it meant to be a neighborhood. He didn't have any family, no one to take care of him. His friends in the neighborhood rallied. We set up schedules and signup sheets. Donal was never alone from the time he told us about his cancer until the day he died. We took him to his appointments, got his food and sat with him through his time in hospice. His great fear was to have an empty funeral and when they rolled his coffin into St. Patrick's Church there was a standing-room-only crowd. A neighbor- hood did that, not any government program. I thought that that was the way it should be. If you just pay your taxes and expect the government to do those things that we did as a neighborhood, you lose so much because it'll never happen."

Mike thought for the first time that he was reaching some in the audience.

"That's all I wanted to say. I want to be mayor because I think that if we rebuild our families, our neighborhoods, our caring for one another, the rest will follow. And I know politicians are told to stay away from religion, but I don't think it would hurt if a few more people in the city went to church more often. When you believe in something greater than yourself a lot of good things can happen. Thank you."

The applause started slowly but built and lasted until Mike had to raise his hand to quiet them.

The questions weren't bad from there, with Mike sticking to the theme he had established. He recognized the plants with the trap questions and was completely prepared with the right answer. He relished in the real questions and hoped that his sincerity was coming through to the crowd.

They went on for about an hour until there weren't any more people in line.

"Thank you so much," Mike said, "I appreciate your support and your hospitality."

He went over to the cameras and gave a short interview. He couldn't help thinking that some of the reporters looked disappointed that he hadn't been trounced by the crowd.

CHAPTER 99

THE FAT LADY'S WARMING UP

THE SUNDAY before the election the headline in the *Genesee Herald* read "TOO CLOSE TO CALL". Mike's team wasn't surprised by this because Professor Ralph Keating at Seneca University had given both campaigns a detailed explanation on the Saturday before, with all the demographics and locations of the people in the survey that he did for the paper. The best news they received, as Brahm had predicted, was that the people voting for Mike had rated themselves as very enthusiastic, whereas the voters for Mayor Lerner had only rated themselves as moderately enthusiastic.

It was going to be a long three days until the polls closed on Tuesday. There were three dinners to go to that night, each with a speech, which wasn't a problem, because Mike had nearly memorized the "on message stump speech" that Brahm had written for him. The last part of the speech was where Mike gave an almost canned, "I'm one of you" talk from his heart. He had written this himself, although Brahm edited.

"Three more days," Mike said to Helen in the kitchen as he read the paper.

"Then what?" she asked.

"Either I go back to my old life, even though I don't think I can. Or I am the mayor and the things that keep me up at night were just multiplied by a million."

"We will be fine either way," Helen assured him.

"Three more days," he repeated.

CHAPTER 100

LABOR PAINS

ON TOP of all the problems associated with the last days of campaign activities, Seamus was becoming more and more unavailable as Roxanne's due date approached.

"Don't worry," she had told Seamus. "I was a week late with both my kids."

Seamus could put a transmission together blindfolded but he had almost punched a hole in the wall putting together the cribs. But everything was ready, the room was painted, there was a spare room full of clothes and diapers after the half dozen baby showers, on top of all the supplies that the customers of the salon had brought in. Roxanne had worked up until the point that she couldn't cut hair because her arms couldn't reach her customers with the extension of her twin-sized baby belly.

Seamus had mapped out every possible route to the hospital and had three reserve drivers in place just in case. The fact that Seneca University had a home football game the Saturday before Roxanne's due date kept him up all night after he saw the schedule. He wanted her to switch to Community General, away from the University, but she wasn't going to change doctors, so University Hospital was going to be the place. He told her all about the gridlock of a game day and how University Hospital opened their parking garage for the game, but Roxanne couldn't be swayed.

The Sunday before the election, they were meeting early at Quinn's for a planning session for the day's activities.

Mike was going to three churches that morning, he was going to conspicuously sit in the front row and shake hands as people came out after the service. At noon, he was going to a rally at the Teamsters Union hall. At two he was meeting with the Teacher's Local where he was going to give a speech about school discipline. At four he was going to his St. Benedict's Alumni Association, where they were having a ceremony to give him a distinguished alumni award. A dinner with the VFW and American Legion members on the west side where he had a speech ready about Jimmy Quinn's service in World War II. Finally, the cap of the evening, they were having an invitation-only event, drinks with key contributors at Quinn's, organized by former Mayor Dan Halligan.

Murph and Pete were assigned to follow Mayor Lerner for the day and video all her events. The good news was that her first event wasn't scheduled until 2 p.m. "Lack of enthusiasm," Vince declared, holding up the newspaper as proof. The videos they later showed the team told the story of small crowds that clapped politely.

The general mood was upbeat. Before they went out to campaign, they had their daily online meeting with Brahm.

"Mike, I just want to start by thanking you for all your hard work," Brahm said from the laptop. "You listened to everything I told you and you have become a great candidate. You have made me feel what it is like to be back in the trenches and it has been a great experience. After you serve a couple terms as mayor, we can talk about the Governor's mansion."

"Thanks, Brahm, but I am done with politics after this, win or lose. It's not over till the fat lady sings, and I can hear her warming up."

"Don't use that one before Tuesday, all we need is a charge of sexism and body shaming before the election," Brahm warned.

"Don't worry," Vince chimed in, "if I hear him start to say that, I'll give him a quick punch to the kidneys."

"That'll look great on camera," Brahm said.

"We have this under control," Mike said. "Everybody bring it in. Vince, you want to do the honors?"

"Sure," Vince said as he made the sign of the cross and led them in a Hail Mary before they headed out for the big day of campaigning.

As the group of friends said "Amen," Roxanne abruptly sat up in the booth with her hands on her belly.

"You okay," Vince asked.

"Sure, the twins are just excited about the election."

CHAPTER 101

REMEMBER WHEN

THE MONDAY before election day was even more full than the day before. Mike had events scheduled from 8 a.m. until midnight. He was running on just a couple hours of sleep. Helen was already up and ready with a pot of "Sea- mus-strength" coffee for him.

"It's almost over," she said as she poured his coffee and then stood behind him and massaged his shoulders.

"Two more days. They say that being mayor is a lot harder than the running for mayor," Mike sighed.

"Win first, and then worry about that."

"I know," he said. He reached back and patted her hand. "Can you believe all that has happened over the past year?"

"It has been a year to remember. Donal, the goat, Seamus and Roxanne. Now we have twins due any day. You really know how to shake things up."

"Whatever happens, on Wednesday, I'm just going to go to Quinn's, pour pints and be a plain old barkeep for a while."

"Well, Michael Francis Lee, I couldn't be prouder of you. You stood up to a bully, the worst kind of bully, one that doesn't think they have to answer for what they do."

"Thank you. In all the reading that Brahm has given me to get ready for the election and hopefully to run the city, you see it over and over. The cities that have one party rule and have been that way for decades, are almost all in the worst shape. Look at what Detroit has become. Take the worst five blocks in Genesee and that's almost the whole city. There are more vacant houses and empty lots than there are houses. They spend more per pupil in their schools than almost any city and they have the worst results. But so much of it isn't even up to city government, they can't do anything about missing fathers and kids having kids. The drugs. The unbreakable cycles of poverty. It is now embedded in the culture. There's nothing a mayor can do. So even if we win, I don't think we can change any of those things."

"There will be one big difference though," she said as she hugged him from behind.

"What's that?"

"You'll actually worry about trying to change things and you'll be the mayor that'll really want to do something, other than making yourself rich and getting re-elected."

"That still doesn't mean I'll be able to change anything."

"Why do you think Mayor Lerner is mayor?" she asked squeezing him and talking softly into his ear.

"Because if she doesn't go on to run for higher office, the governor, who is the same party as her, will give her a six-figure sinecure State job. She'll retire at fifty-five with a city and state pension and move to Florida, where she won't have to pay taxes on either."

"Sounds like a pretty good deal. You should consider it if you win."

Mike turned around in the chair and kissed her.

"I'll think about it," he said with a wink. "Now, I have a full day today and an even busier one tomorrow. I'll text you and let you know how it's going. I love you, Helen. Thank you."

"I love you, Mike Lee, win or lose. But you may think about staying somewhere else if you lose. I have a reputation to uphold."

"That, I'll consider," he said as he kissed her again.

CHAPTER 102

THE DAY OF DAYS

ELECTION DAY HAD FINALLY ARRIVED.

Angela helped Roxanne get out of the car at the polling place. This was the first time that either of them had voted. Roxanne held her belly when Angela got her to her feet.

"What's wrong, Mom?"

"Just tired from carrying around these twins, I'll be glad when they get here."

The line to get into the polling place was a lot longer than they expected.

"I guess everyone in the neighborhood is here to vote for Mike," Roxanne said and waddled toward the line.

"That's a good thing. Mom, do you think he has a chance?"

"I'm forty-four and voting for the first time in my life. I don't know a thing about politics and haven't cared much until now. I believe in Mike though."

"Roxanne, up here!"

It was Kate, she was at the front of the line.

"I can't cut the line, thanks anyway, Kate," Roxanne called back.

Kate walked over to Roxanne and Angela.

"Does anyone mind if this very pregnant, with twins by the way, goes to the front of the line? Unless there is anyone that wants to see her wait and possibly drop them right here in the parking lot," Kate shouted to the line.

People looked down and a few said "Sure."

Kate took Roxanne's hand, with Angela following, and lead them to the front of the line.

"Wow, I don't know what to do," Roxanne said when they got inside the doors.

"They'll tell you what to do, just make sure you vote for Mike," Kate laughed.

"No problem there. What time are you getting to the hotel?" Roxanne asked.

She was referring to what would be the victory celebration for Mike's campaign they were having at the University Sheraton. The polls closed at nine and they were estimating that all the votes would be in and counted by midnight.

"I think Angela is going to bring me around ten. I don't think I can get there any earlier than that and last long enough to hear the results," Roxanne explained.

When they got to the front of the line Roxanne handed her license to the lady with the rolls. She scanned the lists and saw her name before the poll worker saw it.

"There it is," Roxanne said showing her excitement.

"Please sign here," the poll worker instructed. "You can go to any open voting booth."

"Thank you, this is my first time," Roxanne confessed to her. "Sorry for being excited."

"Don't be sorry." The poll worker smiled.

Roxanne entered the booth and was drawn immediately to Mike's name just as she had seen it in the sample ballot in the newspaper. She ignored all the other candidates and initiatives and pulled the lever for "Michael F. Lee, Independent".

Kate and Angela were waiting for her by the door.

"Do you want to go get something to eat?" Kate asked them.

"Sure," Roxanne answered.

"What sounds good?"

"Everything, they're very hungry" Roxanne said, rubbing her belly.

"Well there's no rush. I have the day off. Seamus and Vince are voting with Mike at noon so they can be there for the cameras. After that, they have all kinds of appearances. Do you want to go out to Madison? The Tuscarora Inn has a great brunch, if you are up for the drive," Kate suggested.

"Oh, I love that drive. There are some great stores in the village. I think I feel up to it," Roxanne said looking at her daughter for support.

"Are you sure, Mom? You look really tired."

"I need something different, if it gets to be too much, I'll let you know."

"Okay," Kate said. "A nice country drive on a beautiful fall day."

CHAPTER 103

READY TO BURST

THE CORNED BEEF hash breakfast had become a campaign tradition and there was no reason to do anything differently on Election Day. Brahm was in town for the morning, as well as Stone Saunders to do a follow up story on the man he had catapulted to national prominence. Mike was late, having spent some of the morning with Helen and then a stop by St. Patrick's to light a candle.

"Where have you been?" Brahm yelled across the bar when Mike finally came in the front door.

"Praying," Mike said.

"Well you'll probably need it then," Brahm said lowering his tone. "Come here so we can go over the schedule. Can someone get Mike a plate?"

Vince loaded up a plate for Mike and put it in front of him along with a cup of coffee.

"Like anything stronger than cream, Mikey?" Vince asked.

"Maybe later, thanks," Mike said. He smiled up at Vince.

Vince leaned in, "I'm so proud of you and what you've done. You showed them Mikey."

Mike looked up and shook Vince's hand.

"It's been quite a ride; we'll see tonight if it was all worth it."

"They don't need to count a single vote for me to know it was worth it," Vince said, putting his hand on his friend's shoulder.

"Thanks, Vince."

Brahm interrupted, "You two done kissing?"

Mike laughed. "I'm done with everything."

"Just one more day. We have a breakfast at the City Club in an hour with the precinct leaders that we have signed up, we're at the polls for the news stations to get their shot of you voting at noon and at three you are going to shake hands at the farmer's market downtown."

"What about Stone Saunders?" Mike asked.

"He can wait for when we are ready. His show won't air until after the election and won't matter. Now if you gentlemen will excuse me, I have paying clients that are up for election today that I have to talk to." Brahm said getting up from the table. "I'm flying back to DC in thirty minutes, but I'll be back for the victory party."

"Have a safe trip." Mike stood to shake Brahm's hand. Seamus took Brahm's vacated seat.

"How's Roxanne?" Mike asked.

"She's ready to burst," Seamus worried. "Between the twins coming any day and the election, it could drive a man to drink."

"Can I get you something for your coffee then?" Vince asked.

Seamus shook his head "no," and then winked as he took a sip.

Seamus' phone rang.

"It's the wife. Hello... you're going all the way out there?... Well at least Kate's a nurse.... Check in during the day...be careful, love you."

"What's going on?" Vince asked.

"They just voted and now they are going out to Madison for brunch," Seamus replied.

"That's a hike," Vince said. "At least it'll keep them busy for part of the day till we have the party at the hotel tonight."

"Is everything ready at the Sheraton?" Mike asked. "You worry about what you have to do, we have everything else under control," Seamus answered.

"Well, look who's here," Mike said causing everyone at the table to turn toward the door.

Piersky stood at the door, his usual rumpled condition, with the addition of an old fedora.

"Get yourself a plate," Mike offered.

"No, I can't, it might look like I'm playing favorites," Piersky said, eyeing the full plates in front of everyone at the table.

"Murph, get a plate for our friend here, please," Mike called out.

"Well, if you insist, but this will not influence any of my columns," Piersky said, grabbing silverware from the middle of the table. "Coffee too, Murph. Black."

"Make yourself at home," Seamus said, rolling his eyes towards Vince.

"You gonna come by after all this is done, Piersky?" Vince asked.

"You guys have grown on me. And when Mike wins, I'll want all the inside scoop from the mayor's office. It'll help me win a local Pulitzer."

"You really think I'll win?" Mike asked.

"I thought you were crazy when you got into this race. I thought the mayor would scare you away without any effort. Then we heard she wanted you in the race, but she underestimated you in a big way. You wouldn't back down or play her games. You kept fighting. I admire that. I'm not sure if you'll win but if you excuse me for a second, I'm going to lose my impartiality, off the record, I really hope that you win."

"Thanks, Piersky, that means a lot. Does a mayor have a press secretary? You can have the job if there is one," Mike said.

"You can't start handing out patronage jobs until you're in office, Mikey," Vince reminded him, "and by the way, I've penciled myself in as Public Works Commissioner."

"Okay, let's get this show on the road then," Mike laughed, looking at his untouched plate.

"Eat something first," Vince suggested.

"Okay, Mom." Mike took a few bites.

CHAPTER 104

BOUNCING BABIES

THERE WAS a lot of road construction on Route 5 through the town of Savona that bounced the ladies around in Kate's minivan.

"I need to get Vince to take this over to Seamus and have new shocks put on," Kate said as they hit several potholes.

"I hope I have an appetite left when we get there," Roxanne said.

"Are you okay, Mom?" Angela asked from the back seat.

"I'm fine, I see the end of the construction up there."

"I'll slow down a little till we get through," Kate said, looking behind her to see how much traffic was piling up.

They finally made it to the Inn and thankfully there wasn't a line on this quiet weekday.

"You sit down, Mom and I'll get your plate," Angela said leading Roxanne to a table and then heading to the buffet line.

"What do you want to drink hon?" Kate asked.

"Bring me a pitcher of mimosas please," Roxanne smiled.

"Okay," Kate said. "Coffee it is."

"You're no fu..." Roxanne winced before she could finish.

"What is it hon?" Kate said taking her hand.

"A big contraction. I have to be honest; this isn't the first one today. I was hoping it was just false labor. But..." Roxanne smiled.

"But you think you are going into labor?"

"I don't think they'll pop out before we can have a nice breakfast, so don't worry."

Okay then, but don't eat too much" Kate said looking at Roxanne closely. "You tell me right away if you have another contraction. It's now 9:58 so I'm timing you."

"Okay, please get me decaf, two sugars and cream."

"Should I call Seamus?"

"No, he's so busy today. Calling him now would just send him into a panic. There would be twenty ambulances out front before I could eat a piece of bacon. And don't tell Angela when she gets back, please."

"Okay, but I'm watching you," Kate said, and she went to get the coffee, turning back to look at Roxanne every few steps.

Angela came back with a plate piled high with bacon, blueberry muffins and a made-to-order western omelet.

"I'll be back with more in a minute, Mom," she said putting the plate down.

They ate and chatted about the election. Kate looked

at her watch, it had been twenty-five minutes since Roxanne's last contraction. She smiled and showed Roxanne the stop- watch she had started. "A good nurse is always prepared," Kate winked.

SEAMUS PULLED the rented Chevy Suburban into Mike's driveway at exactly 11:30 per the plan. Helen was sitting on the porch, reading a book.

Mike rolled down his window, "Hey gorgeous, ready to smile for the cameras?"

"Are you sure you want me to go along for this?" Helen asked without looking up from her novel.

"As long as you vote for me," Mike said getting out and walking up to the porch.

"Okay, I've been practicing my princess wave for an hour, I think I have it down."

"Well then, you're ready, let's go."

Mike took her hand and led her to the car and opened the front door for her. He jumped in the back seat.

It took less than a minute to get to the polls, that were fittingly in the gymnasium of St. Patrick's where Mike's life had really started.

Seamus pulled up to the curb and sat there until the news crews recognized Mike getting out of the car. They scrambled over but deferred to Lacy Turnstone because they knew she would get Seamus to let her go first anyway.

"Mr. Lee, how do you feel this morning?" she asked as she put the microphone in front of Mike.

"I think we have run as good of a campaign as we possibly could. We have reached out to people all over the city and let them know what we want to do if we have the privilege of being elected by the people. Win or lose we are very happy."

Mike answered all their questions for a few more minutes.

"Thank you for your reporting over the past months.

We'll see you tonight at the University Sheraton."

Mike held Helen's hand as they walked into the gym. He looked up at the faded championship banner from his senior year. He closed his eyes and inhaled the smell of the place that he never thought would continue to build memories for him.

They signed in and Mike deferred to Helen to go first. The cameras were ready to get the shot of Mike coming out of the booth where he was supposed to give a big thumbs up, but he decided that he would just smile.

Helen finished and Mike went into the booth and closed the curtain. He looked on the second row and saw his name. He ran his fingers over the letters and thought of his father and then all that his mother had to do for the family after he died. He pulled the lever for himself and then voted in all the other races. Brahm had made a point of telling him this three times today, "in case anyone leaks your ballot." Mike had asked why it would matter because that would be after the election.

"The election was over a week ago, we are in governing mode," Brahm had replied.

Mike couldn't see anything past today. He opened the curtain and stepped out.

"What took so long?" a reporter called out.

"Couldn't make up my mind," Mike joked.

"How does it feel to see yourself on the ballot?"

"To tell you the truth, it is more the fact that we are here in St. Patrick's gym. It really drives home what made me run. You can dismiss this if you want to be cynical, but I love this place. It made me. This city made me and I love it so much that I put up with all the headaches, the doubt, the money, to get here to be talking to you guys today. Because I truly, in my heart, want to make our city better."

The stunned reporters couldn't ask another question.

"Thanks," Mike finished as he put his arm around Helen and walked back out to the car.

CHAPTER 106

UNION CONTRACTIONS

KATE PULLED into Roxanne's driveway after making it back from brunch without any further problems and just a few contractions.

"They're getting closer together," Kate said looking over at Roxanne.

"What are closer?" Angela asked.

"Your mom's contractions, sweetie."

"Her what?" Angela yelled, almost climbing into the front seat.

"Contractions," Kate repeated. "Your brother and sister want to come out in time for the election results."

"Oh, my GOD!" Angela said and fell back into her seat. "I'm calling Seamus right now. Where's your bag? Which hospital are we going to?"

"Wait, wait" Roxanne tried to turn around. "We still have time. Let's go inside. We can make sure we have every- thing and then go to the hospital. Kate will call Vince and warn him, before we call Seamus. Sound like a plan?"

Angela looked at Kate.

Kate smiled. "Your mom's right, we have time. There's no need to worry right now. But we aren't going to dilly dally in the house and we should be at the hospital in about thirty minutes."

"You good now, Angela?" Roxanne asked.

"Yeah, I can't believe I'm going to be a sister."

"And what about your brother Pete?" Roxanne asked.

"Oh, right, I forgot all about him." Angela laughed.

Thirty minutes later Kate and Roxanne were back in the car. Roxanne made Angela stay at home so she could open the salon in the morning.

"I'll be fine and Kate will let you know what is happening every minute sweetheart," Roxanne said in answer to Angela's protests. "And tell Pete he needs to stay with Mike. They can't afford to lose both him and Seamus on election day. And make sure you check the appointment book when you open tomorrow to make sure everyone is covered."

"Okay mom, I can handle it, call me right away, love you."

Kate had called Vince while Roxanne was getting ready and made him promise to wait until he got a text from her that it was good to tell Seamus. They were just getting ready to meet with the Police Union group, so they were only minutes from University Hospital.

They made it to the hospital without any problem and Kate called a friend of hers to get them through admissions quickly. As they wheeled Roxanne into a delivery room, Kate sent the text to Vince that they were ready.

CHAPTER 107

FREE BEER FOR LIFE

VINCE SNUCK a peek at his phone when he felt it vibrate in his hand. Mike was at the podium talking about his plan to bring law and order back to the city. It was based on the same Manhattan Institute principles that helped Rudy Giuliani turn New York City around, start with the "broken windows." He talked about all the positive changes that happened to New York once the city was deemed safe. How it all started with law and order.

"It all begins with you, the ladies and gentlemen in this room. I know that your goal is to do your job, protect the law-abiding citizens and go home to your families at the end of your shift. And you want to do all that and know that if you have to make a split second, justifiable, lawful, life-or-death decision, that you will have someone at City Hall who will back you to the end of the earth. That, ladies and gentlemen, is me."

The room exploded into a standing ovation. Mike looked over to Lacy Turnstone and looked right at the camera next to her and motioned to the police chief to stand up next to him. This increased the intensity of the applause.

"It's easy when you know half the cops from Quinn's," Seamus whispered over to Vince.

"Seamus," Vince said pointing to his phone.

Seamus took the phone and held it close so he could read the text. It took him a second to react to what he was reading. When the message finally made it through the synapses in his brain, he looked at Vince. Vince nodded.

Seamus turned toward the door and then stopped and ran back to the microphone where Mike was still standing with the police chief.

"Which one of you bastards has a car outside and doesn't want to pay for another beer at Quinn's for the rest of their lives?" he screamed into the microphone.

A dozen hands in the room went up immediately.

Thirty seconds later Seamus, Mike and Vince were in Pat Quilty's cruiser with all the sirens blaring and lights flashing, going sixty miles per hour up towards University Hospital.

Pat pulled right up to the front door of the hospital, sending the people in the small, roped-off smoking section diving for cover.

The guys jumped out.

"Thanks, Pat," Vince yelled while Seamus ran ahead like a man possessed.

"Tell Roxanne congratulations and tell Seamus he picked the wrong guy to promise free beer to."

Vince and Mike caught up to Seamus and he ran back and forth from every elevator hitting the buttons until one finally opened. He hit the button for the fourth floor continuously until the doors began to close. The other people waiting for the elevators took one look at Seamus' manic disposition and stepped back, away from the doors.

When the elevator opened, Seamus yelled "Four twenty-three" to the unsuspecting nurse at the front desk. She pointed to the left and Seamus ran in that direction. He saw four twenty-two and tried to stop but he slid all the way to four twenty-five and had to scramble to regain traction on the waxed hospital floor to get back to Roxanne's room.

He ran inside and slid past the bed all the way to the window.

"Where's…the…. Babies?" he barely had enough air to ask.

Roxanne looked up from her magazine and pointed to her belly.

"Right here where you left them this morning, sweetheart."

"But…but…but," he managed to say as he fell into the chair at the foot of the bed trying to catch his breath.

Mike, Vince and Kate walked in.

"She's only at five centimeters, we still have some time," Kate said going over to Roxanne and giving her a cup of ice.

"What?" Seamus wiped sweat from his forehead.

"Dr. Desimone, just popped in. She'll be back to check on me once they get the baby heart monitor set up," Roxanne said. "I hope we didn't worry you. Vince was supposed to make sure you knew everything was all right."

Seamus looked at Vince.

"I wanted to see you go crazy. But I never thought you'd steal a police car."

"What?" Roxanne and Kate said in unison.

"We didn't steal a police car, we just had an escort to the hospital," Mike reassured them. "Now if you'll excuse me for a second my phone has been vibrating non-stop since we left the police union."

A technician wheeled the heart monitor into the room, pushing Vince out of the way without asking. She started to hook up the leads to Roxanne, pulling up her gown and wrapping the straps around. A second lead was wrapped around her belly before the machine was turned on. There were two charts on the screen, the first labeled "BABY 1" the second "BABY 2". The tech adjusted and readjusted the pickup until there was a rapid heartbeat in each chart.

"I'll let the doctor know you're all set up" she said before leaving the room.

Dr. Desimone came into the room clapping her hands. "There's my favorite patient with twins and her crazy Irish husband." She looked at Seamus and stopped smiling. "A police car? Isn't that a little cliché?"

Seamus shrugged and smiled.

"Was that the future mayor I saw in the hallway?" Dr. Desimone asked.

"Yeah, that's Mike Lee, he's a friend of ours," Vince answered.

"Good, but he'll have to wait because these two have a few years before they can vote. Why don't we take a look? Seamus, you can stay. Kate, you can stay. And you, Mr. Kate?"

"Vince Di Pietro." Vince extended his hand.

Dr. Desimone looked at his hand. "I'm a doctor and that thing is full of germs."

"Sorry, I've been campaigning with Mike too long."

"Well Vince, you are the one who has to leave."

Vince waved and walked out joining Mike in the hallway. Dr. Desimone went over to the monitor and watched the screen for a few minutes. She hit the record button on the screen and dual rolls of paper began to print out the heartbeats.

"Well, well, looking pretty good," Dr. Desimone said as she looked at each roll.

CHAPTER 108

SOFT TEDDY BEARS

MURPH WAS WAITING in front of the hospital to bring Mike and Vince back to Quinn's so they could readjust the schedule now that Seamus was out of the mix. There were still five hours until the polls closed and there wasn't much left to do, other than look at the turn-out by precinct and try to make some calls.

The city bus they rented had been busy picking up senior citizens and bringing them to the polls. Mike had polled very well in their demographic because of his tough on crime message. They were hoping for one of Genesee's famously dreary, cold, rainy days to keep the less enthusiastic Lerner supporters from voting. Mike's voters had shown they were more enthusiastic and were more likely to brave bad weather. But it had been a gorgeous, Indian summer type day.

The back-dining room was filled with volunteers on disposable cell phones making calls from the lists that Brahm's people had provided. If a person had already voted they tallied those numbers and if they hadn't, they offered to send a car to take them to the polls.

They were anxious to see the after work turn out numbers because Mike led the mayor almost 2-1 with employed voters.

Mike grabbed a chair and watched the action. It all seemed surreal, but at least in a few hours it would all be over and he could either get back to his old life or get on to his new life of trying to figure out how to be mayor. Brahm had assured him that he would give him one of his best young staffers, that needed seasoning, for his administration that would serve as his chief of staff to keep everything straight.

Mike got out his phone and called Brahm.

"What's wrong?" Brahm blurted out without saying hello.

"Hello to you too."

"You never call me unless I ask you to call me, so hopefully you are calling with unexpected good news."

"No, I just wanted to call and thank you. I wouldn't have been anything other than a clumsy novice pretending to be a politician if you hadn't materialized."

"Well that's a first," Brahm laughed. "I've never had a candidate thank me before they found out whether they won or lost. And only the winners call to say thank you."

"Well, this has been the ride of my life and you know, watching all the things going on today, all the excitement and action, you know, Brahm, I really want to win this thing."

"Why didn't you sound like that four months ago?"

"Because in the beginning I didn't want to be mayor, I

just didn't want Lerner to be mayor. I hope that makes sense?"

"It does. Listen Mike, I need to thank you. You've worked so hard, did almost everything I told you to do and without your genuine love of the city you want to lead, none of this would have happened. I wanted to resharpen my teeth by helping you and they are now like razors. I've regained the enthusiasm I had from twenty years ago. You know how often I work with a sincere, genuine politician? Never. You are my first Mike Lee. Thank you."

"So, when I'm interviewed after the election and they ask me about how it was to work with the great Brahm Barbour I can describe you as a soft teddy bear?"

"Don't you dare. I still need to make a living. No one hires teddy bears to run presidential campaigns. Back to business, before you tell me you love me. My plane leaves DC at eight and I will be in your backwater burg a little after ten. By the time I get to the hotel, we'll have some numbers to go over."

"See you then, Brahm, love you, big guy," Mike smooched into the phone.

"I'm hanging up, go out and campaign, you are campaigning until the second the polls close," Brahm said and hung up.

Mike looked at the time on his phone, still time to make some calls. He grabbed one of the lists and started dialing.

CHAPTER 109

TIME FOR THE BIG NEEDLE

ROXANNE WAS PROGRESSING THROUGH LABOR, wincing with the contractions and watching the matching heartbeats on the monitor.

"I think it may be time for the epidural," Roxanne told Kate after the last contraction finished.

Kate had stayed at Roxanne's request because she said she wanted a nurse in the room with her "because Seamus was pretty much useless."

It was true, Seamus paced back and forth in front of the window during each contraction. He was sweating more than Roxanne.

"It probably is a good time to ask for the epidural since they have to get the anesthesiologist on call and they make take a while. I'll go talk to the nurse's station," Kate said leaving the room.

"Come here," Roxanne said to Seamus as she patted the side of the bed.

Seamus did as instructed and walked over to his wife.

"It's going to be okay, stop pacing like a crazy man." Seamus leaned over and kissed her on the forehead.

"You've been through this twice, I'm new to the game. I can't help but worry. You've got to pop out two of them and all I can do is pace and watch."

"We have Kate here if anything happens and Dr. Desimone said she won't leave the hospital until the twins are here. I'm sorry also."

"Sorry for what?" Seamus said, a little surprised.

"You're going to miss all the fun at Mike's party."

"Ah, I don't care about that right now, are you kidding me? Mike has all the help he needs. They don't need me, you do."

"Oh no, here comes another one," Roxanne breathed out as another contraction started.

Seamus went to the door and looked for Kate. She was at the nurse's station and came to the room when she saw Seamus.

"They've called for the epidural, it shouldn't be long," she reassured him.

"The epidural's coming," Seamus said to Roxanne as they went back into the room.

"Not (breath) a (breath) minute (breath) too (breath) soon," Roxanne said.

Ten minutes later the anesthesiologist was in the room preparing Roxanne for the epidural. Seamus took one look at the size of the needle that was about to go into his wife's back and turned to look out the window. He could see the University Sheraton a couple blocks away. He looked at his watch, the polls had just closed.

CHAPTER 110

THE COUNT BEGINS

THE BALLROOM at the Sheraton was packed even though the polls had just closed. A huge "Mike Lee – Mayor" banner was hung behind the podium where Mike would be giving his acceptance speech or conceding to his opponent in a matter of hours.

Mike worked the crowd, shaking hands and thanking people for coming out. He made his way to the podium for his quick welcoming speech.

"Hello, everyone," he said and waited for everyone to settle down. "Welcome to tonight's gathering. The polls have closed and the results will be coming in shortly. It'll take a few hours but hopefully we'll know by the end of the night if you have to put up with me as your mayor or put up with another four years of you-know-who."

The crowd laughed and cheered.

"I have learned one thing in this campaign and that is that a politician and a bartender are very similar. They both tell you what you want to hear so you'll keep buying what they're selling. At the end, you wake up hung over and out of money. Thank you again for coming out."

Mike tried to leave the podium, but the applause and cheers weren't dying down. He kept saying "thank you" into the microphone and waving until he felt he could walk away.

Brahm showed up in time for the first precinct results. It was the 2nd, that included Liberty Hill.

"My sources tell me that the mayor forced the Board of Elections to release the precinct results in order of her weakest to strongest. She wants everyone watching, especially the people in Albany, to see an amazing come-from-behind victory. My source also reassured me that the Board has all the mail-in and absentee ballots from the Post Office so they will be included in the numbers. There may be some stragglers though but we'll worry about that if there is a recount," Brahm told Mike as the results started to be posted.

There was a big screen to the left of the podium with the tally of votes. Vince walked to the podium with the counts.

"Ladies and gentlemen, we have the first results. They are from the 2nd Precinct which includes Liberty Hill."

The crowd cheered at the reference to Liberty Hill and they turned their attention to the screen. The numbers flashed up. Lee 7,444 – Lerner 842.

People started to jump up and down. They were hugging and dancing around the room. Mike ran up to the podium. It was Rocky knocking Apollo Creed down in the first round, there were still fourteen rounds to fight.

"Everyone, everyone," Mike yelled into the mic.

"Every- one, this is our neighborhood, we expected this. There are still eleven more precincts to go. Thank you for your enthusiasm but we still have a long way until it's over."

Ten minutes later two more precincts reported, the 7th and 9th, both had polled strongly for Mike. As the results were posted the totals stood at Lee 19,070 – Lerner 3,415. More cheers erupted and this time Mike let them cheer.

"So far, we're tracking very close to the polling," Brahm said as he studied the results. "We are about 2% behind though, so let's hope that trend doesn't continue."

It was another thirty minutes before the next results came in, three precincts: the 3rd, 8th and 11th. The crowd quieted as they watched the board. Lee 27,191 – Lerner 7,292.

More cheers.

"Well, we are back on track to the polling, we made up the 2%," Brahm said while punching numbers into his phone calculator.

"It shows one thing clearly," Mike said in a tone that made everyone around him look up.

"What?" Vince asked.

"The city is clearly divided. There is no middle really," Mike lamented.

"It's that way across the country. Why would you think Genesee would be any different?" Brahm asked.

"I didn't," Mike said. "But you would hope that at a city level there would be some common ground for people to rally to."

"If you can lower crime and bring some business back

to the city, the other side will just call you a fascist, and not a dirty fascist," Brahm joked.

"If that's progress then we're in big trouble," Mike said. More results pinged into the computer.

"Four precincts this time," Murph said. He typed the results into the tally as they popped up on the screen.

Lee 38,855 – Lerner 23,144

"Three left," Murph said looking at the precinct list.

"Yes, the 5th, 6th and 12th. Lerner's strongest. If the polling holds true, she'll catch up with those three. This is going to be too close to call," Brahm said, rechecking his math.

"It's going to be a long night," Vince said, then checked his phone to see if Seamus had texted.

CHAPTER 111

TIME TO PUSH

DR. DESIMONE CAME in and turned on the printout of the heart monitor and studied the paper for a few minutes.

"Okay, let's check your cervix to see how much progress you've made," she said. She walked to the end of the bed and put on a glove.

Seamus took out his phone and typed a text to Vince: *"How is it looking?"*

His phone buzzed a second later: *"Mike is up but the mayor's strong areas have not reported. It will be close."*

"Well, we're there, ten centimeters. Let me gather the troops and we can get ready to start pushing and see if we can get these babies here."

Seamus sat down in the chair. His phone buzzed. Vince: *"How's Roxanne?"*

Seamus: *"Time to push, I'll let you know"*

Vince: *"Ok, I'm saying a prayer and wishing I could be there with you. Good luck. I'll send the results in as soon as they come in."*

Seamus put his phone back in his pocket. "What's the news from the party?" Kate asked.

"Mike's in the lead for now, but the mayor's strong parts of the city haven't reported yet."

"He's winning?" Roxanne asked.

"Yeah, but don't worry about that now," Seamus said. "Let's get those kids out here so they can go over to the hotel for the celebration," Kate laughed.

CHAPTER 112

CATCHING UP

"THE FIFTH IS IN," Murph said.

"The Heights, where the mayor lives," Vince said, looking over Murph's shoulder.

"Not great," Murph said. He typed in the results, Lee 40,816 – Lerner 29,736.

Before they had a chance to go over the details the next results popped up.

"The twelfth is in too," Murph yelled even though everyone was right next to him.

"Oh boy." Murph typed in the numbers: Lee 42,739 – Lerner 36,768.

"One left, the sixth, the Southside," Brahm said checking his polling data again. "She polled at close to 90% in that precinct. Holy cow, this is what keeps my blood flowing. It's going to be so close. Now remember, Mike, anything under a one-percent difference means an automatic recount. We might not get a final answer tonight."

Brahm's excitement was tempered by Mike's sullen appearance.

"What's wrong, the recount thing?" Brahm asked.

"Mikey, what's the matter?" Vince seconded.

"Just a bad feeling," Mike said. "Probably just the stress of all of this. And I would rather be down the block at the hospital with Seamus and Roxanne."

"They don't need us sitting in the waiting room," Vince reassured him. "Besides, we would just be in the way over there."

"I know," Mike said as he looked through the room for Helen.

Helen was sitting at a table with a group of the phone volunteers. Mike walked over and sat down.

"Anything new?" she asked. She smiled at her husband. "Just this mayor thing."

"Not that. Any word from Seamus?"

"Yeah, it's almost time to start pushing." Mike squeezed her hand.

"Good. It's turning out to be quite a day."

"Mike! Last precinct's in," Murph yelled over the crowd.

Mike got up and kissed Helen.

"This is it," he said as he walked over to his team as they hovered around Murph's computer.

CHAPTER 113
WHAT'S WRONG

DR. DESIMONE CAME in and inspected all the equipment setup that the nurses had done. The room was crowded with people and everything they needed for the twins. A nurse handed her a glove. "Okay, let's check to see what the babies are doing," Dr. Desimone said.

She did her examination and looked up and smiled. "Let's get started, Roxanne. Seamus, you ready?" she said, laughing.

"Me?" Seamus asked.

"When you faint, try to fall away from all the equipment please."

"Ah, come on now Doc, I'm not going to faint. I hope," Seamus rocked back and forth on his feet to test the strength of his legs.

"Okay, Roxanne, when you feel the next contraction we'll start pushing. You've been through this before, you'll do great. Are you ready?"

"Do I have a choice?" Roxanne looked over at Seamus. "I guess not," Dr. Desimone said. "But don't worry, we'll take care of you and the babies, I promise."

The pushing started as Dr. Desimone checked Roxanne's progress and kept an eye on the monitors. She calmly gave Roxanne instructions while directing the nurses.

After the second round of pushing finished an alarm sounded.

"What's that?" Roxanne asked, her voice full of concern.

"Doc, what's wrong?" Seamus said feeling the strength in his legs wobble.

"Hold on. Get the sonogram ready," she directed a nurse.

Dr. Desimone moved the transducer over Roxanne's belly as she studied the screen and then rechecked the heart monitor.

"Okay, Roxanne, Seamus, there's a change of plans. The first twin that is in the birth canal is fine. The second one is in distress. We cannot let you deliver the first without endangering the second. We are going to have to do a C-Section right away."

"Oh God," Roxanne cried. Seamus froze.

The room was suddenly a rush of activity. People appeared and moved through the room with practiced efficiency. Within minutes, Roxanne was being wheeled out into the hallway.

"Come with me please, Mr. Corrigan," a nurse said taking Seamus' hand.

Seamus was led into a waiting room.

"Please stay here, Mr. Corrigan. The surgical area is right through there. I will be going back and forth and I will let you know everything that is going on. Please don't worry, your wife is in good hands. Dr. Desimone is the best in the city. Is there anything I can do for you?"

Seamus tried to process everything that was going on.

"No, just please, take care of my wife. Please."

"We will, Mr. Corrigan."

Seamus pulled out his phone and started to send a text, but he couldn't see the screen through the tears in his eyes.

CHAPTER 114

AND THE WINNER IS

MURPH LOOKED at the numbers and tried to do the math in his head but he couldn't add two plus two at the moment.

"What are they," Mike asked.

"Lerner 7,052, Lee 1,497. Let me enter them in," Murph said. He tried to stop the shaking in his hands as he typed in the numbers into the computer and looked up at the screen for the totals.

Lee 44,236 – Lerner 43,820

"The Southside, we got almost twenty percent of the vote. I did reach them. I made a difference." Mike smiled.

It took a second for the numbers to sink in before a huge cheer went up through the room.

"You won Mikey!" Vince cheered as he grabbed Mike in a bear hug and danced him around.

"Congratulations, Mike, don't worry about the recount. I'll have a team of lawyers watching every ballot." Brahm said. He grabbed Mike's hand and tried to shake it as Vince carried him around.

Murph was trying to do a combination victory-River-dance that would make any Irish step dancer cringe.

Reporters swarmed around Mike as their camera lights made him and Vince look like a couple doing their spotlight dance at the Prom. He was looking over Vince's shoulder and waving to Helen to join him up on the stage.

"Mr. Lee, a comment please!" they yelled.

Vince let Mike go so he could give Helen a big hug. The reporters were still circling waiting for their chance to talk to Mike.

"You did it, you did it," Helen said. Mike buried his face in her shoulder.

Vince grabbed his phone to text Seamus the news. He looked and there was already a text from Seamus.

Trouble.

CHAPTER 115

BURNT CELLS

THE GOVERNOR of the Great State of New York sat in a big leather chair in the mansion in Albany, eating popcorn and watching the election results from around the country. The disposable cell phone in his pocket buzzed.

"Did you see?"

"Yes, it made the national news unfortunately," the governor responded.

"Fix it or I'll get very chatty."

"Done."

The governor hung up and shook his head.

"Goddamn loser," he muttered.

CHAPTER 116

TIME TO PRAY

KATE CAME into the waiting room and found Seamus sitting there with his head in his hands. She walked up to him and rubbed his back.

"I checked with the surgical team; everything should be okay. We should know pretty soon. Do you want me to let everyone know?"

"No, they're busy," Seamus said without taking his head out of his hands.

"Nonsense, they would want to know."

"Okay, call Vince please," Seamus said looking up at her.

Kate called Vince.

"What's wrong, Seamus texted there's trouble," Vince said quickly.

"One of the twins was in distress and they didn't want to take any chances, so they are doing an emergency C-Section," Kate said and walked out into the hallway.

"Oh God." Vince did the same, trying to get away from the noise of the celebration.

"They'll do their best. This isn't all that uncommon since she's a few weeks early and because of her age."

"Where are you now?" Vince asked.

"We are in the Maternity Surgical waiting room, 7th Floor."

"I'll be right there." Vince hung up.

Vince ran back into the ballroom and found Mike. Mike took one look at Vince and knew that something was wrong.

"The hospital? Are the twins okay?" Mike asked.

"Um," Vince didn't know how to answer, "I don't know, there's trouble. Emergency C-Section, I just talked to Katie."

"Let's go." Mike ran over to tell Helen what was happening.

Helen grabbed her coat from the back of the chair, "Let's go."

Mike explained to Brahm what was going on.

"We'll hold down the fort here. Let me know once everything is okay. I'll have Murph talk to the press from here, they'll love that."

"What about the recount? How is that going to work?" Mike asked Brahm.

"Go take care of your friend."

CHAPTER 117

INAPPROPRIATE HUGS

MIKE, Helen and Vince hurried down the block to University Hospital, chased by a couple reporters who wanted to know what was happening.

Vince turned around and with a menacing look said, "Not now, this has nothing to do with the election, this is private."

That was more than enough to stop the reporters in their tracks.

Kate was waiting for them by the elevators. She hugged Vince then explained what the situation was in more detail, telling them about the monitor alarm and the baby being in distress.

They went in to see Seamus.

Seamus stood up and hugged Helen.

Helen kissed his cheek, "It's going to be okay."

"I hope so," Seamus said barely audible.

Vince looked at his best friend, the mountain of a man that he had never seen show any fear and he saw in his eyes the near panic just below the surface, as Seamus tried to hold himself together.

Vince hugged Seamus hard. When he let him go, Vince made the sign of the cross and nodded. "They will be all right."

Seamus hung his head.

It was Mike's turn to give Seamus a hug. When they parted, Seamus held him by the shoulders.

"Well, Mikey?"

"We won, by four hundred and sixteen votes."

"What?" Seamus asked.

"We won, Seamus. But let's focus on you and your family," Mike said trying to smile.

"You did it, Mikey, you did it." Seamus gave him another hug.

"We did it," Mike said. "You pushed me into this thing and carried me through the campaign. I can't thank you enough."

The nurse came in and everyone turned to look. She walked to Seamus and held his hand.

"Mr. Corrigan, the first twin is here and he is fine. They are sending him to the NICU just to be safe but his APGAR score was good and this is just so he can be under observation. They are working on your daughter now; we'll know in a few minutes. I'll be right back."

She disappeared back into the operating room. Seamus sunk into a chair.

"Okay, we're halfway there, everything's going to be okay," Vince said.

Everyone agreed.

Kate sat down next to Seamus. "How are you doing?"

"I feel so helpless, I want to take care of Roxanne and I can't do a thing."

"She's in good hands," Kate replied.

Before she could say anything else, Dr. Desimone came through the doors. Everyone stood up immediately.

"The second twin is here and she's going to be fine. She's up in NICU with her brother. They are closing up Roxanne now, she was a champ through the entire operation and she'll be fine. She'll be in recovery for an hour or so, then you can see her. Congratulations, Mr. Corrigan, everyone is alright."

"Thank you, Doc," Seamus said, too exhausted with relief to do anything other than give Dr. Desimone an awkward hug.

"Thank you, Mr. Corrigan, you can let me go now."

Seamus let her go and then went to hug her again, but she ducked out of the way and went over to Kate.

Kate talked to Dr. Desimone and got all the details. "Congratulations, Dad," Vince said slapping Seamus on the back.

"What a night," Mike said.

"That's the biggest understatement ever made," Seamus said making everyone laugh.

CHAPTER 118

CONCESSIONS

MIKE AND HELEN walked out of the hospital to head back to see if anyone was left at the celebration. He called Brahm.

"Yeah, the place is still full. The mayor hasn't conceded. She said she is looking forward to the recount. The reporters are still here too, they'll be very happy to see you. Come back to the party. Murph is driving them crazy and they want the new mayor."

"Be there in a few minutes," Mike said. A voice came from behind them.

"So, you did it, congratulations Mr. Mayor."

"Piersky! I was wondering when you'd show up." Mike shook Piersky's hand.

"You cost me a fortune in lost bets though. I'm sure Brahm Barbour told you about the recount?" Piersky asked.

"Yeah, I know all about it," Mike said. "But we're not going to worry about that tonight."

"Barbour going to bring in lawyers?"

"A team." Mike laughed.

"Good, you'll need them. I wouldn't trust Lerner. I'll bet you anything that she's going to pull something," Piersky said.

Mike looked at Helen, "We aren't going to worry about that tonight."

CHAPTER 119

DR. LEE, I PRESUME?

MIKE, Helen and Piersky walked into the lobby of the Sheraton, the noise of the celebration spilling out of the ballroom.

"Shall we?" Mike asked his companions.

"Mr. Mayor?" a voice behind Mike asked for the second time in a few minutes.

Helen let out a scream, "Kit!"

She grabbed her daughter in a hug, "You came, you came," she repeated.

Mike joined in the hug, kissing the top of his daughter's head. Helen let go and Kit fully embraced her father.

"I'm so proud of my dad, the mayor of Genesee. I knew you could do it."

"Kit, I can't believe you came all the way up from Florida," Mike said holding her out to look at her.

"Surprise! I wouldn't have missed it for the world. Although I thought I was going to miss it because my connection at LaGuardia was delayed for hours and it didn't look like I was going to get here tonight."

Mike realized Piersky was still standing there.

"Kit this is Devan Piersky, he's a reporter for the *Genesee Herald*. Piersky, this is our daughter, Doctor Catherine Lee."

"Doctor?" Piersky said extending his hand.

"PhD.," Kit replied, "I teach Shakespeare at the University of Florida."

"Shakespeare? I got my degree in English from Union College. Let me see if I remember... 'If I could write the beauty of your eyes And in fresh numbers number all your graces, The age to come would say, This poet lies; Such heavenly touches ne'er touch'd earthly faces.' Was that right?"

"Why yes, Sonnet 17. It's one of my favorites. I'm very impressed, Mr. Piersky."

"Devan, please."

"Piersky, I hope I'm not seeing what I think I'm seeing," Mike interjected.

"Leave him alone," Helen cut in smiling at Piersky's attempt to impress Kit. "Just two young people meeting each other. Why don't we go in and join the party?"

"Of course," Mike said as he opened the door for his wife and daughter. He turned and looked at Piersky. "I'm watching you."

The crowd saw Mike and a cheer tore through the room. He followed the applause up to the stage and the microphone.

"Thank you everyone, thank you. Well, it's been a long night and it's going to be a while before we know the outcome of the election. I have spoken with the mayor's people and they are going to press for a recount."

Jeers and boos echoed off the walls, louder than the cheers that greeted Mike.

"Now, everyone please, please settle down." He waited for quiet.

"I'm okay with the recount. I wouldn't want it any other way. I want there to be no doubt in anyone in the city about who won the election. Unfortunately, we'll have to bring in lawyers on our behalf and we'll do everything we can to make sure that the recount is fair and legitimate."

Applause filled the room.

"Now I want you to continue to have a good time. There is still plenty of food and drinks. We have rides for anyone who thinks they may have had a few too many. I want everyone home safe tonight. I want to recognize a few people that without their help and support I would not be up here tonight. Helen, Kit, please come on up. Actually, I want all of my team to come up on stage."

Helen and Kit walked up on the stage, followed by Murph, Pete, and Brahm.

Mike continued.

"Most of you know my wife Helen. Helen, I couldn't have done this without all the support you have given me since the first time I saw you in the gym at St. Patrick's. I love you honey. Thanks. And this is our daughter Catherine, she flew all the way up from Gainesville, Florida to be here tonight. Please join me in applause for these lovely ladies."

The crowd cheered and whistled.

"I want to thank my team, first the boys from Quinn's, John Murphy, Pete Piontek, Vince Di Pietro and Seamus Corrigan. Vince and Seamus are over at University

Hospital because Seamus' wife Roxanne gave birth to their twins tonight. A boy and a girl. Mother and children are doing fine."

"Seamus! Seamus! Seamus!" the crowd chanted.

"And Pete here is Roxanne's son so congratulations Pete, you have a new brother and sister."

"I want to thank Devan Piersky from the *Genesee Herald*, Lacy Turnstone from Channel 9, they gave me a fair shake in the paper and on TV and I appreciate how they withstood the pressure to tell a different story.

"And finally, my Washington D.C. pro, Brahm Barbour. Brahm came in and turned us into a real campaign. He taught me more about politics in the last few months than I ever learned in school. No offense, St. Benedict's."

Mike stepped to the side of the microphone and applauded his team.

"Now, have a great evening, thank you."

The room cheered louder and roared until Mike took a small bow. He waded into his people, shaking hands and accepting hugs.

CHAPTER 120

WRAPPING IT IN A BOW

THE REPORTERS ASKED questions for almost an hour as Mike patiently answered each one honestly and with good humor. Brahm finally rescued him because he needed to talk.

"I have to go back to D.C. My team will be here tomorrow afternoon. They'll make sure everything is handled correctly. Now, Mike, that doesn't mean she can't pull anything. It'll take at least a week for this to play out. Call me anytime day or night."

"Thanks, Brahm, have a safe flight back. I'm going to head home here shortly and maybe I'll be able to get to sleep."

"How are Seamus and Roxanne? And the twins?"

"Just got another text, Roxanne's almost out of recovery. The twins are still in the NICU. I'll let you know as we find out, but it really looks like everything is fine."

"Well, Stone Saunders has been caught up in the celebration and has had a few too many, you should talk to him before he finds some young lady to pull into the coatroom."

"Thanks, Brahm, I'll do that. We did it, didn't we?"

"Go talk to Stone Saunders," Brahm said as he looked at Mike before breaking down and embracing him in a bear hug.

CHAPTER 121

A KICK IN THE PRIVATES

STONE'S TEAM had him set up in a smaller meeting room in the hotel. A producer was feeding Stone coffee while another staffer tried to apply make-up. Mike sat in the make-up chair and asked the young lady to take it easy on him.

The lights went on, which caused Stone to come to life. When the countdown finished Stone was one hundred percent Stone.

"So, Mike Lee, you did it, you beat all the odds, you quieted all the critics. How did you do it?"

"Well Stone, I owe a lot to you and the exposure your show gave us. Without you, Brahm Barbour doesn't walk through my door, so I owe you for that."

"That's what I do Mike Lee, I am a kingmaker, that is why I have the highest rated program on cable TV," he said winking into the camera.

"Yes Stone, you were a big part in getting our message out to Genesee, to New York and to the country. I hope you come back and check in on us."

"But what about the recount? Aren't you worried about what can happen with that?"

"Yes, Stone, I am. There are plenty of instances in the country where the candidates with the right connections and the right amount of money have played shenanigans with the recount. It wouldn't surprise me in the least for something to happen here."

"What can you do about it?"

"Brahm will help with the legal assets and we'll take it as it comes."

"Mike Lee, it has been a pleasure working with you and I hope you'll have us back to check in on how your administration is doing. But if you aren't getting the job done, we'll hit you hard on the issues."

"If I'm not getting the job done then you can come back and metaphorically kick me in the privates," Mike said getting up and then shaking Stone's hand.

CHAPTER 122

FLOWER POTS ON THE BALCONY

AGENT BALSAM'S phone buzzed while she was reading the *Genesee Herald* online. The number was unknown but the area code was from Genesee.

"Agent Balsam."

"I'm ready to meet."

"I thought I would be hearing from you today."

"Today, 2 p.m., top level of the Sheraton parking garage."

"I'm going to have to bring my partner Agent Kamholz with me, so don't get spooked."

"Just be there before I change my mind."

CHAPTER 123

TALKING BOOBS

SEAMUS WAS WAITING in the room when the orderly wheeled in Roxanne.

"There's my champ," Seamus said as he went to her and held her hand as the orderly helped her into the bed.

"Have you been up to see the twins?"

"No, I wanted to see them with you," Seamus said. He kissed her on her forehead.

"Dr. Desimone said when she released me from recovery that she'd be down soon."

"Is there anything I can get for you; did they say whether you could eat or drink anything?"

"Let's wait for the doctor. But when they say I can eat, I want you to go over to Wimpy's and get me a double bacon cheeseburger."

"Done. You deserve it love, for what you've been through."

Dr. Desimone came into the room.

"How's my tough patient doing? You made us earn our money today."

"I feel good even without the pain killers."

"No painkillers? Doc, get her the pain killers right away," Seamus pleaded.

"No, I don't want any, Seamus. I can't feed the twins if I'm all doped up," Roxanne said.

"What?" Seamus asked.

Seamus looked at Roxanne as she pointed to her breasts. "Feed the kids," she said again.

"Oh, I get it. Sorry, I'm new to this game."

"Okay, if you two are done talking about Roxanne's breasts, we can talk about the kids. I've released them from the NICU, they should be on the way down here."

"They are?" Roxanne asked. "Thank you, Dr. Desimone. Thank you for getting the twins here okay."

"Yes, thank you, Doc," Seamus seconded.

"Knock, knock," a nurse said as she wheeled in the first baby. She was followed by another nurse with the other twin.

"Here, Mom," she said as she handed the first to Roxanne and then the second.

Roxanne held the twins in each arm. "Look how beautiful they are, Seamus."

"Aye, they're the most beautiful sight I've ever seen."

CHAPTER 124

HIS CITY

MIKE THOUGHT he would be able to get to sleep, but when he got home, he felt like he'd had a triple shot of espresso. He turned on the news that he had set up to record. He fast forwarded through the parts where he was being interviewed, to the interviews of Mayor Lerner. He wanted to hear what she said. Maybe he could get an indication of how the recount would turn out. What he saw disappointed him.

Mayor Lerner seemed too happy about the outcome and the recount. She looked like a candidate who had won by a landslide. Mike felt his gut tighten as he saw her smiling image on the screen.

He turned off the television and went onto the porch. There was a strong northerly breeze that gave Mike a chill. He went back inside and got his varsity jacket from St. Benedict's and his favorite Seneca University hat. He was going to be a walking billboard for the city whether or not he was going to be the city's mayor.

He walked up to Quinn's and stood across the street and looked at the place where he spent almost all his time.

He thought about the first time he went in there to meet Jimmy Quinn after he had asked out Helen. He knew Jimmy wanted to size him up. He laughed at the thought of how Jimmy, at 5'5" and 125 lbs. intimidated him.

When Jimmy asked him if he wanted anything to drink Mike had answered, "a pint."

Jimmy laughed and poured him a Coke.

He walked down the hill to St. Patrick's where he grew up, won a championship, met and married Helen, and this morning voted for himself for Mayor of Genesee.

He kept walking down the hill to the railyards where his great-grandfather worked after he came from Ireland and where his grandfather worked unloading trains until he got a job at the Soda works out in West Genesee. His father followed his dad into the Soda works, where exposure to the chemicals he worked with put him in an early grave when Mike was a kid.

He walked along Erie Boulevard, on to downtown. He went through the revitalized section of Veteran's Square, old factories and warehouses turned into trendy shops, restaurants, and bars. This area showed what was possible for the city. Veteran's Square attracted the monied people from the suburbs and students from Seneca University. It wasn't enough to turn the city around, but it was a good start. Of course, the politicians didn't do this, one entrepreneur bought a building for nothing and opened a restaurant. A couple people followed and soon the area was revitalized.

A few blocks later and he was on Genesee Street, the heart of the city. When Mike was a kid Genesee Street was the center of everything. Huge department stores lined both sides of the street for blocks. The sidewalks were always full of shoppers and workers. At Christmastime, Mike loved to come down and see the decorations and lights. The smell of the caramel corn store, the bell ringers, and the Christmas music playing from the stores.

All the local department stores had been swallowed up by national chains and had moved out to the malls. Only a few storefronts were being used and those were cheap discount stores. The sidewalks were cracked and damaged, garbage overflowed from the city trash cans.

If he hadn't seen the city in its glory when he was very young, he wouldn't believe that what he was looking at today was the same place.

Mike headed three blocks northeast to City Hall.

He sat on a bench across the street from the old stone building that he might occupy if the recount went his way. He thought about when he and Helen went in there to get their marriage license and how she didn't think it was funny when he got in the next line that was for dog licenses.

Sitting there he wished he had brought a flask of Jameson's, but then he saw the headlines in the paper, "Mayoral Candidate Arrested for Drinking in Public."

The walk home seemed twice as long as the walk to City Hall. He got home just as the sun was coming up. He got into bed with Helen and pulled her close to feel her warmth.

CHAPTER 125

COMING HOME

A FEW HOURS later Mike was up and dressed. Kit was still asleep, she and Piersky had gone out to eat after the Election party wound down. They left her a note on the kitchen table that they were going to the hospital to see the twins. He and Helen were waiting on the front porch for Vince and Kate to pick them up so they could all head to the hospital to see the now doubled Corrigan family. This time Mike didn't forget the flask even though he knew Helen would skin him alive if she caught him with it.

Helen had a gift, matching Irish lace baptismal gowns that she ordered the day she heard Roxanne was having twins.

Vince pulled up front and honked even though Mike and Helen were on the porch. Mike laughed when he saw Kate reach across and hit Vince on the shoulder for the unnecessary honk.

The hospital room was filled with pairs of gifts, one for each twin. Mike thought to himself that he didn't need the flask to see double. Roxanne was holding Caedance with her pink cap and Seamus was holding Declan wearing his blue, when the visitors entered.

"Seamus, you look like a natural holding that baby," Kate said seeing Declan wrapped in Seamus' huge arms.

"As natural as a suit on a monkey I'd say," Seamus said shifting his son a little, so he was more visible for the visitors.

"You should have been here earlier when Pete and Angela were here to see their brother and sister. If you think Seamus looks nervous, Pete was twice as bad. Angela looked very natural though," Roxanne laughed.

"Oh my, they're gorgeous," Helen cooed as she leaned in to look at Caedance.

"They are so beautiful," Roxanne agreed. "May I?'

Helen held out her arms and Roxanne passed the baby over to her.

"Thank God they look like Roxanne," Vince chimed in, earning another swipe from his wife.

"May I hold a baby too?" Kate asked Seamus as she leaned in for a look.

Seamus handed his son to Kate with the exaggerated carefulness of a first-time father.

"Oh, this makes me want another one." Kate sighed as she rocked Declan in her arms.

"I hope you're kidding," Vince said. He held out his finger for Declan to grab.

"They are just so precious. How are you feeling, Roxanne?" Kate asked.

"Very sore, but also very happy."

"When are they letting you go home?" Helen asked.

"Tomorrow morning, but I want you to take that one home

today so he can shower and change," Roxanne said pointing at her husband.

"Don't worry, Mike and I will drag him out if he won't go," Vince chimed in.

"Any news on the recount?" Seamus asked.

"I don't know, I'm taking a day off today," Mike said. He looked over Helen's shoulder at the baby.

"Everything's ready at the house. Refrigerator's full. I turned the heat on for a little while so wouldn't get that old furnace smell," Vince said.

"Thanks, buddy," Seamus said.

"Do you want me to get the cops for the escort home, like your ride here to the hospital?" Mike asked.

"Naw, I think I got that one covered." Seamus laughed.

"I brought over your truck this morning, it's in the garage, third level, spot three-fifty-one," Vince said.

"Wow, this is all starting to feel real." Seamus sighed. "I could use a drink."

Roxanne chided him about the drink, but he laughed when he saw Mike patting his jacket pocket.

"Kate, why don't you take Helen home?" Vince handed her the keys. "We'll get Seamus home and cleaned up."

Once in the car Mike handed Seamus the flask as he sat in the passenger seat. Seamus opened it, "Slainte," he said, and took a drink.

"It's been quite a few days, huh?" Mike asked.

"I don't think we'll ever be able to top it." Seamus took another swig,

"Let's go home," Mike said. He took the flask from Seamus and took his own drink.

CHAPTER 126

LAWYERS, GUNS AND MONEY

BRAHM'S LAWYERS descended on the city the next day as he had promised. They filed a stack of motions and briefs with the city board of elections to try to protect Mike from the mayor cheating. The ballots and machines were secured at the board of elections in a locked and sealed room. A meeting was scheduled for 9 a.m. on the Tuesday following election day for all the parties involved. There was a rumor that the governor was going to send in a team from the state.

Mike arrived with Brahm's lawyers at the appointed conference room in City Hall, expecting to meet with the mayor and her local lawyers. Mike knew right away that the lawyers that were already seated in the room were not local.

"That's Reed D'Alesandro, he worked on the Minnesota Senate recount a few years back. That's bad news for us," Brahm's lead lawyer whispered to Mike. "I have to call Brahm and let him know."

Seated at the mayor's table was a team of pros from the National Committee.

The meeting went badly from the beginning. Every motion that Brahm's team had filed had a counter motion.

The team from the National Committee had lawsuits ready to challenge the votes in the precincts that Mike carried by large margins. They also had challenges to the access to the recount by independent observers, they only wanted the people from the board.

To challenge all this Mike would need a lot more lawyers and potentially millions of dollars.

They retreated to Quinn's after the meeting for a conference call with Brahm.

"They got us, Mike, I don't know why they brought out their biggest guns for a mediocre mayor like her, but they did. She must have something on the Governor or maybe that walking disaster of a Senator that you constantly see on the news," Brahm said.

"Is there anything we can do?" Mike asked.

"I'm sorry, I don't have the resources that they can muster. We'll fight what we can but they'll either knock out enough voters to give her the lead or some other tricks, like they used in Minnesota, that's why D'Allesandro is here."

"I knew I was up against a dishonorable woman, but I had no idea," Mike said shaking his head.

"You did an amazing job. I'm surprised they didn't make up something before the election to knock you out. As you can see, they won't let anything stop them from stealing back the election."

"Someday they'll pay the price for selling their souls for the power."

"That is what politics has become. I might think about retiring, this isn't what this country should be about. Getting elected, staying in office, career politicians. The city needed you Mike. You need to challenge her in four years."

"Well, if I ever do decide to run again, I want you to send your best guy up here to Genesee to knock me out with a two-by-four," Mike joked.

"That's a deal." Brahm laughed. "I'll have the lawyers let you know when this is over. There's still a small chance they won't be able to steal this though."

"What kind of chance?" Mike asked. "About five percent," Brahm conceded.

A week later, Mike got the call from Brahm.

"They came up with a voting machine that they missed counting the ballots from the 4th precinct. Over three hundred votes, all but two for Lerner. And another from the 12th, same thing, almost all for Lerner. Even more mailed in ballots that were somehow received before the initial validation by the board. They just appeared. She's up by over four hundred after the official recount. All of the found votes are a statistical impossibility, but they don't care. The press won't investigate, so that's it," Brahm informed him.

"What should I do now?" Mike asked.

"Call a press conference and concede the election. Feel free to call into question the means by which the mayor won this thing. It stinks. She can't protest too much and hope- fully it'll leave a bad taste with the people in the city. At least she will have some people watching her for the next four years. You didn't win officially, Mike, but you did beat her."

"I'll call them now and get it over with," Mike said. "Thanks again, Brahm. Please don't be a stranger. I want you up here at Quinn's for St. Patrick's Day."

"It's a deal, Mike."

CHAPTER 127

FORCED CONCESSIONS

MIKE CALLED Piersky first so he could put a story up on the newspaper's website before anyone else from the press. The television stations saw the article as soon as Piersky put it up and their trucks were out in front of Quinn's within a half hour.

Seamus directed them to set up their cameras in the same spot where he announced Mike's candidacy all those months ago.

Lacy Turnstone called Seamus over.

"You want an exclusive interview?" he asked her.

"Sure, if it isn't too much trouble. If he doesn't want to, I'll understand," she said.

"I'm sure he'll do it, maybe not today though" Seamus said. He turned to walk back into Quinn's to get Mike.

"Hey Seamus," Lacy called.

"Yeah?"

"You guys were robbed."

Seamus looked at her and nodded.

Mike came out to face the cameras a minute later.

"I am very proud of the campaign we ran. When we started this race on this very spot, no one gave us a chance to even get on the ballot. And in the end, it came down to the ballots that miraculously appeared a week after the election. I congratulate Mayor Lerner on her reelection. I am willing to work with her in any capacity because my goal remains to make the city a better place. I would also like to announce my retirement from politics. I am returning to my life as a bar owner and businessman. I love the city of Genesee and I will continue to work and live in the only place I have ever called home. Thank you."

Mike didn't take any questions. He walked back into Quinn's, poured himself a pint and asked Seamus to tell the story of his fiftieth birthday party and the exploding goat.

EPILOGUE – I GIVE YOU THE FBI

A FEW MONTHS after the election, the FBI knocked on Mayor Lerner's door at 5 a.m. as they served warrants across New York state. She was being arrested for allegedly taking kickbacks on the building projects in Genesee as part of the Governor's "ReNEW YORK" initiative. They built an empty research center, an unused movie studio and a renewable energy plant that didn't produce enough electricity to keep the lights on. Finally, there was the Grover Cleveland Middle School Public Housing project, all just to funnel the money to their friends and themselves.

The governor was untouched of course, but the list of fall guys that took the bullet for him was long and full of well-known businessmen and women.

Carter got a text from Agent Balsam saying the arrest was done and to be prepared for the next step of testifying.

Nancy Elliot saw the news alert on her phone when she got into her office in Washington where she was working for a Congressman from Georgia.

Quinn's was packed for the 12 o'clock local news. The news trucks were parked outside and the reporters that Mike knew so well now had already been into Quinn's begging for Mike to come out and make a statement live before the news was over.

Mike, Helen, Vince and Katie sat at their regular table. Seamus, Roxanne and the twins sat at the next table with Pete and Aoife, who was sporting a Gerry Marra engagement ring special. Angela was in the booth across from them with her new boyfriend, the captain of the Seneca University hockey team who had just been drafted by the New York Rangers.

Seamus was feeding Declan and looking at his untouched pint and wondering if he could ask for a straw. Murph was at the bar, right next to the television. He had turned the sound up all the way and had turned on the closed captioning just to be safe.

The noisy bar hushed as the news came on. The video of Mayor Lerner being perp-walked into the Federal Building filled the big screen, her knowing smirk gone and her pale, make-up less face was tear streaked.

Mike couldn't help but feel sorry for his old opponent. He also felt completely justified in his attacks on the political class and the fact that the city would be better off without her. Helen put her hand on top of his and kissed him on the cheek.

"I'm going to go talk to them," Mike told Helen.

"Of course you are," Helen smiled.

Mike walked out to the cameras as the lights turned on and reporters crowded in front of him with extended microphones.

Mike turned back and saw his friends and family looking out of the windows.

He took a deep breath and faced the cameras.

"Thank you for coming out, I can understand why you want me to give you a statement. Well, today is as sad a day as there ever has been here in Genesee. If you love the city you are sad and you know we are better than this. Last year during the campaign we convinced the city that there was a better way. I knew we were right then; I didn't need the events of today to tell me otherwise. I just pray that a lot of eyes are open and that we can use these unfortunate embarrassments to decide to change direction and get to work fixing things. If we can't agree to that now, then, well, we don't stand a chance of doing anything. That's it, thanks."

Mike didn't take any questions, he just slowly walked back to the bar.

Before the month was out, the City Council had voted to remove Mayor Lerner from office and set a special election for June 6th.

The same day as the council vote, Mike set up all the chairs in his living room. All of his friends were coming over to the house.

THE END

ABOUT THE AUTHOR

Tom Cosentino lives in Indian Rocks Beach Florida. He is a graduate of Syracuse University and the Rochester Institute of Technology. He served in the US Army as a Field Artillery Officer. He has published several short stories; this is his first novel.

BACK COVER PHOTO

The neighborhood guys and friends for half a century
    L-R: John Wutzer, Luke Grealish, Dan Halligan, Tom Cosentino, Eric Heitzman Ed Downes. (Photo by the late Jim Heitzman)